ISRA
ISLE

Falls of Niagara
Grand Niagara
Schlosser
Navy I.
GRAND ISLAND
Ararat
BUFFALO
Ferry
Black Rock
Waterloo
Fort Erie
BUFFALO
MAP
OF THE
COUNTY
OF
ERIE
By David H. Burr
Published by the SURVEYOR GENERAL
pursuant to an Act of the Legislature

ISRA ISLE

A NOVEL

Nava Semel

TRANSLATED BY JESSICA COHEN

MANDEL VILAR PRESS

Supported by "Am Ha-Sefer"—the Israeli Fund for Translation of Hebrew Books
The Cultural Administration, Israel Ministry of Culture and Sport

Published by arrangement with the Institute for the Translation of Hebrew Literature.

This book is typeset in Monotype Waldbaum. The paper used in this book meets the minimum requirements of ANSI/NISO Z39.48-1992 (R1997). ♾

Publisher's Cataloging-in-Publication Data
Names: Semel, Nava. | Cohen, Jessica, translator.
Title: Isra Isle / translated Nava Semel by Jessica Cohen.
Other Titles: Ísra'el. English
Description: Simsbury, Connecticut : Mandel Vilar Press, [2016] | Translation of: Ísra'el.
Identifiers: ISBN 978-1-942134-19-0 (print) | ISBN 978-1-942134-20-6 (ebook)
Subjects: LCSH: Jewish refugees—New York (State)—Grand Island (Island)—Fiction. | Jews—New York (State)—Fiction. | Newly independent states—Unites States—Fiction. | Grand Island (N.Y. : Island)—Fiction. | Alternative histories (Fiction) | Jewish fiction.
Classification: LCC PJ5054.S24939 I8713 2016 (print) | LCC PJ5054. S24939 (ebook) | DDC 892.437—dc23

Printed in the United States of America
16 17 18 19 20 21 22 23 24   9 8 7 6 5 4 3 2 1

Mandel Vilar Press
19 Oxford Court, Simsbury, Connecticut 06070
www.americasforconservation.org   www.mvpress.org

ACKNOWLEDGMENTS

THIS EDITION is supported by Joey and Carol Low; it is dedicated to Edward and Hannah Low, and Marcel and Mignon Lorie, children during the Second World War, who, despite all their personal travails, managed to build large families who are devoted to the well-being of Israel and the Jewish people.

In memory of my beloved father,
always my helping spirit.

CONTENTS

PART ONE

Grand Island 1

PART TWO

Ararat 113

PART THREE

Isra Isle 167

Always in your mind keep Ithaca.
To arrive there is your destiny.
But do not hurry your trip in any way.
Better that it last for many years;
that you drop anchor at the island an old man,
rich with all you've gotten on the way . . .

—Constantine Cavafy, from "Ithaca"
Translated by Daniel Mendelsohn

PART ONE

Grand Island

SEPTEMBER 2001

WITHOUT A trace.

Every missing person notice ends with this succinct phrase that is part desperation, part acceptance of an extraordinary event.

Like an actor in rehearsals, Simon T. Lenox recites the inevitable next line: "As if he was swallowed up by the earth." His face adopts an expression his ex-wives all perceived as a highly effective weapon because it perfectly disguised his intentions.

The earth only swallows up dead people, Lenox scribbles in his notepad, *but man swallows up himself.* He rips the page out and shoots it into the wastepaper basket. He will have to tell the commissioner to give the case to someone else. He has no intention of wearing himself out on a wild-goose chase for some Israeli gone missing in America. Not at his age. Not in his position.

Still holding the pad, he can't help catching the missing man's photograph out of the corner of his eye. He instantly imprints the Israeli's image in his memory—an aptitude he was born with, or perhaps acquired during his many years of hunting people down. The man's eyes are narrowed; he looks startled by the sudden camera flash. His hair is neatly trimmed except for a few stray locks that might have grown back too quickly. He has a square, rigid chin and sunken cheeks. He gives off a faint whiff of defiance. A man of Lenox's own age, more or less, looking formal. No special markings.

When Lenox holds the page up, he notices a stain above the NYPD commissioner's handwriting: "Urgent! Special request from State Dept."

If only he could shred the piece of paper into tiny scraps, including the trite phrase "without a trace." How futile to search for people the earth has swallowed up, leaving nothing behind for their loved ones except the uncertainty of their death. He's not going to bear this weight on his shoulders. The home-grown cases are bad enough—now he's supposed to worry about the Israelis, too? Fuck the Israelis.

HIS PROTESTS are met with indifference in the commissioner's office. Simon T. Lenox pounds his fist on the desk hard enough to make his notepad jump. His colleagues peer out from behind their partitions. There's nothing new about a confrontation between Lenox and the commissioner, but such violent outbursts are rare. Some colleagues have been recommending early retirement, and there is persistent gossip about the celebrated investigator who has lost his magic touch.

What is so special about this Israeli man that makes the United States government want to find him? Has he committed a crime?

The commissioner shakes his head.

Then why is he wanted? Is he going to be extradited to Israel?

No.

Perhaps he is privy to top secrets that can't be allowed out? Or is he working for a hostile entity?

The commissioner doesn't bother to reply.

Might the Israeli be an embarrassment to his country, or a threat to US security? Because if all he is liable to do is hurt himself, then that is none of their fucking business.

Once the shouting stops, the commissioner makes sure the door is closed.

It's a delicate matter, Lenox. I need an expert on this case. We have our reasons.

But Simon T. Lenox does not walk into the flattery trap, or the duty one: You can send someone else. And anyway, an Israeli is a case for Immigration.

The commissioner insists: We're just following orders from above. We've annexed you to the Secret Service. They have all the materials on Israel. And if you crack this case . . .

Then what? Israel will give me a medal? Thanks, but no thanks. Who needs honors from a foreign country?

Forced to accept the commissioner's decision, Simon T. Lenox is swiftly vacated from his office and resettled in another office on the eighty-fourth floor of the North Tower of the World Trade Center—stuck in a place where he doesn't belong, struggling to tamp down his anger. He has better conditions here, ample space—an office designed to win him over, furnished with an executive leather chair and a state-of-the-art laptop. But all these props serve only to underscore how foreign he is in this new domain. Where are the incoming and outgoing mail trays? Where is the picture on the wall commemorating the much-publicized arrest of a suspect who was caught only because Lenox recognized her perfume? And what about the framed letters of appreciation, and his target-practice outfit, and his tailored suit on a hanger for when he is unexpectedly summoned to testify in court?

Who wants an obscure case and someone watching over your shoulder?

Simon T. Lenox stares at the partitions. Outside, the windows are drizzling: 43,600 tearful glass eyes. Inside, the phones are ringing. Crimes and misdemeanors occur constantly. In recent years he has lost something of the hunger, the joy of the hunt. Even when he solves a case, he does not feel the elation anymore. Back in the day, he used to finish off two bottles of Jack Daniels to celebrate a closed case.

At his age. In his position. He's seen it all and heard it all. Nothing can surprise him. Not even foreigners who go missing in a country that isn't theirs.

Without a trace. A phrase meticulously designed to mask the grief. As it should.

The place may be foreign, but the notepad is familiar. Simon T. Lenox pulls himself together and starts to write:

> To: Brig. Gen. Yoav Rosen-Vardi, Israel Police Attaché
> to the United States, Washington, DC
>
> I was requested by my supervisors to investigate, on behalf of the State of Israel, the disappearance of Mr. Liam Emanuel, and have happily accepted the assignment.
>
> Incidentally, does the subject not have a middle name, as is usually the custom with us?
>
> I hope to be able to locate the subject. I am honored to serve a true friend of the United States.
>
> Yours sincerely,
> Simon T. Lenox, Chief Inspector
> Senior Investigator, Missing Persons
> Annexed to the Secret Service
>
> PS Kindly forward the affidavits you collected in Israel, as well as any relevant materials I may require during my investigation.

THE LAST person who saw him was the flight attendant on the red-eye from Tel-Aviv to JFK. She remembered the subject only because he shut himself in the bathroom for an unreasonably long time. She was about to break in, but then he suddenly emerged, seeming calm, and asked her whether she knew Yuri Gagarin. The flight attendant assumed he was suffering from some kind of mental disturbance. She'd once caught a couple going at it in the bathroom, and another time there was a man who had a stroke on a flight.

Transatlantic sex. Simon T. Lenox leans back in his executive leather chair and holds his notepad to his chest. This case might turn out to be more interesting than he'd expected.

Opening scene in a play: A man bursts out of a tiny cabin and fishes out from some hidden level of consciousness the name of the first man who broke through the gravity barrier. Did the Russian cosmonaut suffer from space sickness? That is what the missing man asked the flight attendant. Or was he troubled, during that single orbit around Earth, by his bladder? He was finally free, the son of a bitch—Columbus of the cosmos. That was what he said to her.

She was convinced he had lost his mind. Would you like a valium? she asked, and picked up the internal phone to the cockpit.

The passenger said: What a shit job, babysitting three hundred people on a jumbo jet who'll do anything to hide their terror of death.

Ever since that day, every time she demonstrates the emergency procedures before takeoff, the flight attendant remembers that passenger. She straps on the inflatable life jacket, pulls down the oxygen mask with the dangling tubes, and his defiant face jumps up at her. Unshaven. Fresh stubble. She remembers the stubble clearly.

Did the passenger appear frightened? Might he have gone into the bathroom to cry?

No. Flight attendants are adept at spotting tears. There are people who lose their equilibrium when the rug of solid ground is pulled out from under them, she told the investigator in Israel. Simon T. Lenox presumes something of that shock, the shock of the earth falling away, afflicted her as well.

The subject pointed at the darkness swaddling the plane and asked: How do pilots learn how to control their bladder?

The flight attendant thought he was joking.

What made her ask if he was going on a secret mission?

The subject kept on about Yuri Gagarin. What had the Russian cosmonaut taken with him on Vostok 1? he wanted to know. He had the placid voice of a curious boy holding back his teacher after class. The choice of objects, he continued, must have been made with the clear knowledge that if he never came back, neither would they.

The flight attendant lost her patience and instructed the passenger to return to his seat immediately and fasten his seatbelt.

Yuri Gagarin? Who the hell is that, anyway? Lenox has trouble deciphering whether she had spat out that question at the bothersome passenger, or at the investigator. He sighs, suddenly aware of his age, albeit not of his position.

In the end he crashed. Three years after the daring spaceflight, the cosmonaut met his death in a foolish jet accident. This fact was not recorded in the affidavit from Israel, but Lenox scribbles it in his notepad as a footnote.

A possible destination for the subject: Houston, Texas: the NASA Space Center.

Only then does he allow himself to relax into the soft leather chair.

THE NYPD website lists dozens of missing people. Simon T. Lenox knows each of them by name, as well as their families, acquaintances, and enemies.

If he himself were to suddenly disappear, who would notify the authorities?

Such contemplations are best quashed early on. Self-pity is a luxury, and personal involvement only sabotages an investigation. He will do what is required, no more. He doesn't owe the Israelis anything. He doesn't even know any Israelis, except the ones he sees on television. CNN. Breaking news! They occupied us! We occupied them! They killed us, they're killing us, they'll kill us! He has no interest in the endless Middle Eastern blood cycle. Troubling the whole world with their problems for over a century already. Whenever Israel's name comes up, he quickly flicks over to the nature channel. A river beaver building a dam. The white-tailed deer's mating habits. Those are the only scenes that can lull him to sleep.

Yet here he is, with a missing Israeli.

Israelis are a type of Jews, aren't they? What kind of Jews are they?

The FBI's central computing system aggregates data about missing people from all law-enforcement authorities. Innocent and less-innocent people who walked out one fine day from their homes and never returned. Lenox, unwillingly, has become an expert—a dubious title, since he has failed to get most of his subjects home in time, or in one piece.

Since the last time he logged into the site, three bodies have been found, among them that of a six-year-old girl who was murdered with her mother by the mother's boyfriend, in a motel near Albany. He killed them both with an axe. A particularly horrific case, if there is even any reasonable way to rank such horrors. Lenox remembers being notified about the disappearance of the woman and her child, who'd gone to spend the afternoon in the park. He remembers trying to get the neighbor woman to talk on the phone, but all she could do was shriek at him. The girl and her mother had no one else in the world.

Now Lenox wonders who attended the double funeral.

The hardest moment is facing the person who comes to notify the police about a disappearance. Although it is a fairly consistent scenario, variations on the same scenes and events, Lenox has still not managed to build up adequate barriers between himself and the grief. At first they shut themselves up at home and wait for news of any sort, even the news of death. Then come the phone calls in the middle of the night, when Lenox pretends to be encouraging, murmuring hollow clichés pulled from his reservoir. And of course the despair, a companion that grows more and more constant as time goes by. Even when the notifiers stop visiting the police station hoping for information, Simon T. Lenox can't stop seeing their eyes. They are nailed to his consciousness, as though he holds the key to these people's happiness or calamity. When he tries to fall asleep, he is pierced by that gnawing longing in the loved ones' pupils. He will be spared of all that with this case, thank God, because the State of Israel has no eyes.

Most of the missing people eventually turn out to be dead, as Lenox informs the department rookies year after year. He warns them to prepare for the moment of identification by arming themselves with any defense mechanisms they can muster to prevent the outbursts of pain and compassion. Above all he loathes the "floaters," the ones spat out by the ocean and the rivers, whose faces have been washed clear of any human expression. The first time he had to identify a floater, he puked his guts out. He's built up immunity since them, although the thought of the Israeli's face sends shockwaves through his body nonetheless.

This is his twenty-eighth missing person. Why does he count them, categorize them, and shuffle them?

His first Israeli. He was preceded by the Irishman who

jumped off Mount Rushmore, the seventy-year-old Greek who left his wife, children, and grandchildren and ran off to Reno where he married a seventeen-year-old waitress, and the New Zealander who just forgot to call home. Who came first? Lenox can't remember.

And the Israeli?

Without a trace.

THIS ISN'T my Israeli.

It's not anyone's Israeli.

Simon T. Lenox wakes up in the middle of the night. If he dreamed, the dreams are gone. He stands over the toilet but the urine takes its time. The pressure cuts through his groin. Like a tomahawk strike.

Fuck the Israeli.

THE SALESWOMAN at the Duty Free shop in Ben-Gurion Airport also recognized the missing man. Her affidavit was taken in her native Russian.

A tiresome business, the medley of foreign languages in the Middle East. Lenox is planning to ask for overtime because of this case. Had he been present at the interrogations, he would have monitored the witnesses' body language, all the hidden signals that reveal what they themselves do not even know is important information.

Did the subject bother the saleswoman about Yuri Gagarin, too? Lenox skims the affidavit wearily, disappointed to find no mention of the Russian cosmonaut. But since the encounter preceded the incident with the flight attendant, it is possible that it was the saleswoman's Russian accent that jogged the subject's memory with Vostok 1.

What language did they talk in?

Hebrew.

Lenox is impressed by the young Russian woman's quick mastery of a new language.

She is a “New *Olah*”—the Hebrew term is noted in the margin. Lenox will have to find out what that means. Why not just “immigrant”?

A deceptive language, Hebrew.

Moving on.

The subject purchased a pair of sneakers at the Duty Free, and made a point of confirming that they were waterproof. The soles would have to withstand a slippery surface, he explained to the saleswoman. But the sneakers weren’t the reason Valentina remembered him. The pair he chose was simple and unembellished, although she tried to talk him into getting a newer model, with air cushions.

Valentina. The name flashes through Lenox’s mind—distant thunder—and he circles it.

The subject told her that if she had immigrated to Israel thirty years ago, they would have made her change her name to Vardina or Adina.

Why? Lenox wonders. The Israeli investigator had not bothered to explain.

It was the boarding pass that made the subject stick in Valentina’s memory. He was clutching it the whole time, and inadvertently tore the stub off.

A façade of serenity, Lenox notes, and looks at the photograph again.

The man paid in cash, dollars. He put the new sneakers on at the store and left his old pair by the checkout counter. When the final boarding call for flight 001 to New York came over the speakers, Valentina found the boarding pass stub sticking out of one of the customer’s old shoes. At first she thought it was a note, and she had a moment of doubt: opening strangers’ letters was a rude invasion of privacy, and she was a well-bred young woman from Saint Petersburg.

Did you abandon your post? asked the Israeli interrogator.

Simon T. Lenox hopes Valentina wasn't fired.

She ran to Gate 3 and found her customer holding up the line with a long trail of grumbling passengers behind him. She was so excited that she had trouble explaining to the flight attendant what had happened. All that came out of her mouth was Russian. The flight attendant was furious. At first she refused to match the two parts of the pass, but finally she inserted the stub in the machine and scolded the passenger.

Did the man thank Valentina? Without her, after all, he would not have been able to get on his flight. Or perhaps he had changed his mind? Was this a desperate attempt to sabotage his own disappearance?

In the document faxed from Israel, the silences are not recorded. Lenox is convinced that Valentina paused for several seconds before answering. Either way, the text is blurred and he cannot decipher her reply.

OLD-FASHIONED SNEAKERS. It's doubtful that is what Yuri Gagarin would have chosen to take on Vostok 1 for his voyage beyond gravity.

Sipping his third Jack Daniels later that night, from a bottle whose label reads, "Every day we make it, we'll make it the best we can," Lenox scans his apartment and cannot find a single object so precious that he would be unwilling to part with it. Even his notepad is replaceable. What's already written is less important than what has yet to be written.

The glass in his hand is cool. A cheap tumbler—he bought three of them at the drugstore across the street after his third wife left with the entire contents of the apartment.

If he were going on a voyage beyond gravity, all he'd take would be a bottle of Jack, so he could have a few sips while he watched the bluish-green ball from above. A once-in-a-lifetime opportunity to piss on everyone.

The pain in his groin again.

Israel is so small that you can barely see it from outer space.

Fuck Israel.

Irritating raindrops tap on the window, but even the drizzle doesn't open up his bladder.

HE NEVER files his notepads. He promised the commissioner that on the day he retired he would box them up in sequential order and deposit them at the archive. Behind his back people make fun of his techniques. He always starts by collecting testimonies in reverse chronological order—going back in time—and then he examines each one discretely, as if they did not form a series of events in one person's life. Simon T. Lenox believes that every human encounter is an autonomous event, a closed circuit, which can only be assigned meaning when it is over, in the light of previous events.

The theory of traces.

There are those who believe he inherited the approach from his Native American forefathers, but Lenox dismisses this idea out of hand. His wife—the second one, if he recalls correctly—claimed he was the reincarnation of a coyote: he could smell blood. But she said that during a vicious fight, shortly before hurling every glass in the kitchen at him.

This won't be a complicated case. The sloppy Israeli will leave plenty of tracks. After all, he left his old shoes at the Duty Free, and even forgot his boarding pass stub. He'll be easy to find.

Or his remains will.

Everything points to a spontaneous, unplanned decision. A rebellious kid playing hooky.

This is the first conclusion Lenox presents to the commissioner, and he doesn't bother trying to disguise his smugness.

LENOX IS under pressure. Nothing is spoken outright, but he picks up whispers from behind closed doors. Someone from the Israeli Embassy in DC calls to find out if there's any progress on the case. They don't want anyone talking, otherwise the subject will find out they're tailing him. And as soon as the press smells any blood . . .

Impatient fucking Israelis. Convinced they have the whole world eating out of their hand. If their missing man is in danger, why don't they say so clearly and name their suspects? Keeping their dirty little secrets to themselves.

But the commissioner is on edge. He is also being pressured to report up the chain of command. Hit the road, Lenox. Don't bury yourself in paperwork. Fill in the details as you go along.

But Lenox has yet to read the Israeli's résumé, a series of dry data he intentionally leaves for last, burying the subject's official curriculum vitae at the bottom of the pile. When he entered the US, he wrote "business trip" on his arrival form. His handwriting is clear and his English seems fluent. No signs of anxiety. The immigration authorities report that his passport is valid. Everything seems to be in order. And yet . . . Doesn't a man have the right to shake his life off? Like a dog getting rid of a tick?

Perhaps the Israeli was in debt. Statements from three Israeli banks attest that he had emptied his accounts out, one after the other, shortly before the flight. He mailed his life insurance policy to a post office box in Jerusalem. There is not a casino in the world that will not roll out the red carpet for him.

Lenox makes a note: "Possible destination: Las Vegas." He looks at the window. The rain on the eighty-fourth floor of the North Tower is puny, or perhaps the drops have not gained enough velocity at this height. The window-cleaning machine is operating. The windows are smaller than the standard size, to prevent the tower from becoming a heat trap. Despite the downpour, the cleaner has not deactivated the washer.

Idiot, Lenox thinks. It's pointless. Perhaps the window washer also keeps a precious object with him as a memento? If he ever gave any thought to the abyss gaping below him, he'd quit immediately.

Idiot. Or a hopeless optimist.

Lenox devotes another second of thought to the cleaner and plunges into the next document.

WHAT CAME before what came before? Some people in the department dispute the unique investigation method Lenox has developed. "Shuffling the deck," they call it. Why not go about things sequentially? Examine the testimonies chronologically until you get to the intersection at which things went either this way or that? But Simon T. Lenox prefers to chronicle events before they occur. To him, going backwards is the most logical direction. Putting toe to heel is not a regression, because it allows him to uncover the clues from which the future actions of the subject will derive. In previous cases Lenox has been able to predict the subjects' destinations fairly accurately, and then he can lie in wait for his prey a step or two ahead—this on the basis of a cluster of clues gathered retroactively. It's not prognostication. It's not exactly science. Just a simple human talent that he has refined over time.

How unfortunate that his methods are not widely adopted—going backwards while facing forwards. The only steps Lenox seems unable to predict are his own. When he tries to chart the various branches of his life, whether by following the conventional theory of traces or using his own variation, he cannot reconstruct what came before what came before.

Sometimes he thinks his third wife left him before his second one did.

IN THE middle of the night, Simon T. Lenox sits up in bed and looks at the numbers glowing on the clock. Sleep has left him, and he lies there gazing at a drizzling Manhattan—Eighty-Seventh Street and Third Avenue—and thinks about suitcases. He pads over to the bathroom and squeezes a few drops out into the toilet.

If his wife had seen him remember to lift the seat and put it down again, she might not have left. Was that the second one or the third one? They all used to complain.

He pours the remaining Jack Daniels into the toilet, hoping the stream will awaken his bladder.

VALENTINA.

With his boxers still halfway down his legs, Simon T. Lenox bounds out of the bathroom to his computer. It's getting light. Downstairs they're collecting the trash. Black plastic bags piled outside the main doors.

Like bodies. That's what one of his wives used to say. The one who got up early.

Soft pecking sounds emerge from his computer as it connects to the network. Sometimes he feels as though he himself is a search engine.

Valentina Vladimirovna Tereshkova. A Russian cosmonaut aboard Vostok 6. The first woman in space. How many times did she orbit Earth?

Lenox thinks he's starting to get the Israeli mindset. He goes back into the bathroom and purposely dribbles on the toilet seat.

THE MISSING man had something else to say to the flight attendant when he came out of the bathroom: he complained about the faucets.

It's a crazy system. Either your hands freeze or they get scalded, and you waste a lot of time trying to reach a lukewarm compromise. Not only that, but passengers are requested to wipe away the grayish residue in the bottom of the miniature sink, "In consideration of your fellow passengers."

Simon T. Lenox highlights that paragraph in the affidavit with bright yellow.

A LUGGAGE carousel slowly revolves in his mind. He peers into his bedroom closet and takes out a small suitcase, then tosses in a pair of socks and a shaving razor. None of his wives were very good at packing. He would always find something missing and have to stop in some godforsaken town to buy underwear or a toothbrush.

The suitcase gapes at the foot of the bed like a mouth with its false teeth removed, and he kicks it shut and shoves it into the dusty darkness under the bed. He's not going to set off without finding out his destination.

Not at his age. Not in his position.

Outside, in the rain, he realizes he's forgotten an umbrella.

THE COMPLAINTS from Israel soon land on the commissioner's desk: Why is your detective wasting our time with trivialities? What difference does it make which kind of suitcase the man used? What matters is what was inside it!

Lenox yells at the commissioner: What is up with these Israelis always being in a hurry? Why are they demanding results before they've even lifted a finger? They're asking us to guarantee that some crazy theory they've concocted will turn out to be true. They should be grateful we're helping them at all and shut up. We're doing their dirty work and they sit there in their bloody Middle East and have the gall to complain.

The commissioner cuts him off. Listen to me carefully, Lenox. This is a mutual obligation, at least as long as our interests are aligned. And you're the one who should be thanking me, because I'm the dam holding back the pressure from upstairs. A Republican congressman from Indiana has already intervened. What's going on with your Israeli, Lenox? What is he up to? Where is he headed?

When Lenox demands once again to know why he is being asked to turn over every stone for this Israeli, the commissioner blurts: Maybe they count them over in Israel, like a herd of buffalo.

HE CAREFULLY copies the inventory faxed by the Israelis into his notepad:

> One faded brown leather suitcase full of old records. One zipper torn, the other rusted. The strap used to tie it is on the bathroom floor.
>
> One gray Samsonite. The inner pocket contains an old Hebrew-English pocket dictionary. One wheel broken. A ten-year warranty affixed to the side.
>
> One gym bag with a Los Angeles Olympics logo. In the side pocket is a ticket for the javelin throw finals.
>
> One empty cosmetics case.
>
> One military duffle bag. At the bottom, two cheap towels and a pair of khaki underwear.
>
> One red suitcase with every zipper torn. Inside are gas masks, twenty rolls of adhesive tape, and a package of rubber gloves in various sizes.

SIMON T. Lenox sends an urgent fax to the Israeli Embassy. When no reply is forthcoming, he sends another. That evening he is informed about the emergency kit that every Israeli citizen has been required to possess since the Gulf War. Every so often the kits are "refreshed." They must be joking, Lenox remarks to the commissioner. But the Israelis didn't trust their authorities, so they added a few of their own items to the official survival kit: a rag soaked in bleach and baking soda, rubber gloves, and muck boots. If the Iraqis invade, they'll assume the Israelis are busy washing dishes and cleaning bathrooms.

At first the police thought the house had been burgled because there was such a mess. Closet doors and drawers were open, the floor was strewn with belongings, the toilet was clogged and dirty water had flooded the bathroom. But there was a row of suitcases and bags lined up underneath the opening to the *boydem*. Another unfamiliar term in this document stamped "State of Israel." Lenox circles it and scribbles a question mark. Then he says it out loud to make sure he hasn't missed something in the pronunciation. Could they have meant *Boy Damn*? But what would that mean?

He'll end up having to go see Jackie Brendel, the woman known in the Secret Service as "the Jewish Question." But he's worried he might hurt her feelings and get a complaint filed against him. That's all he needs, just before early retirement.

My luggage inheritance, said the son who was brought in from Jerusalem by the police to identify the apartment contents.

So the missing man has a son.

But he wasn't the one who notified the police about the disappearance.

AT EVERY stage of the investigation, Simon T. Lenox calls

up images and attempts to construct a scaffolding of the missing person's drama.

The Israeli stands in his bedroom with its entire contents scattered around him, and looks at the containers in which his life has been repeatedly packed and unpacked. In his mind's eye Lenox sees the Israeli untie the suitcase strap, kneel down, and rummage through the collection of LPs he couldn't bring himself to throw out. *The White Album*, *Dark Side of the Moon*. The mementos he chose to take with him might shed some light on his mood before disappearing. And how fortunate that vinyl is back in fashion—Lenox will advise the Israeli to sell the collection for a handsome profit.

He must have an interest in sports, since he traveled to the Olympics. But why did he choose a marginal sport like the javelin throw?

Lenox goes back to the photograph. The Israeli's shoulders are hunched; he does not look particularly athletic. Lenox envisions a javelin floating through the air toward the rainy horizon.

Gravity. An important detail—or perhaps a dead end.

WHAT DOES he have so far?

Yuri Gagarin. A one-way plane ticket. A torn stub. Sneakers. Nonskid soles. Valentina. A pair of faucets in an airplane bathroom. The Vostok spacecraft. Gas masks. A javelin.

There is also a large backpack, the kind favored by serious hikers. That is the item missing from the luggage inheritance, according to the son.

Lenox does not have any children.

HE GATHERS the traces carefully, like precious relics. As the assembly floats around his mind, he has trouble separating the shards of information and ranking them by importance. He has learned to wait patiently for the collision that will direct him to the start of the route, with the understanding that even the slightest random detour could throw him off course.

Don't give up, Simon T. Some clarity has to emerge from all this. When archeologists gently blow the dirt off their findings, they take into account that the wind might scatter a few blinding particles into their eyes.

Lenox contacts the sneaker manufacturer and asks for samples of nonskid soles. He wastes an hour on futile lines of questioning until he finally identifies the right model.

Sir, why are you so insistent on finding an outdated pair? This model was discontinued long ago. But Simon T. Lenox does not give in, going from one store to another until he can top his stack of documents with an imprint of the sole.

The eighty-forth floor of the North Tower is empty. Everyone has gone home, except the officer on duty. Lenox sips mineral water from a bottle he found in the hallway and scolds himself for being too cowardly to smuggle a bottle of Jack Daniels into the office.

The Israeli has not checked in to any hotel in New York, nor has anyone matching his description rented a vehicle in the last few days. Lenox marks the items still needing clarification, and uncomfortably shifts the papers around, right to left, right to left. The pen hovers, and his hand is tempted to write his name backwards, the way it would be written in Hebrew. His letters come out crooked, clumsy, like a child learning to write.

What made those people in the Middle East choose right-to-left for their alphabet? What kind of Jews are these Israelis?

Jackie Brendel will know, but who wants to get mixed up with the Jewish Question?

He packs up the documents and puts his raincoat on. At

the liquor store near the subway he buys a fresh supply of Jack Daniels. His hands fondle the bottles and the papers.

His bladder has calmed down. For now.

Every detective insists that there is a tendril binding all the clues together, and even if it is merely the product of their contemplations, they spread out the net and do anything they can to declare that they have fished out a meaning.

But Lenox believes that the clues he gathers enable him to track the human mind while it is still bubbling, zigzagging among the fragments of its past and future acts. Lenox walks softly through the thicket, stealthily approaching the unknown land, an estate anyone can claim. He patiently awaits the right explanation, the one and only possibility—yet he does not reject all the others.

He falls asleep at the kitchen table, covered with a mound of clues.

Someone is throwing water in your face, Simon T. It's washing away the traces. How will you find the way to the island, White Raven?

When Lenox wakes himself, he finds his clothes drenched. For a moment he thinks he has wet himself like a baby, but it's only sweat.

He plunges onto his bed, his whole body aching from the javelins.

Visions.

His grandmother claimed they were flashes of the past or the future, encoded messages sent by the spirits. Unexpected images that come in dreams or hallucinations, during sickness or intoxication.

Perhaps that was the old woman's way of justifying

Lenox's weakness for Jack Daniels. When he once shared a vision with her, she was ecstatic. First she celebrated the fact that her grandson, the man who had left the reservation without looking back and studied in the finest white institutes of education, was still graced with hidden powers. She viewed this as decisive proof that the river of time cannot sweep away ancient gifts.

But the visions contradict Lenox's perception of himself as a rational, measured, reasoned man. At first he thought he might have "Korsakoff's syndrome," which makes people confabulate to compensate for their memory loss. Then he concluded it was a by-product of his overworked brain.

Is the event that occurred the complete opposite of the event that did not occur?

That's a crock of shit, said the old woman.

As a last resort, he tried to explain to his grandmother how computer games work, but she dismissed him with a wave of the hand.

The earth is the same earth, White Raven; it is only the people who are different. Or at least they appear to be. And when the presence of prior incarnations is denied . . .

She sounded like a New Age preacher.

And don't use my Indian name, he told her. Definitely not in public. They'll come looking for my feathers and tomahawk.

JACKIE BRENDEL is reticent when people ask about her religion. It underscores the fact that she is the only Jew on the eighty-fourth floor of the North Tower. Lenox understands her. He also gets angry when his investigative talents are attributed to the heritage passed down from his forefathers.

The Jewish Question works as an accountant for the Secret Service. A busy bee, she sits hunched over her desk for long hours, surrounded by numbers and only rarely taking breaks. Her hair is dyed auburn. She has twice been named Most Valuable Employee.

Hey, Lenox, have you heard the latest one?

Lenox smiles.

What's an anti-Semite?

Someone who hates Jews just a little more than necessary.

And what's an Israeli?

Someone you can hate a little more than a Jew.

Lenox laughs. Of course he does.

Except for the occasional hello, they have never spoken. He ran into her twice at the coffee station where she was pouring muddy liquid out of the carafe very slowly, as if calculating how much she could take before being obliged to make a fresh pot for the other employees.

Lenox tries to catch her in the hallways, but she always slips away. Finally, he sends her an e-mail:

Dear Ms. Brendel,

I have willingly accepted a request from the State of Israel to help locate an Israeli citizen who entered the US legally and has not been seen since.

I would be very grateful if you would be kind enough to answer a few of my questions related to your people.

Yours sincerely,
Chief Inspector Simon T. Lenox
Senior Investigator, Missing Persons,
New York Police Department
Annexed to the Secret Service

From Lenox's notepad:

> After condensing the clues, what is left?
>
> A Russian female cosmonaut. Duty Free. Night flight. Military duffle bag. Khaki underwear. *Boydem Dark Side of the Moon.* Hiking backpack. Javelin.

EVERY TIME he writes down a group of clues, the javelin annoyingly reappears.

IN THE second stage of his investigation, Lenox always experiences distress at the prospect of invading a stranger's private domain, probing the miniscule habits and daily routines of a man he has no intimate connection with. Only later does he become aware of the percolating pleasure, the joy of voyeurism. To cleanse his conscience, Lenox pretends the subject is a fictional character whom he will never encounter face to face. But for some reason, this case does not surrender to the familiar pattern. No distress. No conscience. Not even any pleasure.

Lenox is suspended in a physical state somewhere between gas and liquid, while his feelers work hard to capture the true nature of the man he is looking for—the bone marrow that quivers inside the rigid formal uniform worn by a person when he goes out into the world. His offenses, the ways he repays those who mistreat him and sometimes spurns those who favor him. The strategies he employs to climb up the ladder. The fine threads of deceit, the fawning before supervisors, the deposit of resentments that amass into an impenetrable stratum.

Lenox is a lightening rod for weaknesses.

The nose pickers, the ball scratchers, the zit poppers, the hair pullers, the nail biters. The ones who hit, the ones who ogle at young girls, the child rapists, the incestuous. He has exposed them all during his career. A river of Jack Daniels has flowed through the NYPD hallways.

Does the Israeli remember to put up the seat when he pees?

Lenox writes the question in his notepad.

Jackie Brendel does not write back. Lenox stands at his computer angrily and types:

Dear Ms. Brendel,

In using the term "your people," I had no intention of casting doubts, heaven forbid, on your absolute loyalty to our country.

Yours,
S. T. L.

Simon T. Lenox has always been able to figure out the reason for a person going missing early on in his investigation. The spectrum of human motives is fairly limited: jealousy, narrow-mindedness, revenge, fear. None of these fit this case.

Assuming the Israelis are not keeping some essential piece of information from him, the subject has no enemies, no debts, no criminal involvement; he is not a foreign agent, not under the influence of medications, not depressed, and not suicidal.

Not, not, not.

But there must be something that he *is*.

The questions melt in Lenox's boiling brain. He can barely observe his own condition.

Perhaps, unwittingly, Lenox is not conducting a search but a hunt. His request to publish the missing man's picture in the press and put him on the front page of the missing persons' site was met with firm refusal from the commissioner. As was the suggestion to offer a monetary reward for information. If only he knew why this Israeli was not being treated like other missing persons.

They look out at him from the website, rows and rows of faces. An innocent web surfer would think he'd come across a family photo album. Their digital eyes flicker on the screen. No desperation or pleading. Those are reserved for the circle of loved ones waiting in torment. Lenox does not bother to ask for updates anymore.

Which of these people will never be found?

IF THERE is a son—that must mean there was a wife.

A wife, however, is no guarantee of sons.

Lenox's second wife told him: You don't deserve it. His third wife blamed his faulty sperm. And the first wife? What, if anything, did she say?

Dear Inspector Lenox,

I have never been to Israel, and not all citizens of the state are Jewish.

Respectfully,
Jacqueline Winona Brendel
Chief Accountant, Secret Service

ALTHOUGH HE could easily look online, Simon T. Lenox chooses to open up an atlas he finds in the Secret Service storeroom, where they pile up the books no one uses anymore.

The atlas is dusty. Hasn't been opened for years. Outdated geographical boundaries stretch over the pages' inner hinge, which is as loose as the perforation on a boarding pass. Lenox's forefathers used to winter in one area and relocate in summer. Yet they viewed themselves not as nomads, but as dwellers of everyland.

Israel fits under his pinky finger. He swipes at the image

as though it were a spill and instinctively licks his finger, expecting to taste blood.

His fingers start to walk. He surrounds the sea, passes wearily over Europe, plods through Asia, crosses the Bering Strait with two fingers, and goes down from Canada to the US border.

On a whim, he calls an outdoor gear store and gives them a description of the Israeli.

The young woman laughs: Have you lost your mind? Do you have any idea how many nature buffs we get in here?

Lenox insists. He can fax a photograph over—maybe someone will remember.

He hears her mutter: Some asshole is posing as a cop. She hangs up.

Simon T. Lenox's fingers are still on the map. America is between his thumb and his pinky, and the continent sprawls beyond his hand.

The fax chatters and spits out another affidavit. Lenox reaches for it with one hand while his pinky finger remains in the atlas, blindly probing for the estimated location of Israel.

I HAVEN'T seen Dad since my grandfather's funeral.

That is what the missing man's son said.

And it hasn't occurred to the fucking Israelis to tell him this until now?! What were they thinking? Are they trying to manipulate an American detective the way they maneuver the whole world? Lenox refuses to be their pawn. He'll close the case and be done with it. They can go find their lost son themselves.

He hurls the atlas onto the windowsill. The drops outside tremble from the impact, but quickly resume their course.

Fuck you, Isra—

He sips his Jack Daniels and slowly calms down.

Orphanhood.

The javelin that slowly slices, scalping away the last remaining trace of childhood.

Here is a logical explanation: the Israeli is removing his grieving self from his familiar environment. He is going far away, somewhere where he will not be consoled, where no one will sympathize and pat his shoulder and utter clichés about having to be strong and how the show must go on.

Lenox's grandmother said: The dead are always following you. Indians are excellent trackers in their next lives, too.

He corrected her: in their deaths.

He had cultivated his characteristic expression when he was a child, and it really was a very effective way to disguise intent. Lenox even insulted his grandmother under the guise of politeness. Folklore is a business for old ladies on the reservation, not for a citizen of the New World. We've crossed into the next millennium, and despite all the fanciful prophecies of doom, the world continues to suffer the usual calamities. The same endless bickering. Always us against them. Yawn.

And the world record goes to the Israelis. Addicted to their tedious quarrel. They and their neighbors were offered a chance to put down their weapons, but they missed it.

Fuck them all.

Before the police arrived, the missing man's son assumed his father had shut himself away in his home for the duration of the bereavement period. The discovery that he had left the country without observing the custom of *shiva* horrified him. He found it hard to believe that his father could trample Jewish tradition so crudely. He accused the police detective of provocation, and the poor man had to swear on his children's lives that the father had really left Israel the night after the funeral. The son made a point of noting how sacred he himself held the customs, and talked emotionally of how he had gathered his friends from the *yeshiva* in Jerusalem to say prayers for his late grandfather's soul.

If a person dies without leaving enough relatives, the newly religious grandson explained to the secular investigators, people could be paid to say Kaddish over him.

Lenox scatters question marks over the document: *shiva*, *Kaddish*—terms vaguely familiar to any New Yorker, but what is their significance for members of the map-stain nation?

The son had called his father a few times after the funeral, but naïvely assumed he had disconnected his phone for the mourning period. As a rule, they did not speak often. Ever since he became a *ba'al teshuva*.

The Israelis haven't bothered to explain this term either, and Lennox circles it.

He's given up on Jackie Brendel. What is that Jewish woman afraid of? That he'll plunder her precious faith? Why would anyone want to join up with the Jews anyway? Chosen people my ass.

At that very moment, a note is slipped under the door. Simon T. Lenox is in no rush to pick it up, feeling tired and troubled by his bladder.

Dear Inspector Lenox,

All Jews are responsible for one another.

Yours,
Jackie Winona Brendel

He sits there pondering, rolling the bottle between his hands without taking a drink.

Does this mean they have some sort of fraternity? Or

has Israel become a closed enclave where no stranger can set foot? What is it about this map-stain nation that has it ruffling feathers all over the world for more than half a century? Other states barely get a mention on the evening news, even when they are the sites of massacres. Maybe the Jews themselves are not yet accustomed to having their own sovereign entity, and they're still trying to lodge it in the world's consciousness.

Lenox puts off a trip to the bathroom. His bladder is ringing false alarms anyway.

THE SON felt that his father wanted to be left alone at the cemetery, and he recalled watching him hunch over the grave, his pants cuffs getting dirty.

There is nothing odd about that. Every person has his or her own way of saying good-bye.

The missing man placed small stones on the dry clods of earth while his son stood nearby, hidden from view, watching as his father demonstratively removed his yarmulke and put it in his pocket. The last of the mourners had left and the son lingered, swallowed his pride, and approached his father. He wanted to get through to him.

Dad, he who does not obey the ancient laws will be punished.

Stop reciting slogans, son, the man replied. Look at us. I'm the older one—running ahead, and you, the younger one—you're going in the opposite direction.

Unable to avoid a graveside argument, the son declared that the Jewish faith was eternal and had no backwards or forwards.

Something seems to be clearing in Lenox's mind.

The father said: I feel sorry for you, my child.

Child. As if he had not been through his own journey of learning.

The missing man dug through his pockets. For a moment

the son hoped his father had changed his mind and was looking for his yarmulke, but instead he pulled out a crumpled piece of rolled-up paper and said: This is our property. Granddad left us an inheritance.

When he held out the paper, the son turned his back. Now he regrets that, he told the investigator. At the time he thought it was blasphemous to speak of an inheritance at the newly dug grave. Desecration of the dead.

He could still hear the echo of the body sliding into the grave.

Lenox reads this over and over again, to make sure there is no mistake. The body—into the grave? But where was the coffin?

Dear Ms. Brendel,

Why not, "All humans are responsible for one another"?

Yours,
S. T. L.

LENOX THINKS back to the only Jewish funeral he ever attended, at the elegant funeral home on the Upper West Side. The commissioner himself eulogized the deceased—a senior fraud investigator who died of a heart attack in the middle of the second act at a Broadway show. He enumerated the man's virtues in great detail, elevating his stature to sublime levels, while the mourners shifted uncomfortably in their seats facing the coffin.

Lenox represented the unit. Wearing his smart suit, the one that always hangs in his room for court appearances, he placed a wreath of red carnations, ordered specially, on the dais. He noticed the dissonance immediately, and later learned that Jews do not bring flowers to a funeral. He felt misled. To relieve the boredom of the eulogies, he stared at the coffin and considered its composition: restrained elegance, no superfluous copper or velvet adornments. Fine oak. The decay would take years.

He was relieved to find the coffin closed. He would not have to stand over the dead man's face, and his breath and droplets of saliva would not descend with the coffin into the earth as a promissory note, a reminder that Lenox too would one day arrive in that same nameless no-place. He wondered for a moment whether the Jew was wearing his finest suit and a pair of shoes cobbled especially, as was the Italian custom.

A sealed coffin. How convenient.

Lenox, accustomed to seeing butchered bodies, prefers not to look at natural death straight on. He didn't even go to his grandmother's funeral.

He doesn't remember who instructed him to press the widow's hand and murmur, "You should have no more sorrow." A ludicrous phrase. After all, if there is one thing in the world that is not only probable but certain, it is sorrow.

Jews haggle with the future, using idioms passed down from generation to generation like whispered spells that have lost all power, although they refuse to admit it.

As ordered by the commissioner, Lenox accompanied the convoy to the Jewish cemetery in Queens. The coffin was gently lowered into the grave without a sound. The dead man vanished with no exposed face frozen in death, no expression of relief or torment, no outline of the body that once was. No unnecessary sounds that keep echoing out.

But in Israel they put the dead person straight into the earth, like a burden to be gotten rid of.

YOU WILL have sorrow and your children will have sorrow and your children's children will have sorrow.

Lenox, though, being childless, will be spared the sorrow.

There will be no one to have sorrow after him.

Perhaps that would be his consolation, were he to allow himself to wallow in self-pity. It's a good thing he is not one of those naïve people who beg for life to stop moving after they are gone. The way he sees it, any remnants of grief are tossed into the grave, with or without a coffin, and that's that. As though they never existed. As far as Lenox is concerned, it would be best to have no mourning at all.

Reconstructing that Jewish funeral, he suddenly recalls Jackie Brendel's presence at the Queens cemetery, like a detail swallowed up in the investigation that now suddenly emerges, surrounded with a soft halo. He remembers her standing outside the circle.

Which of his wives did she remind him of . . .

When Lenox starts pacing, with his notepad between his teeth, his colleagues beyond the partitions always know he's reaching the critical stage of an investigation.

PROFILE OF an Israeli. Intermediary Report:

Frenetic. Control freak. Delusions of invincibility. What happened will not happen again. Charges ahead.

How come these Israelis never get tired? Or perhaps in this case the tables have turned, and it is the javelin that is launching the thrower.

Simon T. Lenox waits for a signal, like a buffalo who senses a hunter closing in on him, weapon aimed, yet still the beast does not move.

He murmurs the missing man's name for the first time: *Liam Emanuel.* It sounds foreign. And yet . . .

WHY THE javelin throw? A sport so devoid of glory. Lenox pounces at the computer and sucks out data. The challenge is to throw the javelin in mid-sprint, since even the slightest deceleration will slow the spear's velocity and result in a huge waste of effort.

If only he knew what the destination was. Deep down, he admires Liam Emanuel for pushing his own limits, as though he has trained for this race his whole life. From whom was the Israeli expecting applause?

Lenox paces up and down the hallways, reading and rereading the printout, tempted to put his own body to the test, even if his colleagues scoff at his clumsy movements.

His body is ungainly. His belly folds over his belt, and the flesh on his arms is flabby. It's a pity he never joined the cult of physical fitness worshippers. If he tries to throw a javelin he might end up hitting someone behind him.

A legal throw must be over the shoulder or the upper arm, he reads out loud. The thrower may not turn his or her back on the direction of the throw, and in order for the throw to count, the javelin's tip must penetrate the ground and leave a mark.

He is suddenly visited by an image: A blazing javelin soars toward the window, aiming its fiery tip right at him.

In his new office, Simon T. Lenox flinches and almost falls, then bursts into laughter that makes the windows shudder. Hallucinations! How he mocked his grandmother for them. Once he told her she had a Jewish disease—and he didn't want to catch it.

Jackie Brendel is stingy with her information. Keeping her cards close to her chest. Maybe that is the common thread linking the Jewish source with its Mediterranean offshoots.

Still, there is something charming about this woman, though he has never been willing to admit it before.

LENOX SPENDS the day studying the marginal sport.

In the "American grip," the javelin is held diagonally along the crease of the palm, with the pinky finger and thumb wrapped around the top and bottom, and the three remaining fingers gripping the cord.

Complicated? No more than a manual for a DVD player or a newfangled washing machine, which manages to obfuscate even the simplest tasks.

Is there an "Israeli grip"? He has already learned that the Israelis never settle for what already exists, always feeling the need to reinvent the wheel.

The person who notified the police of Liam Emanuel's disappearance was his ex-wife, who had not loosened her grip even after they were formally separated. Here is the key to the mystery: she probably wanted to make sure she wouldn't be left out of the inheritance, that her former partner wouldn't make off with a treasure. Greed—the most common motive for all crimes and misdemeanors. Why would he have thought the map-stain nation's members were any different?

Intermediary Conclusion: Liam Emanuel turned his apartment upside down because he was looking for his father's will.

Before he shuts down the computer, Lenox writes:

Dear Ms. Brendel,

Do you know what a *boydem* is?

He does not sign the message.

He's not sure if the pressure in his groin is from his bladder or his erection.

Profile of an Investigator. Final Conclusion:

Frenetic. Control freak. Delusions of invincibility. Charges ahead.

Just like the Israelis—a patently discomforting comparison.

He has to close this case, soon.

Lenox paces back and forth, biting his notepad. Behind his back they always gossip: it's his Indian blood. They never say it out in the open, not wanting to be suspected of racism. For a moment, Lenox allows himself to take pleasure in the sweet pressure in his loins.

TAKING ADVANTAGE of Lenox's trip to the coffee station, Jackie Brendel slips another note under his door. Her handwriting is less neat this time, and the letters wander onto the margins. She does not bother with polite openings.

A Jew is buried in a coffin in the Diaspora, but in Israel only the shrouds separate him from the earth.

There is no sign-off either.

How can she respond to a question he has not asked, and yet not answer the question he did ask?

AT THE end of the son's affidavit there is something else. He quoted the last words Liam Emanuel told him at the cemetery. They were standing some distance apart. The son had started walking out on a different path than the one he entered on, since a person must not enter and leave a cemetery the same way. Liam Emanuel, scorning such superstition, demonstratively turned to leave the same way he came in. He shoved the crumpled paper into his pocket with his earth-stained hand.

And then he said something to his son.

A meaningless mumble, the Israeli investigator determined.

If only this were a different case . . .

THERE'S NOWHERE to go from here. He'll have to call it quits. Even though the commissioner has finally eased up on him, and the Israelis in DC have stopped breathing down his neck too.

A miserable case. Who cares about a piece of real estate that some old Jewish guy once bought as an investment and left to his Israeli descendants? Is that all there is? Some drama!

Not at his age. Not in his position. He will not babysit a petty Israeli who won't share his property with the other heirs. What sort of treasure are we talking about, anyway? Probably some moldy dump in Brooklyn or Queens. Big fucking deal. A real find. Liam Emanuel is holed up there, sitting on his Israeli ass downing Jack Daniels and laughing at everyone. You gotta admire the Israelis—wrapping the whole world around their little finger. The ex-wife managed to keep two governments—including one superpower—on their toes just so she could sink her teeth into a juicy piece of the pie. Inheritance squabble. That's the whole story.

Lenox leans over the fax machine and feeds in his intermediary report. At least he'll be spared having to identify the body.

Attn: Brig. Gen. Yoav Rosen-Vardi, Israel Police
Attaché to the United States, Washington, DC

Re: Israeli Missing Person

Dear Sir,

Following a vigorous investigation into your case, I have found no evidence that the Israeli citizen Liam Emanuel is involved in any act of a criminal nature, or has fallen victim to a hostile plot. The earth has not swallowed him up. It would be more accurate to say that he is the one who has swallowed the earth.

I must therefore conclude that there is no justification for further involvement of US law authorities. Your missing person wishes to enjoy the fruits of an investment in an American asset. I advise notifying any of his relatives who may still be concerned about his well-being that the evidence points to a person

> who acted lucidly, and, if I may be permitted, out of sound financial considerations. Your man is not mixed up in anything un-kosher.

Kosher. Finally a Jewish word. Lenox has such fun typing it.

IN THE dimness that is never completely dark, Lenox places his report on the commissioner's desk. Manhattan glows outside the windows. An arrowlike city shining bright. For Lenox, it is an unimpeachable place, although he has always been reluctant to award it the overwrought title of "home." His eyes have stopped taking in its beauty. He has grown accustomed to it, as one does to a pair of tattered slippers. An island bought for twenty-four dollars from Indians. His naïve forefathers. He wouldn't have walked into that trap.

He gives his tower's southern twin a farewell glance. A French tightrope walker once tiptoed over a cable strung between the two towers. Twelve mountain climbers have scaled their walls. Three parachuted down safely, and George Willig was arrested and fined one cent for each of the hundred floors he climbed.

Lenox permits himself a moment of sentimentality at the sight of this urban evergreen forest in its seductive packaging. The spirits of hunters and herds of buffalo and coyotes, assuming they exist, are now roaming the mazes erected by white people in an island of rock. The Israeli, who is not his at all, was not swallowed up by the earth; he probably wanted to be buried in a coffin rather than thrown straight into a grave.

A barbaric custom. There's no understanding them. Israelis, Jews, same thing. As far as Lenox is concerned, the affair is over.

The Israeli's photograph, still perched on the stack of

paperwork, reflects the Manhattan glow. His narrowed eyes seem to be winking.

Bye-bye, you Israeli fucker.

A QUICK nod at the night watchman, and Lenox is out on Fulton Street, corner of Greenwich. Flooded with relief, he skips the subway station and decides to walk uptown.

Pain in the ass of a nation. With their ancient death cults. After all, the solution to the mystery is always less complicated than one thinks. You have to look at the first circle of acquaintances, because the harasser is almost always someone who knew the victim. But Lenox hasn't exposed a perpetrator in this case—only the missing man's well-wishers who were suffocating him under the pretext of concern.

Digging through his coat pocket for his jangling bunch of keys, he finds a note from Jackie Brendel. When did she sneak that in? He angrily unfolds the paper and reads under the light that glows from the Towers.

A *boydem*, the Jewish woman wrote, is a hidden opening. A place of shelter inside a house. A Yiddish term that made its way into Hebrew.

The letters start to bleed in the rain and Lenox has to huddle close to the building to read the rest of the note.

At times of trouble, one can seek refuge there.

WHAT IS she talking about? Refuge from what? There was no apparent threat.

Lenox himself is starting to toy with the idea of disappearing. When you disappear, no one has any idea what you're doing, and you are free to navigate beyond the awareness of those who would encircle you. What is there to bind Lenox to his present existence except the shackles of habit? His time card, a handful of friends as worn out as he is, and the occasional fuck. The familiar stomping grounds of life. Even his youthful yearning to bring about revolution is no more than a feeble flicker when he awakes, and it quickly fades into daily routine. How tempting to just cut away. To run and throw the javelin at the same time. On the empty streets of Lower Manhattan, Simon T. Lenox practices. He doesn't get very far from the Twin Towers before he starts panting. He tries to gain momentum, reciting the rules:

The javelin must be gripped above the ear, higher than the head, with the tip aimed forwards and tilted down. The most common mistake is to swerve before letting go, which makes the javelin miss its target.

Who would eventually notify the authorities of his disappearance?

Who gives a fuck.

The advantage of not having an inner circle is the freedom to act without guilt. He mustn't become a cliché. If there's one thing Lenox has learned from the Israeli, it is that.

The end of this case also means no more dealings with Jackie Brendel and her impenetrable gibberish. Why does he feel as if the Jewish woman is rebuking him? He did everything by the book, he wasn't sloppy, and he reached his conclusions honestly and unbiasedly. The Israeli is alive and well, either here or somewhere else. Let's respect his choice and leave him alone.

Lenox holds the note out and lets the rain soak it. Jackie Brendel's words melt away. He balls up the soggy mess and launches it overhand at the Hudson, without knowing whether or not it hits the target. The dark waters lap at Manhattan. According to the official definition, it isn't even a river, because it is deeper than the body of water into which it flows.

THE RUN did him well. Lenox can't resist calling the commissioner at home to announce that he's cracked the case. Beneath the façade of praise, the commissioner is clearly annoyed, perhaps by the invasion of his privacy. The conversation does not go as planned. Lenox is left with a bad taste in his mouth. Maybe Jackie Brendel is meddling behind the scenes, trying to get ahead at his expense. Even if there are still a few unanswered questions, the final conclusion is unaltered. The Israeli has come to no harm, and if he alienated his relatives and left home slamming the door behind him, that is no business for the authorities.

Jack Daniels is an excellent cure for doubt, but the shops are closed. Maybe he did not study all the data properly and unwittingly went off track. Perhaps he should have, from the start, sailed backwards along all the branches of the winding generational path, and kept rowing towards what came before what came before. Liam Emanuel and his son. And the late grandfather. He had died of natural causes and been given a proper funeral. Why should Lenox be expected to go back to the intersection at which the Jews and the Israelis parted ways?

Lenox's grandmother had a long-standing allegation: Your father's bones were never removed from the ground for a final burial, as is the tribal custom. She attributed the failure of Lenox's three marriages to his having prevented his father's entry into the eternal hunting ground.

Out of respect for the old lady, Lenox made do with gentle mockery: American—that's what he was. If he were to yield to superstition, he would be undermining the ideal of one nation. He sounded like a politician on the stump. Still, he asked her not to downplay his accomplishments: a satisfactory albeit not glowing career, imminent retirement with a comfortable pension. He had achieved all this through his own hard work, without any special favors or affirmative action.

It's just old age that attacks them and makes them slaves

to nostalgia. His grandmother never got used to life outside the reservation. She demanded that he find shamans for her, even in Manhattan, and wasted her money on witch doctors who promised to help her communicate with the spirits. Toward the end, she was so disoriented that she stopped speaking English and mumbled in an indecipherable language. Yet still she demanded—though it wasn't clear from whom—reparation.

Lenox's Indian grandmother and the missing man's Jewish grandfather. That could have been quite a *shidduch.*

Shidduch. Another Jewish word.

Matchmaking for the dead—a flourishing industry. A genetic admixture that could spur the spirits of the races, or the nations, or whatever they are.

All people are responsible for one another. The only phrase that will survive this case for him. That's what he should have written on his application for the police academy when asked why he wanted a law enforcement career.

Lenox tries to hail a cab, but because of the rain they all pass by without stopping. Having no choice, he makes his way on foot, his muscles weary from running. From time to time he stops to wipe the rain off his face.

ARE YOU the officer, Mister?

Yes.

Did you call yesterday? Looking for someone?

Lenox rattles the cell phone to get better reception, and identifies himself in his most authoritative voice.

Your guy was just here. I think. I'm almost sure.

Where?

In our store. Outdoor gear. He talked with the sales girl.

Are you certain?

He had an accent. You thought he was an Arab, right Keisha?

A female giggle is heard in the background.

Where did he say he was going, Keisha? You helped him. Tell the cop, Keisha. Hey, Mister, is there a reward?

The young woman in the background tries to backtrack. She's not even sure it was the right guy. She didn't want to get the cops involved. Why go looking for trouble? But the chance of a reward . . . Maybe the grateful family would contribute a few bucks?

They giggle again. Lenox suspects they're playing him. The caller does not answer his detailed questions about an athletic build or stubble. He only insists that the man was Israeli, in contrast to Keisha's opinion. The two argue but eventually reach an agreement: You can smell Israelis a mile away. They always drive you crazy, turning the merchandise over and over without ever buying anything. Except this guy did, and he paid cash.

What did my Israeli buy? Lenox asks.

Only tomorrow morning will he consider the fact that he has appropriated the Israeli. At this moment he is simply aware of the tension building in his muscles as he awaits the answer.

A map and a raincoat, says Keisha. Jesus, I was so sure he was an Arab.

The line goes dead.

LET GO, Simon T. Let the man wallow in his anonymity. His reconstructed, recycled life is not your own life returned to you. The Israeli is merely movement in space, something that passed over your head and vanished. Let go, Simon T. Do not give in to the romantic notions about the traces a man leaves behind merely by being present. You are only the audience in this race, and you didn't even pay a dime to watch it.

The Israeli case is closed, just as it was before you crudely stepped into it. After all, you can't expect thanks from Liam Emanuel, and don't be tempted to believe you are his savior, from others or from himself. The sense of intimacy between you and him is inevitable, and all too familiar from other cases. You already know it's a false intimacy. If you met him face to face, you would be complete strangers to one another. He would scoff, and rightly so: What do we have to do with each other?

And let's say he was from a different nation—would you dare trespass his borders for your own needs, like you're doing now? French, for example. Or Hungarian. Is it only because he is Jewish, or Israeli, that his borders are a free-for-all? And is the solid evidence of him being alive not enough to halt your voyeuristic desires? Or maybe that's a side effect of the bladder problems.

Let go, Simon T. Give this man a final burial, as is the tribal custom.

Your bones mean nothing to him either. It's best to stick with mutual ignorance.

Boydem. Boydem. Boydem.

A foreign word taps to the beat of the raindrops. The sky is pierced with holes. It's a pity Lenox didn't become a doctor, like his grandmother wanted him to. Then he could have diagnosed an enlarged prostate and recommended emergency surgery.

As a child on the reservation, the old lady told him an ancient Indian version of the creation myth, whereby the Raven pissed out the world.

A *boydem* inheritance. A road map. A raincoat. A patrimony.

This is our pastpresent, the missing man murmured on his father's grave as he clutched the property title. And Lenox, an experienced detective, had walked into the trap and accepted the Israeli investigator's opinion that it was just a meaningless mumble.

Or maybe he said *presentpast* . . . How had that detail escaped him?

Lenox walks out in front of a taxi and waves his arms dramatically. He tells the driver to hurry to the outdoor gear store. When they arrive, he hands over a fifty-dollar bill and rushes to the glass door. The store is closed, but he spots employees inside, locking up the cash registers and arranging merchandise in piles. Lenox holds his badge up to the glass and bangs.

When he is let inside, he finds Keisha standing meekly behind a stack of discounted sleeping bags. She is no longer giggling. She just keeps saying, "I dunno," and glaring at the young man who made the stupid mistake of calling the police.

Lenox adopts a friendly demeanor and tries to get them to talk.

Sneakers?

They don't remember.

Backpack?

Maybe.

Stubble?

Shrug.

Finally Keisha mutters: Poor guy forgot to take his change. I ran after him. Didn't want him saying I was a cheat.

She got so wet. It was stupid. Chasing after a stranger in the rain to give him back three miserable bucks. She caught up with him just as he was starting his car. Dumbass. He could have put on the raincoat he just bought. She'd tried to sell him an umbrella. But he'd said: I don't mind getting wet in the waterfall. Thundering water, that's all it is.

His car was parked just outside the store, further proof that he wasn't from around here, because every local knows that's a gamble. They'll slap you with an $85 fine and another $125 for towing. They get away with murder.

Such profligate use of the word, Lenox thinks. That is something only people who don't have to spend their lives looking at butchered bodies can afford to say.

The car model—do you remember by any chance, Keisha?

With that tone, biting yet gentle, he had won over three women.

Off-road, Keisha says. Four by four. Jeep Cherokee. Olive green. Her favorite color.

The customer had a foreign accent. When she found him outside, he told her to keep the change.

She answered: And you keep dry.

The stranger smiled at her. The jeep door was wide open and the seat was soaked from the rain.

Then he added: Everything that could have happened has already happened.

An illogical sentence. Certainly not the usual way of hitting on a woman.

Picking up a spark in Keisha's eyes, Lenox becomes aware of a twinge in his lower body. Was this young black girl tempted to leave it all behind for the promise of an olive green Cherokee?

After me, the flood.

Who said that? Lenox asks.

Keisha recoils. Lost her confidence all of a sudden. Maybe she got confused and it was actually *Before me, the flood.*

Who said that? Lenox insists.

I don't know. It's an expression, isn't it?

She looks in vain for support from the young man, who has joined them, but he is impatient, rushing her to close up the store. She ignores him and turns her dark, warm doe's eyes back to Lenox.

Is this guy important to you, Officer?

Lenox nods his head involuntarily. His muscles tense up

again. Keisha's giggle is back too. Nervous, yet full of charm.

You and him look alike. You related?

The young man turns off the lights in the store, and the three of them feel their way out in the dark, past the blinking alarm light.

IN HIS mind Lenox sets up a matchmaking business. An old dead Jewish Israeli and an old dead Native American wade through the mist, and Lenox records their negotiations in his notepad.

The Raven is the Creator, says the dead Indian woman. He is the one who pissed out the world.

And why should he create a world? asks the dead Jewish man to get the conversation going.

Out of boredom, the dead woman answers. His wife was badgering him—she was sick of living in the void.

The Great Spirit, the one responsible for the match, follows the disputation closely from up high.

LENOX'S GRANDMOTHER always insisted that when he was a child, she told him all the ancient secrets. He remembers nothing. Murder stories were far more interesting to him than native folklore.

She lay on her deathbed in a Jewish nursing home in Riverdale, in the Bronx. A lone Indian among Jews. He got her a room there through his connections with the commissioner. If you have to die, then do it in good company. Jews die gracefully. They leave the world without protest. Whereas Israelis—judging by this missing-person case—go out kicking and screaming, hoping their departure will arouse waves of remorse.

Bullshit! There should be equal law for Israelis. Lenox is unwilling to attribute any special virtues to them, in life or in death. Were he the celestial matchmaker, he would advise the deceased couple to find some common interests. They could rattle their bones, gossip about who has been taken out of his grave, who's coming up soon, and who's going down. For his grandmother, a final burial is the only way to get to the eternal hunting ground. But on this point, the match is doomed. The dead Jewish man will be horrified by the desecration of graves.

Lenox's grandmother did not give an inch even when she was fading into complete delirium. Drugged up and dying, she still would not let go. A pathetic grip. Or perhaps it was extraordinarily brave?

Right before the end, Lenox was called to the nursing home. He stood under the Star of David engraved above the front door, clutching a few tobacco leaves in his fist. If his dying grandmother could have seen him observe the ancient Indian custom, she would have been pleased. Hearing everyone around her speak Yiddish, he wished he had tried harder to find her a more suitable place. But at least he made sure she got a room with a view of the Hudson.

He walked into her room with the nurse close behind him. His grandmother's body was emaciated. Only her hands remained fleshy and pink like a girl's.

Simon T., my White Raven, she murmured, looking out at the river through the window.

He gave instructions for her burial and never went back. Thirty days later he received a FedEx package from the Hebrew Home for the Aged. Inside were her false teeth. But where was her pipe? He meant to send a letter demanding a thorough search, but it slipped his mind. It was just a beat-up smoking tool.

She had also owned a faded belt, which was once embroidered with colorful beads. Lenox told them to throw it out. Later, he vaguely remembered that his grandmother had called it a "wampum belt."

White Raven, she called him before the end.

Simon T. Lenox refuses to believe in a world excreted or a Creator unable to control his sphincters.

FULLY CLOTHED, he steps into the shower and turns on the faucet at full power. The scalding flow washes away the late-summer sediments, and Lenox allows the water to untie the knots in his muscles. He drops his clothes on the wet floor, where they block the drain, and the small cubicle starts to overflow. He thinks he might have peed, but the temperature blurs the difference between the fluids.

He doesn't hear the phone chirping in his coat pocket. Only when he steps out of the steaming shower and enfolds himself in a fragrant towel does he see the screen: New Voicemail from Unknown Number.

INSPECTOR LENOX? It's me, Keisha. From the outdoor gear store. I remembered something. Sorry if I'm making you crazy, 'cause this might just be nothing. Even though it's none of my business, and I don't even know what the guy's called, the one who bought a ten-dollar raincoat and a map of New York. But I'm telling you, Inspector Lenox, if that asshole did something bad, then he deserves to be punished, and I don't want him to get away, 'cause we can't always recognize the assholes when they look like good guys. I knew this dude once with a sweet baby face, and then it turned out he was into hitting women with a baseball bat. So if this guy of yours is not what he looks like, and even if I'm wrong and he's just your long lost brother, then I just want you to know that when I said his Cherokee was olive green, he laughed. He said he couldn't tell 'cause he's color-blind. That's some kind of disease, isn't it?

A short giggle.

Beep.

WHAT A headache.

Lenox plans to take two painkillers and dive into a white slumber, free of dreams about dead people who'll never find their *shidduch*. Tomorrow he'll take the day off. That Israeli and his olive Cherokee can end up wherever they end up. He would call Keisha back now, but his battery's dead and he's too exhausted to recharge it. Huddled in his towel, Lenox leans on the wall and calculates the steps required to reach the nearest Jack Daniels, when his brain picks up a buzz at the door.

Why didn't the doorman let him know someone was coming up? Maybe it's a neighbor.

Lenox crouches, hoping to make himself vanish. This is not the time for borrowing an egg or coffee. His fridge is empty anyway. He wraps the towel, which feels less soft now, around his waist and looks through the peephole. For one mad second he expects to see his Israeli.

At first he doesn't recognize her. She stands there erect and tense, like a school girl sent to collect donations for the Salvation Army, her auburn head bowed.

A woman at the door.

A strange woman at the door.

A Jewish woman . . .

When she reaches out and raps on the door with her knuckles, Lenox finally opens it and realizes he doesn't know what to call her.

JACKIE. JUST Jackie.

Why are you here?

To help you.

Lenox remembers his manners, but he can't shake her hand because of the towel. Clumsily, aware of his bare private parts under the fabric, he chatters meaninglessly.

But you wrote Jacqueline on the note.

My mother adored Jackie Kennedy.

And your middle name? Winona? It doesn't sound Jewish.

He's rusty. Completely forgotten how to engage in flirtatious small talk.

But Jackie Brendel ignores the question and walks in.

It doesn't occur to Lenox to ask why she has an Indian middle name.

SHE SITS down at the kitchen table and starts speaking in Yiddish.

Es hot zich oysgelozt a boydem! Nothing will come of this.

Oyf a boydem is a yarid! Much ado about nothing.

Boydem klots! They have nothing to do with each other.

Zogn boydem! A bunch of hokey.

Shlepen di ku in boydem aroyf! Treading water.

An odd language. The code of dead Jews. Moses Brendel was the one who passed down the secret Jewish language's finer points to his daughter. The only thing to make its way into Hebrew was *boydem*.

And what remains of the lost Indian languages? Lenox wonders as he listens to the Jewish woman's soft voice scattering its warmth through his empty space. She turns down the Jack Daniels, and he feels uncomfortable drinking in her presence. They are trapped in forced intimacy, separated only by the towel.

Aren't you writing this down? Jackie asks urgently, as though offloading a burden.

A *boydem* is a narrow, elevated space, usually above the bathroom ceiling, where Israelis keep old items they don't use anymore. It's also where the hot water tank is often housed. *Boydem*: a wasted overhead space that gathers mildew. *Boydem*: an excellent hiding place.

So said Moses Brendel, from his resting place in the Hebrew Home for the Aged in Riverdale.

> Why do Israelis need a *boydem*?
> How many Israelis can fit in one *boydem*?
> What dangers might impel an Israeli to seek refuge in a *boydem*?
> Where could Simon T. Lenox hide in times of danger?
> *Boydem*: a fascinating conversation topic, notes the matchmaker who watches impossible *shidduchs* between dead people.
> *Boydem*: foreplay.

THAT IS what Lenox wrote in his notepad afterwards.

JACKIE BRENDEL gets rid of her remaining cargo:

In Israel, they don't have basements or attics like they do in Europe or America. In the Middle East, there are no wide expanses to spread above houses or burrow beneath them. Moses Brendel visited Israel as a tourist only once, and his daughter has no intention of going there. She buys Israel Bonds, and that's enough. Fifty dollars a year. It's tax deductible, and will eventually be repaid with two-percent interest. Not a bad investment, her accountant says. Jewish. Of course he's Jewish.

The room goes silent, and the two inhabitants consider various options for advancing the conversation. Finally Lenox gets up, remembering to tighten the towel around his dangling parts, and floats a hypothesis:

Maybe Israel is the Jews' *boydem*?

The tension instantly shifts and dissipates. Jackie Brendel promises that next time she visits the nursing home, she will ask her father, a German refugee, to translate that phrase into Yiddish for her, since it is a commonly accepted wisdom that Jewish humor gets lost in any other language.

Lenox is infected by her rolling laughter, as though they are accomplices in an impending crime.

God forbid. Sex is no crime.

HE CAN'T exactly call it "lovemaking," yet he is reluctant to dismiss it as just a fuck. At first he recognized a blend of sadness and fear, followed by mutual thirst with perfect timing. He is unable to reconstruct the precise moment at which her clothes were removed. He, on the other hand, had only to drop his towel.

Perhaps because he was surprised, Lenox had trouble restraining himself, and when she straddled him and guided him inside her, gazing into his pupils from above, the semen suddenly burst out. Without making excuses, Lenox stared at it oozing out on the two of them and then pooling into a dimple.

He forgot about the Israeli. Until morning.

He lay there facing the window, staring at the crisp dawn. Perhaps this was how Liam Emanuel saw the world: gray on gray.

Affirmative action.

HALF-ASLEEP, HE drifts away on a flood of Jack Daniels, kneeling in a canoe, wearing shoes with nonskid soles. He tries to use a pair of javelins to row to a thicket of auburn facial stubble. The sky is clear, though he wears a raincoat with holes in it. He searches for his grandmother's lost pipe. A defaced body floats down the current. Has the disaster already occurred, or is it about to happen? Perhaps it is a cyclical calamity? He cannot find land. He drops the oars and has to row with his hands. The pain is so intense, it's as though they have been amputated.

When he opens his eyes he does not know whether he is

lying on a bed of mud or on the indentation between Jackie's shoulder and her breast, but he knows for sure that he has had this dream once before.

DON'T GO. Stay.

She begs him to let the Israeli man grieve alone. We have to respect his choice. So he's mistreating his son, his ex, and the whole state of Israel. Who cares? If he wanted to commit suicide, he wouldn't have bought a map and a raincoat. Let him lick his orphaned wounds, like animals who leave the pack to focus on their pain and then return. We should admire those who are willing to look finality straight on. He's a big boy, the Israeli. He managed to shake off the herd of comforters with their repository of clichés. Their time will come.

Lenox is almost convinced, but as she talks, Jackie is already shoving spare underwear, a pair of jeans and balled up socks into the tiny suitcase under the bed. She stands on her tiptoes to reach a sweatshirt on the top shelf. He can't remember which of his wives bought it for him; it was a rare show of sentimentality.

She moves through his space as though she had memorized the layout while he slept.

Now she holds his toothbrush as if she's about to toss it to him. A faint odor rises from the bed sheets. He hasn't brushed his teeth yet, and the taste of her orifices—salty mud—comes from his palate.

When he leaves the apartment, he will wonder if he remembered to put the toilet seat down.

ON THE morning after, the partners in sex recede into their fortresses to conduct their private post-mortems. He considers the breasts that made his blood surge, the thighs that kneaded his erection. From close up, at magnifying-glass range, the flesh appeared flawless. But distance allows a sober mutual examination. Jacqueline Winona Brendel is not particularly attractive. Her youth is long gone. Her wrinkled skin seems incongruous with her revelations of passion last night. Nor did she fail to notice Lenox's flabby waist and the mound of his belly, whose outlines she licked up and down and across. On the morning after, there is an unseen presence between them. Perhaps the Israeli is the spirit that ties them together—a matchmaker of sorts.

As Jackie picks up last night's towel to toss it in the laundry hamper, Lenox unzips the suitcase.

If he were Liam Emanuel, he would have gone back to pick up Keisha.

Happy ending. Headlines.

But there was something else that needed to be done.

On his way out, Lenox grabs the last document from the pile—the one he always keeps for the end. Standing at the door, he reads the résumé, while Jackie peers over his shoulder.

> Liam Emanuel. Born: May, 1948, Tel-Aviv. The father, Mordecai Emanuel, is a Holocaust survivor from Manheim, Germany. The mother, Tzippora, a native of Tunisia, was killed in a motor accident when Liam was a child.
>
> 1967: Enlisted in the Israel Defense Forces, served as a soldier in the Six-Day War and the War of Attrition. Reached the rank of captain. As a reserve duty soldier, took part in the Yom Kippur War, the Lebanon War, and the First Intifada.
>
> Graduate of the Theater Department at Tel-Aviv University.
>
> Graduate of the Israeli Foreign Ministry's cadet course.
>
> Political activist. Candidate in the upcoming Knesset elections.

Divorced, father of one—a son, who became religious after traveling in the Far East.

Dry facts: born, lived, will die soon.
All the rest . . .
Life in a capsule.

JACKIE BRENDEL offers an alternative résumé: The missing man is the son of immigrants. Yearns for artistic expression. Possesses diplomatic skills. Ambitious. Seeks power. These milestones, she says, cannot be inscribed on any tombstone. She hands Lenox his suitcase.

At the bottom of the résumé it says:

Special identification markers: color-blindness.

Where are you going? she asks.

Jackie is already showered, dressed, and made up. No one in the North Tower will be able to guess where and how she spent the night.

After a slight hesitation, Lenox picks up the suitcase and answers: Niagara Falls.

SHE WALKS from Eighty-Seventh Street all the way to the World Trade Center. As she steps into the elevator, sweaty, her makeup smeared, she suddenly bursts into uncontrollable laughter. She's never heard of someone inheriting a waterfall before.

The other elevator riders shrug their shoulders and keep staring at the numbers hypnotically. When the elevator stops at her floor she is lost in thought and doesn't get out, and when it lurches again, her blood pitches too and she has a dizzy spell. She waits for the next stop, on the eighty-sixth floor, and gets out. On a whim, she starts walking down the stairs, rolling her laughter down in the darkness.

Before leaving, he debated whether or not to take his gun. At first he put it in his belt, then moved it to a holster on his ankle. Eventually Jackie made the decision. Without saying a word, she took the gun and propped it among his bottles of Jack Daniels.

The fear was gone, he noted. Only the sadness remained.

By the time he gets to his car, he is furious at the Israeli.

You piece of chicken shit! Defector. Emotionally infantile. Is that what they taught you in your celebrated army? In your Middle East bazaar politics? In the theater you so admire? You ducked behind the curtain so you wouldn't have to face the audience spitting at you. You couldn't leave a note on the fridge? A pithy voicemail? Sorry, I've gone out. I won't be back.

Trampling on bodies, that's what you're doing.

That is the real résumé, summed up in three words.

I'll make you grieve, Liam Emanuel. I'll push your unshaven face into the mud. Your body will be upside down, and your man in Washington will have to turn over every stone to figure out what that means to us Indians. You thought I'd give up, that I'd jump into the woman's sticky trap. Well, you listen up, motherfucker: I can't be bought with the promise of second-hand love from your dusty *boydem.* I'm sitting on the tail of your Cherokee spaceship and I'm about to launch you into the sky, in the name of all the miserable people you left behind on both sides of the ocean, stuck here with gravity while you float into space. I'll shove that javelin right between your legs, you arrogant fucker. You thought you'd inherited the sky. Well, fuck you and your country. And fuck your God.

Hey, Lenox, calm down. You're forgetting that the Raven is the creator of the world. He pissed and he shat.

Pieces of shit, that's what we are.

He drives wildly, zigzagging between the lanes. When he crosses the Tappan Zee Bridge over the Hudson, a police car takes after him and pulls him over. The officer marches over, yanks him out and is about to pin him to the side of the car, but Lenox waves his badge and the cop stands back and apologizes profusely.

Excuse me, Inspector Lenox. I didn't know you were on duty. Go hunt down your man, and God bless you.

God again. Is that really necessary?

He gets a police escort all the way to the next intersection.

State Route 17.

It's forty-three miles from Goshen to Liberty, a voyage from slavery to freedom that takes barely three quarters of an hour. Lenox is not aware of this analogy, having virtually no knowledge of the Exodus from Egypt. Even if he were to bother telling Jackie Brendel which road he was on, it's doubtful she would have connected Goshen with Liberty, because, like many Americans, she too skips over the remote little towns that line the asphalt highway going west. Who cares about a handful of Bible thumpers, refugees from the Old World, recycling some promised land for themselves?

If Lenox had time to spare, he might have turned off toward nearby Beth El, and even gone as far as Damascus, just over the Pennsylvania border. But he's in New York State, which has its own Damascus—but this one is a restaurant.

He pulls over at Damascus Diner and walks in. He orders a medium-rare hamburger with baked potato and coleslaw, but immediately regrets his choice. The diner is empty in the sleepy early morning, and the waiter is grumbly. His white shirt is faded from too many washes and his bow tie is crooked. He slams down a huge glass full of rattling ice cubes and a little water, like a miniature winter in a snow globe.

A truck driver wearing faded jeans and sharp-toe boots lumbers in and grunts his order: hamburger, baked potato, coleslaw. This road is heavily trafficked by people longing for someplace, and it runs in both directions. The denizen of Damascus dreams of trading in his provincial, uninspiring noplace for New York City, while the City dweller yearns for some distant, exotic Damascus as a refuge from his battles. The New Yorker and the Damascene will probably never meet. They will merely amuse themselves with imagined exchanges, flexing their desire for an unattainable land.

The waiter can barely conceal his resentment as he goes about his work. Whenever Lenox's cup is empty, he is obliged to fill it up with more of the muddy liquid, which has lost its original flavor from endless reheating. The waiter silently rebukes: Damascus Diner is just a station for me. You'll see, you asshole. You'll see what fucking someplace I get to.

The truck driver wolfs down his food. His hamburger bleeds ketchup. Unlike Lenox, he is served a glass of water with crushed ice.

Lenox dips one finger in his glass and his body temperature slowly melts the ice. The cubes swirl around as the driver watches, wide-eyed, shoveling the rest of his burger into his mouth.

Simon T. Lenox has never been to Niagara Falls.

If he'd had kids, then maybe . . .

One of his wives—the second, if he is not mistaken—liked to travel, but she only wanted to go where it was sunny. Once they took a trip to Florida, a coveted destination dotted with retirement homes for Hebrew elders. After spending one day there, Lenox booked return tickets. They fought the whole way back on the plane. His wife locked herself in the bathroom and didn't come out until landing. The flight attendant claimed she was crying and tried to push Lenox into the narrow cabin, hinting that in-flight sex can do wonders for a relationship.

Someplace Niagara. "Thunder of Waters," in the Indian language. What would have happened if the Belgian monk, the first white man to set foot there, had been hard of hearing and his ears had not detected the massive roar of water? Would deafness have delayed the discovery of the falls and altered the annals of tourism? Sooner or later the site would have been found, and masses of exuberant visitors would have surged to the thundering falls to check them off on their list.

In winter the falls freeze. The guidebooks say it is the most spectacular sight in the world. Ice trunks. Crystal tendrils. Translucent needles. Bold combinations created in the brittle state between liquid and solid. White on white. Only the color-blind Israeli would not see anything extraordinary in this sight. Lucky bastard. He'll never know what he's missing.

But in the first week of September the falls are frothing. Bright gleaming days still abound in the changing weather. And on either side of the border, every evening, there is an extravagant light show.

Except that this colorful spectacle, the jewel in the crown of any visit to Niagara Falls, kitsch at its finest, immortalized in millions of family photo albums, will also be denied to Liam Emanuel.

Just before Lenox left home, Jackie Brendel threw her own question out: So what is he plotting to do there, our Israeli?

Our Israeli?

Fuck.

HAVE YOU seen this man by any chance?

The truck driver shrugs his shoulders and touches the photo with his ketchup-smeared finger.

Why? What'd he do?

He's Israeli.

Lotta shooting over there, ain't there?

Lenox takes back the photo and subtly tries to wipe it off, but the red spot has congealed on Liam Emanuel's cheek, giving him the appearance of a drag queen who did a sloppy job of removing his makeup.

Who is it they're fighting? Oh yeah, the Palestinians.

This man is Israeli.

So? Israeli, Palestinian—same difference.

On his way out of the diner, Lenox thinks he spots the Cherokee. Olive green flashes through his field of vision and vanishes.

The Israeli is ahead of him again. He has to catch up with him before . . .

Lenox is not about to face Jackie and admit defeat.

HOW DID the Israeli suddenly become "ours"? Shared property. Joint ownership.

The question simmers in Lenox's mind as he drives, and he wonders again why he agreed to take the case. What a headache.

Our Israeli.

Our *boydem.*

Our child . . .

Lenox slams on the brakes when he realizes he almost drove past the sign for Niagara Falls, New York. He doesn't want to end up at its identical twin in Ontario.

Earlier, when he left home—rushing to avoid any parting gestures—Lenox told Jackie Brendel: There is another kind of disappearance. The kind for show.

AND THIS is how Lenox summed up Liam Emanuel's résumé in his notepad, ignoring any political correctness:

> Jewish. Only son of survivors. Struggled to live up to their excessive expectations. Shell shocked. Failed marriage. Disappointed in his son. His political future hangs in the balance. Suffers from system overload and an overly dramatic sensibility, like a hyperactive kid stomping his foot: "I'll show you!"

JACKIE BRENDEL wanted to order breakfast in bed. When she leaned over Lenox to reach the phone, her breasts weighed on him. He cut off her call to the restaurant and they made do with bitter coffee. He didn't even have sugar in the apartment. He was relieved to find out that she was also interested in avoiding any farewell displays. Still, she gave off a slight whiff, the faintest hint of last night's admixture of sadness and fear.

Lenox is almost positive he did remember to put down the toilet seat.

THE HIGHWAY traffic calls up a blend of unwanted images:

A foreign object hits the bedrock and he succumbs to the whirlpools. He flutters, blows bubbles, feels himself pulled down by gravity again, and holds onto the javelin as though it were a mast.

The crowds on either riverbank cheer the daredevil on. The Niagara circus. The Israeli, like his predecessors, has excellent survival skills.

Lenox lets go of the wheel.

He wishes he knew Hebrew. When he tries to brush away the images, his grandmother insinuates herself into them, snickering with her bare gums and throwing her false teeth at him.

The pipe . . . Maybe it's not too late to ask the home to give it back.

A pillar of water cuts away from the fleet of clouds on the horizon and sails along like a ghost ship, signaling Lenox's route along the four miles leading to a charmless industrial town: cleaning solvents factory, battery factory, paper recycling plant, hotel signs boasting of their proximity to the prized tourist site.

Lenox slowly realizes that the mushroom, which looks like a nuclear explosion, is in fact the canopy of sprayed water over the falls, which acts as a giant signpost.

He stops at the visitor center, where he is besieged by advertising brochures. On the walls, the falls pose in every possible angle, artificially domesticated and colored in digital hues. Even the Belgian monk would have trouble recognizing the revelation he once kneeled before. In his diary he told of how the frothing abyss aroused in him a keen desire to fly away from the world.

A docent hands Lenox a brochure advertising hot air balloon rides offered by "Flight of Angels." Don't worry, she reassures him: the cables are pegged to the ground, and they carry full insurance.

Lenox shows the woman—middle-aged, albino—the soiled photograph. It makes him miss the friendly, innocent Keisha. With fake enthusiasm, the docent gushes: Would you be interested perhaps in a wedding or honeymoon? We have special deals. A ceremony you won't forget!

She interprets his silence as consent. The company provides a limo to take the happy couple to the bridge overlooking the falls, and of course there's a band, and you can even have hip-hop music. Some couples come back for a second and third honeymoon. Since the first wedding held at the falls, in 1881, when the daughter of the vice president of the United States was married here, they've had fifty thousand love pilgrims. They say the negative ions from the water act as an aphrodisiac.

Jacqueline Winona Brendel.

Until death do us part . . .

Give me a break.

Lenox suggests starting a divorce business. Huge income guaranteed in no time.

Sir, are you joking?

No, ma'am. I'm completely serious.

But we have a very experienced priest.

What about a rabbi? Do you have a rabbi, too?

Is this a joke, sir?

Can I get a wedding gown designed like a waterfall?

Mister, you'd better watch your mouth or I'll call the police.

I am the police.

She doesn't even ask to see his badge.

In one of his notepads, Lenox once documented the moment at which he revealed himself as a law enforcement officer. The man before him descended into groveling and guilt—each hiding a certain fault—while Lenox was suddenly crowned with a halo of omnipotence. If he wanted to, he could ruin this man's life. Or he could forgive.

When he shows the photo to the albino docent, she immediately catalogs the dubious character. Years of working at the falls have made her a keen reader of people. She can spot the eccentrics, the insane, the delusional, the daydreamers. The ones who are willing to risk arrest and pay a steep fine for jumping off the falls, all to put on the best show in town. The last time anyone provided that kind of entertainment was in 1995.

There have been acrobats who walked across a tightrope from the Canadian Horseshoe Falls to the American Bridal Veil Falls. The Frenchman Blondin even cooked an omelet as he sat there suspended between water and sky, and the

Italian Maria Spelterini walked with peach baskets strapped to her feet.

And the cunning Israeli with the flood before him—what is he scheming?

The docent inspects the photo again, and recognizes the stain on the man's cheek. She'd sent the man to the Daredevil Museum. He's an idiot, she pronounces. Or a hopeless optimist.

STOPPED AT the light just before the museum, Lenox updates Liam Emanuel's résumé:

> Born in Tel-Aviv. Sought his death at Niagara Falls in September 2001. Place of death unknown. Threw it all away for one glorious flicker of fame. Like those before him and those who will come after him, he will remain a curiosity. Jew, Israeli, same difference . . . Welcome to the long list of people who shoved their way into history and ended up in a souvenir shop posing as a museum.

Lenox attaches himself to a group of tourists waiting in line and stands quietly a couple of steps behind. This is how surveillance begins.

The first rule of surveillance, Lenox always tells his trainees, is that you must always position yourself in a place where you can pee. The second is that, to be effective, there must be at least two people: the "Eye," who keeps his gaze constantly glued to the subject, and the "Hand," who takes meticulous notes on everything that occurs on the scene and stands in for the Eye only when he needs to go to the bathroom.

Surprisingly, it is often the unfocused and completely random observations that produce the best results. In the case that gained Lenox his reputation, he happened to notice that the suspect had used mouthwash. This innocent act, usually performed by someone about to smooch, was in fact an encoded message to carry out a drug deal.

When Lenox is the Eye, he sometimes has to stay in the same place for hours or even days, and he never relieves the boredom by reading a paper or listening to the radio. It requires total concentration. A quick doze or even a sideways glance at an attractive woman could distract him at a critical moment.

"Passing the time" is an expression with no practical meaning. Lenox is always aware of time as it trickles away like a cancer patient's morphine drip. How do hunters contend with the string of time that ties them to their prey? Some investigators stuff themselves with candy. Lenox likes to warn his trainees that after a long surveillance they will need to go on a diet. Luckily, he never got addicted to smoking like his partner did.

The tourists storm the museum shop, and the tour guide collects his commission from the owners. Lenox notes the successful completion of a business transaction, one of many, and then does something he has never done on any surveillance job: he violates the rule of constant observation and makes a phone call.

JACKIE, YOU'RE disappearing . . . Where the fuck are you?

Beep.

THE ARRAY of data is an isolated island, which the detective must circle but never enter. The attempt to understand the missing person's state of mind must be made from a detached vantage point—as though the investigator stands on the banks opposite the island. But in this case Lenox is desperate enough to break the rules, and he reluctantly steps into the missing man's shoes.

Okay, White Raven, this is your only chance. Try and imagine what it's like to roll down the waterfall in a wooden barrel like the desperate schoolteacher Annie Taylor, or in a barrel lined with fiberglass and liquid foam like Karel

Soucek. Bobby Leach, the Englishman, used a steel barrel that proved a successful survival device, although he ended up in hospital for six months and died years later after slipping on an orange peel.

Lenox marvels at these adventurers' inventiveness as he walks past the exhibits with the hoards of enthusiastic tourists. It's too crowded to take notes, so he is forced to memorize the archetypal daredevil profile. Is Liam Emanuel a member of this rare breed?

The Canadian Jean Lussier's six-foot rubber ball survived intact, while William Red Hill's contraption of ropes and inner tubes could not withstand the pressure and fell apart. All that was left of Charles Stephens was an amputated tattooed arm, and the sole survivor of the Greek chef George Stathakis's escapade was his pet turtle.

Perhaps that is the solution: to share the terror with a partner, like twenty-two-year-old Steve Trotter, who made the plunge twice. A decade after his first successful leap, he and his friend Lori Martin went down the falls in a container constructed of water heaters, with four oxygen tanks attached.

Hey, the Raven also wants a partner.

Moving on. This is no time for the posthumous matchmaking enterprise.

Lenox follows the crowd to a display showing the remainders of Jesse Sharp's kayak. Sharp, who refused to wear a helmet or life jacket, was so confident in his antic that he made dinner reservations at a restaurant down the river. His body was never found.

The final member of the hard-core daredevils with their "floating coffins," as Lenox chooses to call them, was Robert Overacker, who reached the falls on a Jet Ski with an American flag and a sign that read "Save the Homeless." His rocket-propelled parachute failed to open and he screamed as he plunged to his death on live television. 1995. The last flood show.

The tourists rummage eagerly through the souvenir shop shelves. Niagara erasers, Niagara toothbrush holders, Niagara T-shirts. A flourishing production line of objects no one would take to outer space. Weeds spreading through the fields of tourism.

Lenox picks up a plastic frozen waterfall and takes it to the counter.

The tour guide gives the group a five-minute break, and a line stretches out from the women's bathroom. Lenox could teach them a thing or two about holding it in. At the urinal, in between stolen glances at other men's parts, he suddenly spots another footprint next to his own on the wet floor.

A nonskid sole.

Simon T. Lenox charges out of the restroom, barely stopping to zip up. There's no one outside.

Fuck you, Emanuel! He screams himself hoarse.

GOD IS with us. That's what *Emanuel* means, Jackie told him. Lenox let out a half-groan, half-snort of contempt when he heard that. But there was no point in discussing parents who afflict their children with the illusion of a permanent babysitter, a spirit hovering above their heads.

Bagadbanuel. God betrayed us.

Natashanuel. God abandoned us.

Einshumel. There is no God.

That's what he would name his children, if he had any.

What is that twinge he keeps feeling? Could it be that he misses something or someone?

Heaven forbid. Just a lost emotion.

He sits in his car outside the museum and smokes cigarettes from a pack the Hand left in the glove compartment. He fills his lungs with poison as if in mockery of the clean, fresh air. Maybe the negative ions really are an aphrodisiac.

And why should Jackie Brendel want him? A plucked raven, a failed husband to three, an alcoholic. The only thing brimming in him is his bladder. Could be a prostate tumor. When he gets back he'll make an appointment with the urologist.

Liam Emanuel. The twenty-eighth missing person of his career.

Missing inaction.

EVERY JEW is potentially Israeli.

Every Israeli is potentially dead.

Every person is a candidate to inherit death. Lenox does not bother to write this certitude in his pad.

If only he had demanded his grandmother's pipe back from the home. Chain-smoking in his closed car, he reaches a conclusion: fear. That's all they shared last night. If he finds the Israeli he'll get rid of the Jewish woman too.

Why did he push himself into this vortex? He'd be better off drifting away in the current, postponing the inevitable fall.

He decides not to call her anymore.

FINALLY, THE falls.

Like the Belgian monk, Lenox slows down before reaching the sight, so that he may relish the gurgling and thundering. Indians take only what they need from the earth, his grandmother used to say. Perhaps he has betrayed his ancestors by becoming a police investigator, infected by the white avarice, a ravenous consumer of trivialities and accomplishments. Tried to bite off more than he could chew, and ended up choking.

One Israeli less, one Israeli more—what difference does it make? After all, this man is not a leader or a pioneer, whose acts determine other people's fates. Just a two-bit politician riddled with disappointments, addicted to the spotlight. Perhaps what broke him was not his father's death, but his son's life.

The term *ba'al teshuva* still needs to be clarified. *One who returns.* But to what? And from where?

Perhaps they're trying to erase their sins, Lenox whispered to Jackie in bed.

No, no, she said. That's just what they call someone who finds God and starts observing the religious commandments very strictly.

And why is that a problem? Lenox wonders.

It's not what Zionism wanted.

Zionism—like it's a nagging woman. He wanted more details.

But Jackie Brendel got defensive: she was just quoting secondhand information. After all, she was also outside Israel, facing it from the other shore. She was born in America and would die there.

The Israeli: an upgraded model of the Jew.

Lenox chuckled in bed. This wasn't a piece of software.

They shared a heartwarming moment. The fear retreated. Then she fell asleep. It had been years since a woman had spent a whole night in his bed. And she didn't even push him out of his sleeping territory. He lay there in the graying light, listening to the wind.

She was petite. It would be easy to get rid of her. Go forth from my land and my bed . . .

LENOX LOOKS out at the falls, which expose their mouthful of white fangs. He listens to the carpet of water rushing down the cliffs, streaked with ripples of foam.

Ten suicides a year, on average. Maybe the Israeli is already floating over the abyss.

What is an Israeli?

A mutation.

A genetic bifurcation.

A failed laboratory experiment.

Could Jackie Brendel have been Israeli in another incarnation?

Could Lenox have been one?

What?!

Jewindian.

No. Absurdities can only go so far.

Lenox rips out the page and throws it at the frothing Niagara.

BUT IS there a limit to absurdity? Lenox wonders as he bobs along in a *Maid of the Mist* boat on an hour-long ride to the falls. He wears a disposable light blue rain poncho and blends in with a group of exuberant tourists. Unlike body bags, the raingear is made of a thin fabric that allows the body's outline to show through.

Lenox sips in the misty air. He feels sated, and his bladder is also at peace. His face is covered with a drizzle of thorny drops. The ultimate absurdity, he murmurs to himself: people cheering while tears run down their faces.

Lenox is the only one not aiming a camera at the approaching rapids, perhaps because the Eye relies on his memory to carry the burden. He quickly scans the herd of tourists on board, but the Israeli is not among them. There is no point in trying to blind himself to the colors so that he might resemble Liam Emanuel, because as you approach the falls, the world fades into gray anyway. For a moment Lenox himself becomes the biblical Noah, navigator of the Ark, a righteous and blameless man who believes that not far from here is a piece of land that can offer refuge.

The mission is forgotten and Lenox loses himself in the beauty.

Maid of the Mist turns its stern to the falls as it sails back to the riverbank.

Excuse me, Mister, would you mind?

A light blue hood frames a pair of blazing eyes surrounded by a multitude of thin braids dripping with water. Lenox skips a beat.

Keisha?

Excuse me?

Sorry, my mistake. You look like . . .

The young woman with the braids holds out a video camera, shields it with her hands from the water, and asks him to film her and her sweetheart with the receding falls in the background.

I'm Zoe, she says, but does not bother introducing the man.

A red light flickers in the frame, and Lenox has trouble steadying himself on the rocking boat. Zoe forces a hug on her partner and flashes a grin. They both have gold lip rings.

A vision invades the eyepiece: the old Indian woman's empty mouth. Lenox closely inspected every defaced corpse he was ever assigned, but he never saw his grandmother's body. He refused to touch her woody flesh or look into her wide-open eyes. The Jews bound her in their shrouds. What prayer did they say for her soul?

The falls spray water on the lens, and Lenox loses focus. One day, when Zoe shows her children the film, she will blame the photographer when she realizes it's all blurred.

When he hands back the camera, Lenox can't resist asking: Why do you need proof of your love?

The couple exchange looks. The fresh groom's face is mostly covered by his hood; only his lip ring shines out.

Shit, he grumbles. As far as he is concerned, they could have made do with a walk and looked over the falls from the bridge.

Zoe laughs: Proof of our love? That's exactly what the guy who took our picture on the overlook bridge asked. She shakes out her braids like a wet dog. He was really friendly, that guy. Wild red hair. Half-grown beard. We even took a picture of him as a souvenir. When we left, he said, "You should have no more sorrow."

Lenox perks up. In his excitement, he forgets his façade of manners and asks them—almost begs them—to show him the footage in rewind.

You're the first person to watch our wedding video! Zoe elbows her husband and the plastic raincoats rustle. They'll add music and special effects when they get back from their honeymoon, she explains.

Maid of the Mist has anchored at shore, and a new hoard of tourists rushes aboard. Dozens of hands reach for the folded plastic coats, throwing Lenox off-balance as he peers into the camera frame to watch a miniaturized version of his unique investigation method—sped up. Running backwards while facing forward. A dense cluster of images. A brief history of love—in reverse order. Pulling away before embracing.

Maybe it is possible to die first and live later.

THE FILM rewinds all the way back to the wedding ceremony. The priest blesses the union and Zoe and her chosen one kiss with their mouths full of piercings. All that is left of the overlook bridge scene is a few black and white flickers.

It's as if Liam Emanuel never existed.

Zoe is furious: But they said this was the best camera! We bought it at the Duty Free in Canada. We're going to return this and demand compensation!

Did the man on the bridge have a mark on his cheek?

You really think we have time for this bullshit? The groom suddenly blurts out. If your guy was at least a serial killer, we might make the effort. And anyway, hiding out at Niagara? How cunning is that? I mean, he could have crossed over into Canada, or anywhere else that doesn't have an extradition agreement with the US.

So it's good-bye for now. The bride and groom have to make it to their hot-air balloon ride, Flight of Angels, which is included in their wedding package.

Zoe blames the groom: It's all your fault. We paid a fortune for this camera. We would have been fine with the old one. You always get suckered into these deals.

The air fills with negative ions, but not the aphrodisiac sort. The couple is minutes away from a fight. They even forget to take off their plastic coats. The bride shoves, the groom trips. There are several accidents every year at Niagara Falls. People are so eager that they trip and fall. Fortunately for the groom, the bride manages to catch him at the last minute, and shakes him angrily as she grips him.

Which of Lenox's wives . . .

THE WORDS on the damp notepad pages start to bleed:

> What came before what came before?
> Did Jackie come before Liam Emanuel?
> Without Liam Emanuel there would be no Jackie.
> Would there be a Jackie without Liam Emanuel?
> And White Raven—what would he be without Jackie and without Liam Emanuel?

Lenox dials just to hear her voice on the answering machine, but quickly hangs up.

KEEPING HIS expectations low, Lenox scans the hotel

parking lots. Three Cherokees, none olive green. He doesn't bother asking at the front desks. Why show a photograph that doesn't match the real thing? He tries in vain to wipe off the stain from Emanuel's cheek, but the ketchup only gets infuriatingly redder. It's as if Lenox has a rare disability: he sees colors too sharply, especially the bleeding tones.

Apparently the Israeli likes to sleep under the stars. Fine—let him get pneumonia. Serves him right. Maybe that'll bring him to his senses. Heroic end, my ass. There's nothing like a plain old illness to remind you of what you're really worth.

Lenox feels no pain now, but he is fully aware that somewhere in the *boydem* there is a sign waiting: *You shall have sorrow.*

You're the one stuck on the javelin's tip, White Raven. Perhaps you can find comfort in the thought that sorrow is like getting your lip pierced: first it hurts, then you get used to it.

VALENTINA.

Keisha.

Zoe.

Three women. Which of them will complain that her man doesn't put the toilet seat down?

And Jacqueline Winona—what will be her excuse for leaving?

He wasn't planning to run the film that far back. It was all the camera's fault.

One day human beings will be able to trade themselves up. Entire nations will stand in line for upgrades. From Jew to Israeli. Just like they do when they refresh their gas masks over there, from the last war to the next one. But what will the Israelis trade in for when their turn comes? Lenox puts his hand in his pocket and clutches the damp notepad, which is almost disintegrating.

The front desk clerk is surprised when Lenox does not request a room with a view. Unlike the Israeli, he plans to sink into a soft mattress, cradle himself in sheets too stiffly starched for his taste, and not think about javelins or women.

Before he goes under, Lenox feels his way to the bathroom in the dark, rips Liam Emanuel's picture into shreds, and happily flushes them down the toilet.

The seat faces him like a horseshoe, and the Israeli's scraps swirl around in the water.

JACKIE? ARE you there? It's me . . . Pick up if you're . . . Are you there? I wanted to . . . Shit. Personal messages on an answering machine . . . It's not for me. How can I put this? Jackie? Maybe . . . ? *Beep.*

SIMON? I hope I can call you Simon. Or would you prefer T? What does the T stand for? Tyrone? Tibald? Terry? Thorwald? Tobias? Torquemada? Oh God, I'll have to wait for you to get back . . . Will you come back . . . ? *Beep.*

THE WORST seems to have passed.

Lenox feels revived in the morning. He shaves at the steamy mirror, and reminds himself that this is just the crisis that always comes before closing a case.

A strip of photograph that survived last night's downpour lies at the foot of the toilet, and Lenox reminds his double in the mirror that the Israeli case is closed. He throws the orphaned shred into the toilet, but it refuses to go down. The maid can deal with it. Or the plumber. At a hundred bucks a night, he's entitled to leave traces.

You shall all have sorrow.

The phone rings. The Niagara police inform the eminent detective that no unusual events were recorded last night, and the rescue helicopter was not called in to airlift any daredevils from the falls. No intelligence indicating any intrigues or foul play. A gambler was caught cheating the blackjack dealer in a Niagara, Ontario, casino. You can go home now, law enforcer. Everything is in order, with or without you. Someone is out there spending their inheritance like there's no tomorrow. Hallelujah.

The Israelis will be disappointed. This is not the outcome they expected. Lenox suddenly believes he has exposed the true conspiracy of the map-stain nation: they tried to maneuver their American counterpart into telling them exactly what they wanted to hear. Nothing that might contradict their hopes.

Looking at the scrap that keeps circling in the gushing toilet bowl, Lenox believes he has finally figured out the common roots of Jews and Israelis.

ONE NATION, a résumé:

Martyr.
Serial victim.
Prince of the cosmos.
Wind on the water.
A tour guide to nowhere.
The pillar of fire and smoke for all of humanity.
Pretentious load of crap.

LENOX FEVERISHLY searches for notepaper. This will be the last fax he sends Brigadier General Rosen-Vardi in DC. He digs into the nightstand drawer and finds the holy book. Special tourist edition. Dusty cover. Engraved gilded letters. It's doubtful anyone has bothered to look at it since the hotel was opened.

Lenox sends away the housecleaning maid and hangs a "Do not disturb" sign on the door. He leans against the window that does not face the falls, and reads from Genesis.

The rain has finally stopped, and a pale blue veil of light falls on the pages.

JACKIE'S BOOK.

Liam's book.

White Raven's book of books.

That's not possible.

Unless . . .

LENOX SEES in his mind's eye how the dead Jewish man and the dead Indian woman keep bickering in the mist, though they have long ago given up on the *shidduch*—assuming the concept of time has any meaning to them.

The Eye in charge of the matchmaking has also abandoned its illusion of having no more sorrow, yet the couple continues their quibble because disagreement is the living spirit of every relationship, particularly the one between his and her bones.

Lenox hears the dead Indian woman ask:

Why does your book mention the Raven in only one line? With us he is the Creator.

The dead Jewish man knows his Genesis: "And he sent forth a raven, and it went forth to and fro, until the waters were dried up from off the earth." It is an infinite, circular act, he explains. Whereas with you, Creation is a singular occurrence, a quick passing of water and that's that.

Hearing the deceased couple argue, the Eye is satisfied. There is nothing better than a disagreement to rock the boat and cause a small flood. Still, the matchmaker makes sure the couple does not descend into real strife, or, God forbid, come to blows.

Now the dead Indian brings up the issue of trust: If the Raven went before the dove, and Noah chose it first, then we have here evidence of a special relationship. Affirmative action.

But the Raven never returned, claims the Jew.

The Indian's voice pierces Lenox's mind:

Perhaps it was devoured in the windows of heaven. Or, seeing a chance to have no more sorrow, the Raven could not take the pressure. After all, forty days and forty nights of drifting aimlessly in an ark are no small matter. The minute he got out of the pitch-coated ark, he immediately discharged the world again. So the motive was completely different: it was not boredom that led the Raven to create the world, but an irrepressible urge.

And the dove? What about her?

She was handed a ready-made world.

In his hotel room, Simon T. Lenox is positive he's lost his mind. The maid hears him cursing all the way down the hallway, and flees.

To the question of why a respectable police investigator, at his age, in his position, insists on being so foulmouthed, Lenox would reply that "fuck" is a sort of fury rod, a linguistic island in a sentence, at whose shores the waves of frustration and helplessness, and especially sorrow, may lap. No one is there to point out how badly lacking in profanities the Hebrew language is.

Were he required to investigate the repercussions of the lack of "fuck" in Hebrew, Simon T. Lenox would learn that the Israelis borrow their words of fury from Arabic. And he might conclude that in the absence of efficient Hebrew curses, the Israelis' only outlet for rage is violence.

Simon T. Lenox puts the Bible—tourist edition—on the bed. Outwardly, he looks calm. He opens the first page and writes: "Safeguard this. For those who come after you."

As the channel of his thoughts flows backwards to his childhood wounds, he calls room service and orders a bottle of Jack Daniels. If he'd known what sort of whirlpool he was getting into, he would have made the Israeli disappear with his own two hands. And the Jewish woman.

He checks his phone for messages.

A waiter arrives with a sealed bottle and two elegant glass tumblers on a trolley covered with a starched white linen cloth. Lenox tips him generously and bundles the bottle inside the coat he drapes over his arm.

What would you recommend for a boy visiting Niagara?

The waiter is almost at the door. He turns back and stares. Where is the boy?

He's not here.

How old is the boy?

Lenox pulls out another bill and the waiter takes a step back, insulted. Kids like adventures, he declares. He has three. They couldn't care less about beauty. To them it's a given, like happiness. Pretty backdrops aren't enough. Kids want tension, mystery, a scaled-down voyage of risks, so long as their protective parents are supervising. The waiter suggests Cave of the Winds.

Lenox does not ask where the cave is or what kind of winds dwell in it. He shuts the door quietly and walks downstairs.

Before paying his bill, he lights the last cigarette from his partner's pack. The hotel lobby is adorned with massive mirrors, and he stands in a corner where smoking is still permitted. By a metal ashtray stuffed with butts, some with red lipstick marks, Lenox packs in a concentrated dose of nicotine. Surrounded by endless reflections of smoke rings, he imagines himself smoking a pipe. He makes a note:

> White Raven—Black Dove.
> Maybe she is his real partner.
> Could such a union produce offspring?

> The celestial matchmaking business must be shut down and declared bankrupt.

Lenox tears out the page and lights it with the cigarette.

HE JOINS the crowd of yellow coats making their way over the range. The children cheer, the adults pretending to be children cheer, and Simon T. Lenox fakes his own cheer. Like them, he is required to change into soft nonskid moccasins, put on a yolk-yellow cape, and squeeze into the long line straggling outside the entrance to Cave of the Winds.

Lenox easily spots the obsessive thrill seekers, the people whose sole purpose is to accumulate assets and arouse envy. Alongside them are those who find themselves at the falls almost by chance, on their way to some nameless thereplace. The newlyweds on package deals are also easy to identify. But even if these grooms remember to put the toilet seat down, there is no guarantee that the *shidduchs* will be successful.

The guide instructs the group to follow him through a tunnel where water trickles constantly down the rocky walls. The moccasins are as soft as a pair of tattered slippers, and the ground is damp and hard. A frantic boy leans against Lenox's leg, and his mother scolds him when he jumps up and down in the elevator. They might get stuck at the gates of thereplace and not get in.

Kid, you should be thanking us for taking you on a trip. We've given you the gift of this amazing memory. What will you tell your kids, if you tell them anything?

Lenox had no mother to scold him, and now he has no Indian grandmother to claim that elevators are the invention of the white people, who are convinced there is a shortcut to the sky or to the depths of the earth.

The elevator groans and the group is propelled out into

the lit-up entrance. The Indian man agitating inside Lenox longs to kneel down before the sacred waterfall.

A wooden platform leads over the sloped ground to the falls as a sort of gradated maze. Lenox's yellow poncho does not protect him from the roaring streams of water. His skin drips even beneath the layers of clothing. The day is bright, the sky is clear, and yet—a deluge. Preserved disaster, commotion in formaldehyde, a domesticated horror show that anyone can afford.

A white raven set out to see if the waters had gone down, and has never been seen since.

Another uninvited image: the raven did come back, but he couldn't find the ark. His feathers turned black from fear, and then he emitted what he emitted.

What is the world that was recreated?

Lenox has an overpowering impulse to jump.

DON'T TAKE it so seriously, Simon T. Sometimes visitors have daydreams. Travelers' depression is a familiar psychological phenomenon. Take the poncho home as a souvenir for Jackie Brendel. Make love under the yolky canopy. She will be on top, and you on the bottom. Then you can switch.

Lenox remembers to avoid a direct hit from the Bridal Veil Falls, which can be lethal. The boy tugs at Lenox's poncho and squeals. His voice is swallowed up in the din, and only the frenetic motion of his body indicates that something unusual is occurring. Lenox trips on a step, and the moccasins do not stop him from sliding. Only when he sees the rainbow, like a flower suddenly blossoming in the white wilderness, does he realize why the boy shouted. No lighting designer could have created such a perfect rainbow.

Jackie!!!

Lenox shouts and falls down. But he feels as though he is merely floating.

He feels a pair of hands suddenly gripping him, and knows immediately who they belong to.

I've been waiting for you. You're late.

Lenox hears the voice but still does not see the face through the screen of water.

The Israeli's smile beams over his week-old auburn beard. He wears white sneakers, not moccasins.

Fuck you, Liam!

Lenox points to the perfect rainbow, but the Israeli's steady expression implies that he does not understand the commotion. Only then does Lenox remember that he is color-blind. If he were Indian, that would be his name.

Come on! says Color-Blind to White Raven.

Jets of water batter them both, and Liam pulls Lenox to the exit. A faded olive-green Jeep Cherokee is parked outside, covered in a thin layer of dust.

Lenox is so flustered that he forgets to give back the moccasins. A staff member at Cave of the Winds will send a pair of old Italian leather shoes to the lost and found at the end of the day.

LENOX LEAVES a trail of water behind him, like a child who has wet his pants. Here is his Israeli, in the flesh. All his worry was for nothing. All the faxes ricocheting between two continents were just wasted paper. The curses he was planning to hurl at him have evaporated.

Anger, like passion, is a volatile substance. The only thing Lenox's sensors pick up in Liam Emanuel is sorrow, which, like disposable diapers, no one has yet found a way to decompose.

Is the Israeli armed? And is Lenox being kidnapped or taken hostage? What will the Israeli demand as ransom in return for the Indian? A million dollars in unmarked bills? An end to the Israeli-Arab conflict?

A small boat moors by the bushes, and Liam Emanuel reaches his hand out to Simon T. Lenox to invite him in.

Lenox feels weary, deflated. The Flight of Angels trails on, he murmurs.

HE DOESN'T even bother to find out how the Israeli recognized him. They each know who the other is, and that is enough. The photograph was unkind to Emanuel; it aged him prematurely. His eyes are narrowed. His chin is square and rigid. His cheeks are sunken and his red curls are wild, with the occasional streak of gray. Lenox cannot find the stain, unless it is hidden in the *boydem* of stubble. Fiction always magnifies reality when it comes to ketchup.

They still have not conversed, but the threat is gone. It is clear to Lenox that the Israeli has no intention of harming him. Their silence is cloaked by the water's murmur and the rattling boat engine. They haven't even exchanged a look, perhaps to avoid the tacit pact between hunter and prey. When Lenox was promoted for the first time, his grandmother gave him one piece of advice: Silence is the most effective weapon in the investigator's arsenal, because the interrogation subject always assumes that the investigator knows more than he himself does.

Lenox does not press the Israeli to explain his disappearance. He understands now that in the realm of time he inhabits, there is no sooner or later. An Indian will never say "waste of time," his grandmother explained, because time, unlike objects or people, does not get lost. By one route or another, we will get to the destination, she maintained. Her hut on the reservation was located between a substance abuse center and a garish casino. Since Congress legalized gambling on tribal lands, the natives had new economic opportunities at their disposal. Six billion dollars a year in revenue. But his grandmother clung to her hut, surrounded by desperate people who had not adapted to the wounds of the white conquest, until she too was infected by the disease.

Lenox got out just in time. He didn't think he had to ask for forgiveness.

The two men are stuck in an eddy and the boat spins on its axis. Perhaps the emotionally infantile Israeli is fulfilling his dream of becoming a discoverer. Seeking water, to compensate for his arid homeland. A romantic journey in the endless green expanses, which the color-blind man cannot perceive in all their tones.

How can you ask someone born under a harsh sun to enter a covenant with water? Streams, creeks, rivulets, rivers, falls, floods. The map-stain nation yearns for them—they are an unattainable thereplace. Lenox is willing to give Liam some friendly advice: Create your own rain from silver iodide. This will require that you import moisture. America can help put together an airlift—cargo planes loaded with positive and negative ions that will scatter passion or sorrow upon your people.

What are you worth without our help? And you, you arrogant son of a bitch, did you think you'd inherited the sky? Lenox opens his mouth to unload the deluge of curses he'd accumulated on the way from Goshen to Liberty, but the fury refuses to come out.

The Israeli's voice suddenly pierces the silence:

This is what I inherited.

The confused Simon T. Lenox does not know where to look.

Liam Emanuel takes his hands off the wheel and points to a tree-topped horizon beyond the bend in the river.

Welcome to my island.

Thereplace Grand Island.

SOMEONE SHOULD be committed immediately. But it's unclear who has lost his mind—the hunter or the prey.

Grand Island is a resort island near the giant suburbs of Buffalo. Vacation homes for the wealthy. Mansions and yachts. Rest and inheritance, as Deuteronomy would have it, though not necessarily in that order.

Stop, stop! How did I get stuck with a delusional Israeli? We're going off into the deep end soon. I don't want to turn into one of those faceless floaters!

Lenox stands up abruptly and the boat almost capsizes.

An ark of lunatics. A miserable man hallucinating about inheriting a grand island. What he needs is a valium.

Mayday! Mayday!

Maybe it really is better to be born in arid dirt—then you can't die by drowning. But there are all kinds of ways to die. In a firestorm, for example. A man-made glory.

The island looks tranquil as it comes closer to them. Not a hint of calamity.

Liam Emanuel steadies the boat as it floats down the current into a natural anchorage, like a bird returning to its nest.

JACKIE, ARE you there?

I found him.

I'm not sure if . . .

Who found whom.

What difference does it make.

The main thing is . . .

LENOX NOTES that his fear is entirely gone, but he can't tell what is left. While they tie the boat to a tree, he remembers something the Jewish woman told him. At the time, he hadn't paid much attention. It was right after the fuck, which even now he still cannot find a proper name for.

Don't cross the line.

She must have been referring to the rare cases in which an investigator fatally yields to his suspect. She was trying to caution him against making a critical mistake. In retrospect, he thinks Jackie Brendel shed a tear on his shoulder. But that is a patently summoned sense—an initiative of the brain trying to minimize the pain of separation.

Liam Emanuel looks straight at him, at last, and there is no madness or deathly terror in his eyes.

I wanted to step on our pastfuture, he says. His voice is not defiant but childishly curious.

Lenox dislikes the Israeli's use of the plural. Whom exactly is he referring to?

Liam Emanuel takes a thin piece of paper out of his backpack and shakes it as though it were a used napkin. Simon T. Lenox immediately recognizes the certificate that the son rejected at the cemetery. It's doubtful the forensic lab will be able to get fingerprints off it. But finally, here is an original document, written in English.

To my children's children—you who come after me,

I have left you an inheritance, this deed of ownership, so that you may attain redemption on the day of calamity. You shall be beaten and persecuted, consumed by fire, and not a single nation in the world shall come to your aid. Know that there is one place that is yours by law. For your benefit, I have purchased the great island downriver from the Niagara, though I was not able to found the city of shelter on it. I became a laughing stock among the communities of Ashkenaz and Sepharad, and although I publically recanted my plan to gather the lost tribes in the Ararat that is not Zion, still the land is your entitlement, if only on paper. The dimensions of the ark may be in error and it may not have been coated in pitch, yet it shall sail—before it and after it, the deluge—until the raven is dispatched.

Your ancient grandfather Noah,
sailing the way of all flesh,
New York, May 21, 1851

THE LETTER strikes Simon T. Lenox the way a dramatic monologue makes the audience hold its breath at a sharp reversal of fates.

What the fuck is going on?

How can the Native American investigator explain to the Israeli that land is not property and no one can own it? It was given to both the creators and the creatures to guard. We are all temporary guests, and land cannot be inherited.

But perhaps the document is a forgery, produced by a madman insistent on rolling his anxieties and wild hallucinations back up the generational ladder. Why give any credibility to a melodramatic fiction dreamt up by a zigzagged brain? Even hope itself can drive a person mad.

This was also Liam Emanuel's initial response when he read the document after getting home from the cemetery. He took his record player down from the *boydem* and listened to Pink Floyd's *Dark Side of the Moon.* The old vinyl squeaked when he touched it. *When I come home cold and tired, / it's good to warm my bones beside the fire.* A scratch made the line play over and over again in a loop. When Liam moved the needle, it pricked his finger and he bled onto the record.

IN HIS notepad, Lenox transcribes an ancient résumé that was also among the papers in Liam's *boydem.* It will be filed away in a storeroom and only sought out by collectors of oddities:

> Mordecai Manuel Noah, born in Philadelphia in 1785, to a mother descended from Marranos and a father who immigrated from Manheim, Germany. His mother died when he was six and a half, and his father disappeared shortly afterwards under mysterious circumstances. Noah was educated by his grandfather, Jonah.
>
> Lawyer, journalist, playwright, diplomat, US Consul to Tunis, Sherriff of New York.
>
> Married seventeen-year-old Rebecca Esther Jackson at the age of forty-three.
>
> Purchased Grand Island in 1825 as a refuge for the Jewish people. Declared the land "the State of Ararat" and appointed himself "Judge of Israel."

Here is what is not on the résumé: some say he never set foot on the property. He saw the island from the other side of the river, but never bothered to cross over.

LIAM EMANUEL thought the document must be a relic from his drama studies at Tel Aviv University, preserved in the *boydem* as a souvenir. But the paper itself, and the handwriting, the majestic letters drawn with a fine quill . . .

Simon T. Lenox is cautious. There will need to be thorough laboratory tests, but it seems this is not a forgery or a hoax. It's a miracle that the paper was not eaten by moths. It even gives off a whiff of tobacco leaves.

Lenox sniffs the old certificate and holds it up to Liam Emanuel's nose.

Together they breathe in the pastpresent.

WHAT WILL you do with your inheritance? Simon T. Lenox wonders out loud. Is it better to be poor in assets and rich in dreams, or the opposite?

They sit next to each other, dipping their feet in the water. Above them, or perhaps beneath them, the dead Indian woman and the dead Jewish man discover another commonality. For many months, both have been ravaged by cancer, a cruel conqueror that does not distinguish among genders or races. None of the known cures have worked. Liam Emanuel took his father to consult with the finest oncologists. It was no longer clear who was forcibly dragging out whose life and who was refusing to let go. Liam discloses his feelings of guilt.

Faced with his grandmother's deterioration, conversely, Simon T. Lenox created a healing circle in his mind's eye. He poured water onto a circle of twelve stones covered with branches. In the center of the circle he burned pine needles, and surrounded the smoke with his thoughts. He sat in the garden of the Hebrew Home for the Aged imagining a continent free of white people, and blamed them for all the foreign ailments they had brought with them.

Liam tells Lenox that in his father's final days, as the shell of his body continued to flutter and his spirit was still gripped by gravity, he told his son about the ancient deed of ownership that had found its way from one *boydem* to the next. Before the funeral, the document was located in one of the gas mask boxes in an old suitcase. Staring at the boxes and luggage in which the essence of his life had been packed and unpacked over and over again, Liam Emanuel made the decision to fly away. He did not even know whether the island really existed or was merely the product of a dying man's fantasies.

Gas mask? Lenox echoes, and remembers the fax that finally arrived from Israel. He'd written in his notepad:

> Contents: gas mask, filter, syringe.
>
> Storage instructions: keep in a dry, shaded, cool place.

To be opened solely upon explicit orders from the Home Front Command.

Keep away from children.

THE ISLAND'S horizon stretches into the distance. Its soil is covered with a downy layer of weeds, except on the asphalt road that leads off the bridge.

The two men amble along like a couple of retired cartographers. Liam Emanuel looks up at the treetops: maple, elm, white oak, black cherry. He has never seen such trees. Nor had he heard of Grand Island before he came here. There were several other places in the United States with that name, including one city in Nebraska, which had utterly confused him. The person who set him on the right course was the black girl with the braids at the outdoor gear store.

Keisha, Lenox says.

You know her? She told me to be careful. Such a sweet girl.

The two men are in harmony. Lenox points out a beaver, a white-tailed deer, a raccoon, a coyote, wild geese—foreign creatures to the Israeli. Yellow pike and black bass have proliferated in the Niagara waters, making Grand Island an eternal fishing ground. Despite the claims of the name, the island is not large at all.

The Neutral Nation gained its name because it attempted to serve as a buffer between the warring Huron and Iroquois peoples. But although they took no side in the conflict, every last one of them was slaughtered. The name of their village, Ongniaahra, is the only trace left of them, and that is where everything began.

Two generals chose Grand Island as a site for a duel after each accused the other of cowardice. Red Jacket, a Seneca chief, later made a deal with the white people and sold the island for one thousand dollars—an impressive sum compared to the meager twenty-four dollars paid for Manhattan. The most important clause in their treaty, which was also signed by Twenty Canoes, Sharp Shins, Falling Boards, and Man Killer, was the guarantee of fishing and hunting rights to the native peoples.

Man Killer? Who takes a name like that for himself?

Liam feels a shiver. Lenox struggles in vain to hear his grandmother's ghostly voice.

On the information brochure from the Chamber of Commerce one can also read of the island squatters, who were forcibly removed by the Niagara sheriff. It took five days and nights to burn down seventy huts and make a hundred and fifty men, women, and children refugees. Two committees appointed by four states were required to determine the borders and sovereignty of the disputed land. These wounds bled for seventy-five years before healing.

They walk along the western bank, and Lenox can feel every bump and protuberance through his worn moccasins. They stop to rest under the scaffolding of a Holiday Inn that will soon offer resters and inheritors the finest in sorrow-repelling luxuries.

This is the place that was intended for us, way back in the lost Jewish day, says Liam.

Lenox asks: How would the Jews have integrated in the island's history, which has its own bloody résumé, like every other place?

Liam assumes this question also bothered his forefather, who must have feared that his heroes would be alien transplants here—unnatural crossbreeds. After all, how would Jews survive on fishing and hunting? He laughs, and cannot help comparing this land to the thereplace chosen with excessive intentionality in the Middle East. Ostensibly, the Jews are alien transplants in Israel too, and the locals view them as squatters. But unlike Grand Island, Liam Emanuel explains, Israel stems from the original yearned-for land, from which the Jews were forcibly removed. Now they are trying to crumple time as retroactive compensation.

Crumple time? Lenox hears his grandmother groaning—or perhaps it's just one of the faltering hotel's scaffolds—and he confesses to Liam Emanuel that he harbors a desire for Jackie Brendel.

He was not hoping to find love. Not at his age. He did not believe himself worthy of love, and now he must acknowledge that, against his will, love has found him. Still standing under the scaffolding, he takes off his moccasins. He fleetingly sees the dead Jewish man and the dead Indian woman shake hands on the Happy Hunting Ground.

GET THEE out of thy country, unto the land that you could have had.

Liam Emanuel asks Lenox for his notepad and writes the corrupted verse in Hebrew. But his attempts to translate end in failure.

AT A local restaurant, "Village Inn," they order burgers. Simon T. Lenox, barefoot, reaches for the ketchup after Liam Emanuel pushes away the red bottle. But when he realizes that his fellow diner has rejected what he sees as a gray drizzle, he decides to forego his usual drowning of the hamburger.

Although they are only two, they cannot resist ordering three desserts—cherry cheesecake, chocolate cookie pie, and pecan pie—and they finish off every last crumb, to the delight of the proprietress.

With full stomachs, they summon up the cornerstone of Ararat. Mordecai Manuel Noah commissioned it from a Cleveland quarry in honor of the declaration of the Jewish state, engraved it with the date and the inscription "*Shema*

Yisrael," in Hebrew letters, and ordered that the stone be affixed eternally at the foot of the flagpole, facing east.

When did this dramatic scene occur?

On the fifteenth day of September, in the fiftieth year of American independence.

Five days from now we can celebrate the birthday of the Jewish state that never was, Lenox comments in his notepad. Under the table, he puts his moccasins back on.

Can you explain to me, says Liam Emanuel, why inventing countries is so beloved by theater people? Is fiasco in reality better than humiliation on stage? After all, you can barely control the sets, not to mention the props. Stone, for example.

Where is that cornerstone now? Lenox asks.

The restaurant owner hands them the check. Cornerstone? Hebrew letters? What on earth are you talking about? She stacks the empty dishes acrobatically on her forearm, and adds the ketchup bottle.

Are you archeologists?

No.

Anthropologists?

No.

Then what are you?

Liam Emanuel pays the check and Lenox insists on leaving the tip. The proprietress invites them to come back soon and adds, with a grin: You're brothers, right? Twins?

What the fuck are we?

Simon T. Lenox is glad to hear the F-word sliding naturally off Liam Emanuel's tongue.

T? You don't mind me calling you T, do you? I'm worried. Your cell is off, or else you have no reception wherever you are . . .

I'm dying with worry . . .

Maybe that's proof that I . . .

Beep.

Liam Emanuel's father remembered the document just before he died. Liam wonders why he didn't just burn the paper and destroy all evidence of its existence, so that no one would want to trek to the island and re-hallucinate it. Was his decision to roll the island legacy down the generations a form of acknowledging the failure of the Jewish state in the land of Israel? Are fifty-odd years enough to call it quits? Even the Niagara Falls took hundreds of thousands of years to become a prime destination.

What will you do with your inheritance? Lenox asks, putting the cart before the horse. He distractedly sticks his notepad in his mouth.

Liam Emanuel keeps quiet as a fish.

History plays tricks on us, says Lenox, shaking his head. You used to be able to hear the Niagara's thundering waters all the way to Grand Island. But now the deluge falters beneath a cloak of noise. A ritual of tourists taking to the waters.

White Raven wants to wipe the stain off Color-Blind's face, but he resists when he remembers the Jewish woman's warning.

Don't cross the line.

Except that the line has already been crossed.

My father died, says Liam Emanuel. All fathers die, Simon T. Lenox replies. That is the correct order of things. And before them, grandfathers die. After all, your father died of old age—an impressive accomplishment considering the calamities he'd been through. He wasn't born in Israel, but he chose to be buried there.

Straight into the grave . . .

For him that was the only place, Liam Emanuel says dismissively, and gives the Indian a quick Hebrew lesson. You see, Lenox, for us, "place" also means "God."

They leave the restaurant and cross over to the riverbank. A long silence stretches out as the wind whips the treetops.

You have to grieve, Simon T. Lenox whispers, crossing the line despite Jackie's warning.

He kneels under the rustling elm tree and pulls Liam Emanuel down beside him.

Your father was gathered up by Wakan Tanka, the Great Spirit under whose canopy all creatures dwell. Welcome, Wakan Tanka, One Spirit.

MY FATHER died a sad man. His deeds are drowning at sea, and around him they recite poetry.

They stood beside each other at the river and urinated. Some people drink urine as a healing talisman, but no one has ever heard of people who drink their tears.

Thin javelins of bodily fluids turn into glowing arcs in the fading light of Grand Island.

TELL ME, Liam, how do you see darkness?

Black.

Like I do?

Maybe a different black.

Because your vision impairment isn't necessarily a drawback. It might be . . .

COLOR-BLINDNESS RUNS in the family, Liam Emanuel explains. Once every few generations someone is born with the genetic defect. He was extremely relieved when he learned that the gene had skipped his son. The day he was born, he hung dozens of prisms over the boy's crib, but he had to use opticians' books to teach him the colors. The height of absurdity, he tells Lenox, since all that effort was in vain, invested in a boy who walks backwards with his face forward, into a black-and-white world.

He has no intention of apologizing for leaving home

like a thief in the night. It's best to minimize the damages of separation. He knew they would try to stop him. It's so easy to put a man's feet back on a path worn down by many shoes. If he had let anyone in on the secret of the inheritance, his ex-wife would have publically disgraced him and labeled him a madman. The map-stain nation people have developed sophisticated methods to bury a man alive, Liam Emanuel grumbles. Some of his well-wishers would probably have recommended that he solve his mid-life crisis by finding a young lover, perhaps one of the golden-haired beauties who recently immigrated from the former Soviet Union and who are all the rage among middle-aged Israeli men.

Valentina, Lenox says, as he zips up his pants. Liam Emanuel nods.

They both hope she didn't lose her job at the Duty Free.

In his notepad, Lenox writes:

And what about a résumé of love? You can't just keep wallowing in blood.

He dials the number again, without caring that Liam Emanuel can overhear.

Jackie, can you hear me? Where are you?

I have to tell you . . . Grand Island is also a city of refuge for passion. Liam and I—no, he doesn't have a middle name—found out that the island squatters included a couple who ran away to pursue their forbidden love. When the evacuation started, they were desperate, and they went to see the Niagara sheriff. You tell me, what country would give them refuge? It's a good thing the sheriff was a romantic. He let them hide out on the island until the storm blew over. He even gave them two barrels of whiskey, to warm their bones in the terrible cold. Just imagine a dove and a raven in that winter of 1819, on Grand Island, covered with snow and alcohol.

Are you cold, Jackie? There's an extra blanket on the top shelf in the closet.

I promise you . . . I'll try and remember to put the toilet seat down . . .

On Whitehaven Road, between Grand Island's small town hall and the Chamber of Commerce, the two men find a liquor store. They open their bottle of Jack Daniels in a shady spot, without knowing that they are standing under the shelter of the Trail Tree. Hundreds of years ago, the Indians fastened one of its branches to the earth as a road-sign. The tree set down roots, and to this day it points to the east.

Simon T. Lenox and Liam Emanuel lean on the indentation between the trunk and the branch, and drink to life after death. If the lost pipe had been found, they could have smoked some peace together.

By the rivers of Niagara I sat and wept when I forgot Ararat.

They sit on a rock passing the bottle back and forth, waiting for a taxi. In this last leg of the night, they can finally see the world in the same colors: viscous black dotted with glowing white.

If I remember thee Jerusalem on the Niagara. It's the only place in Israel that Lenox can name. He knows it from TV.

If I remember thee Tel-Aviv on the Niagara. The place where Liam Emanuel was born and will possibly be buried.

Sitting on a damp rock, Liam Emanuel outlines imaginary landmarks on Grand Island. In geography class they called it a "mute map" or a "blind map." He draws the street where he was born—Brandeis Street, after an American Zionist leader—and the building: number thirty-one. Three stories. Two entrances. No elevator. A poplar tree in the kitchen window, its roots by the trash cans. And of course, a *boydem.*

Sorry. It has no equivalent in Hebrew or English.

He explains the deceptiveness of the language that came to life after a temporary burial that lasted two millennia, at which point unprecedented calamities occurred and led to the revival of the lost language by the survivors. Mordecai Manuel Noah could not have envisioned these horrific calamities even had he been graced with the wildest imagination. And Hebrew, like a diligent beaver, keeps building a dam of new words to somehow block the cascades of sorrow.

Liam takes one last sip from the bottle that sets his gut on fire.

How many Jews can you fit on a small grand island?

Although Lenox's question sounds like the beginning of a joke, it is a practical query. Like an undertaker preparing a grave, or a woman buying a dress, so the prophet Mordecai Manuel Noah had to consider the ratio between the number of people and the acreage of land. According to his calculations—and it should be noted that he had very little data and only primitive statistical methods at his disposal—Grand Island was well matched to the scale of the Jewish people at the time.

Surprisingly, even current statistics would not rule out its suitability. Except that land, unlike clothes, is not elastic, and borders cannot be stretched out or tucked in at whim. Liam Emanuel compares the country to a chemise, a delicate fabric wrap that must be handled very carefully so that it does not tear.

Still, how many Jews can you fit on a small grand island? Lenox insists when faced with the empty bottle.

Six million—vertically.

Lenox rips a page out of his notepad, pokes it into the bottle, and tosses the bottle into the Niagara.

IT'S NOT too late to claim ownership, Liam Emanuel. You can still redeem the deed. Pastpresent—a justified cause. A herd of seasoned lawyers will be only too happy, in return for a hefty commission, to prove the validity of the title. Almost two centuries late, they will stage the second act of the immortal creation. Deluge: The Sequel.

Simon T. Lenox does not sound drunk.

If Mordecai Manuel Noah were to turn up today, he would option his dream off to Hollywood and save himself the humiliation. Liam assumes one of his heirs dropped the family name "Noah" at some point. They made do with the middle name, so the madman label wouldn't rub off on them. Who wants to pass a mark of disgrace down from generation to generation?

Lenox's predecessors also changed their names, but with them it was additions, not subtractions.

His middle initial, T., stands for Teibele. A woman's name. That's all his grandmother was able to tell him.

Teibele?!

Lenox remembers with chilling precision how he skewered his grandmother when she told him that. It was the day he moved her to the Home for the Aged. He was convinced she was pulling his leg, getting back at him for uprooting her. But she insisted that was the real name, and that she had no idea who chose it—and it must have been chosen very deliberately, in the custom of Native Americans who choose their own prescriptive names when they reach maturity. When Lenox demanded to know what Teibele meant, his grandmother repeated that she had no idea. She turned her back on him and looked out on the river as he unpacked her belongings.

Perhaps that was when the pipe was lost.

A TAXI coasts down the hill toward them, but to Lenox's surprise Liam Emanuel announces that he is staying.

Lenox is outraged. How will he prove to his superiors that he has completed his mission? He begs Liam Emanuel to go back with him, if not to Israel then at least to New York, the safest place in the world. He can live a good life there, far from the incurable Middle Eastern strife.

Instead of answering, Liam Emanuel tells Simon Teibele Lenox to return to the loving arms of Jackie Winona Brendel, the accountant whose red hair dye disguises her roots and who has quite a few wrinkles on her stomach. Lenox described her to him as a woman with stable measurements, and said that any stretches or tucks might endanger their tenuous bond.

Go forth, Liam Emanuel urges him. Perhaps we need to learn how to live with each other before we can die with each other.

He pulls out a yarmulke from his pocket. On his nonslip soles, he approaches the muddy bank, unfolds the yarmulke's edges and scatters a pile of ashes onto the babbling Niagara. Lenox inhales a few specks of the foreign earth and wonders if a seed of aridity has been implanted in him. Although the Jewish phrase "You should have no more sorrow" is imprinted on his linguistic topography, he avoids expressing any commiseration in Liam's grief. He merely repeats the Israeli's prayer, without understanding a word of it.

Ki mayim ata ve'el ruach tashuv. For water thou art, and unto wind shalt thou return. *Yitgadal ve'yitkadash mei raba.* May His illustrious name become increasingly wet and holy.

In his notepad, now missing most of its pages, Liam

Emanuel transliterates the Hebrew words in English characters. Lenox struggles to memorize them. He has to remember. These are the words he will say to Jackie when he gets home.

THE PROPRIETRESS at the Village Inn looks out the window at the two men half hugging half pushing each other. Their stubbly beards, the Israeli's week-old one and the Indian's two-day-old one, rub against each other. Simon T. Lenox slips a plastic frozen waterfall into Liam Emanuel's pocket to weigh things down so they can't fly away.

For a moment Liam seems about to propose founding a new Ararat together. But the fragment of an initiative, if it even existed, evaporates quickly.

If the Israeli were to ask him to stay on the island and perform a historical back flip with him, how would Simon T. Lenox respond? If not for his gnawing longing for a woman—an incurable sort of illness—he might have suggested it himself.

So tempting to live in a make-believe land . . .

Lenox does not ask when Liam Emanuel will return to his real grand island, with its occupiers and occupied. He does not ask because something knocks him off course.

JUST A minute, Liam. Before I leave, I have to ask you something. Are you interested in the javelin throw?

Me?

Tickets to the Olympics?

What are you talking about?

Liam Emanuel has never touched a javelin, nor been to any Olympic games.

And thus they part.

And Lenox forgets his notepad.

THE NIAGARA River is calm, and Liam Emanuel waves

his ash-coated hand at Lenox's figure as the taxi disappears up the road.

In the back seat, Lenox searches for his notepad. There are so many questions he did not have time to ask.

He tells the cab driver that he met a tragic hero who was given a second chance by a casino. Will the hero recognize the opportunity and place the magic chip he was bequeathed on the roulette table?

The driver claims that only compulsive gamblers who still think they can win the whole pot believe in second chances.

A faint smell of smoke lingers in Lenox's car, which is still parked outside the Cave of the Winds. He opens all the windows and invites the wind in.

I'M WAITING for you at home, says Jackie Brendel in a broken voice, and the machine cuts her off.

Home, Lenox thinks. What an overused term, and how we struggle to derive meaning from it.

The ancient ghosts urge him to make do with a soft dimple and a comforting lap as refuge from sorrow. Any further demand is a dangerous stretching of the borders.

Simon T. Lenox takes the highway past the same landmarks he passed the day before, although they look slightly different from this direction. Perhaps the lobes of his brain have switched and he's caught the Israeli disease. Does it have a cure?

He does not stop in Damascus; he sails past Liberty, drives straight through the night, passing trucks and going through intersections without looking at the map. A light tapping sound on the roof of the car announces new rainfall, but the rearview mirror shows a clear stretch of sky. When he passes Goshen, he fiddles with his cell phone to get it to work. He holds it up to the hands-free unit, reinserts the charger, kicks it, and finally tears it apart. The more he strives to bring Jackie to the forefront of his vision, the more blurred the picture grows. He tries to see her straddled on top of him, aiming the seed, and even reenacts their farewell in a different variation, one that offers consolation for the anticipated sorrows—illness, old age, mental exhaustion, bickering over toilet seats.

Finding one missing person does not make up for all the ones the earth has swallowed up.

A matchmaking site suddenly opens up on the screen of Lenox's brain. Keisha, Valentina, Zoe—three women grinning widely, aware they are being immortalized. But Jackie, whose youth is behind her, and whose fertility is in doubt . . .

A child.

Is that still possible?

Don't doubt your decision, says the uninvited image of his grandmother from the rearview mirror.

Grand Island: the last chance after the last chance. The island of survivors.

It could have been a perfect sanctuary, Lenox says angrily to the reflection. Perhaps some of the sorrows of the dead and the living could have been spared. The Indians, the white men, the Jews, the Israelis, the Palestinians . . . All the hawks who keep competing in the suffering-throw.

"If a person does not want to die, he may go to Grand Island and live," the Indian ghost quotes from an 1871 New Age prophecy that floated up from some *boydem.*

Lenox finds the Yiddish word strangely fascinating. He ponders it as he drives, repeating and altering it until it loses all meaning. He barely realizes that he has begun to shed tears and ask his grandmother for forgiveness. He swears he will give her bones a final burial, as is the tribal custom.

Because water I am and unto Wakan Tanka I shall return.

May Your illustrious name become increasingly great in the world about to occur.

Simon Teibele Lenox is going home to drink his tears.

THE POLICE stop him at the Tappan Zee bridge again. This time the badge does no good, and Lenox gets a speeding ticket. Fortunately they don't give him a Breathalyzer test, which would have revealed an elevated blood alcohol level.

Shame on you, man, the cop scolds him. You trying to die?

God forbid. I'm in a hurry. I have an urgent desire to live.

To live.

It's going to be a beautiful day, announces the radio weatherman. Low humidity, high of 77. Perfect weather for a primary election.

As the dawn hovers between black and white, Lenox quickly signs the ticket and accepts the ruling.

ON EIGHTY-SEVENTH Street, corner of Third Avenue, Jackie Brendel cannot sleep a wink. She bought a bottle of Jack Daniels at the liquor store across the street, and could not resist taking a sip, reconstructing the taste of semen on her tongue. To pass the time, she polishes three cheap glass tumblers and scrubs the toilet seat. She does not have time to dye her hair.

On Grand Island, Liam Emanuel curls up in the saturated earth as if he were in his sleeping bag on military reserve duty. His red curls are crusted with dirt and he waits for sunrise with his eyes open. The pink fingers will soon break through, drawing patterns over the water rushing from the falls, but the color-blind man will have to make do with the light that signals the crossing of time's borders.

Mai raba, mai raba, mai raba, he murmurs. *Increasingly wet.* He sails away on a wave of longing for his only son. His reflection gazes out from the water with its beard covered by white froth. He barely recognizes himself.

In Jerusalem, as in New York, there is a temporary fugue from the longing, from the unconquerable urge to change places. But above, or below, the after-living continue to split hairs over what came before what came before. Eventually they yawn; even they need rest.

You finally came back to me, said the raven to the dove when she found him after the sorrowful journey. Her feathers had turned black, while his had whitened. Noah had dispatched her to find out if the waters had subsided. She agreed to go because her heart longed for her missing mate.

The ark of ghosts—with its coating of pitch now full of holes—does not rest on Ararat either, but sails between before and after.

SIMON T. Lenox reaches the tower at the edge of his island in full light and moves with the river of people making their way to their daily jobs. With his worn moccasins and unshaven face, he looks homeless.

In the elevator he tries to reassemble the cell phone. People around him snicker, since there's no reception in the elevator anyway.

First he has to send a message to the Israelis: Your lost son is alive and well.

Then he will be free to write his resignation letter. After all, there has to be some sort of order—first comes first, last comes last.

And then . . .

He's dying to pee.

He signs the paper and puts it in the fax machine, so eager to transmit his news across the Atlantic that he fails to see the blazing javelin in the window. Nor does he hear the phone ring.

Teibele means "dove." That is what Moses Brendel told his only daughter when she visited him in the Home for the Aged. But Simon, who has a Jewish middle name, does not hear the message from Jackie, who has an Indian middle name, or her laughter, which sounds almost blissful.

First his ears detect the terrible rumble, a thunder unlike any other, and then he plunges into a Niagara of fire and jet fuel.

AT FIRST light, Liam Emanuel finds Lenox's thin notepad at the foot of a strange mound. He cannot resist reading the surviving notes. He debates for a long time what to do with the handful of loose papers, marked with a raven's beak-print. Eventually he decides to adopt the pad. He will bequeath it to his heirs, whoever they may be.

In a few hours, on the Tuscarora Reservation, some thirty minutes' drive from Grand Island, a young Indian woman will explain to Liam Emanuel how to throw a javelin and aim it straight into his visions. At the entrance to the casino, a woman with lip rings will instruct him to dab a few drops of water on his forehead and say a prayer of thanks. She will caution him not to look for the water's source.

Get thee out of your country with your face forward, she will tell him, even if your body leans back.

Why? Liam will ask, and the Indian will pull him into the casino, and together they will listen to the waterfall of coins streaming through the slot machines.

The giant screens in the casino will display a loop of images from the ruins in Manhattan, and Liam Emanuel will get down on his knees and rend his clothes in mourning.

The young Indian woman will hold his hand and try in vain to comfort him.

HE READS the last page of Lenox's notepad:

> Dear Liam, no middle name, my twenty-eighth missing person,
>
> We did not have time for much, barely one bottle, and I have no idea what contribution your map-stain nation made to the world of alcohol. Although I could celebrate cracking your case with a crate of Jack Daniels, I know the truth: it was you who were following me, not the other way around.
>
> If only I could tell you where we are going. The earth that seems steady is merely a brittle layer, and everything underneath is fluttering and bubbling, so that any destination we may dream of is inherently precarious. My grandmother, may her visions rest in peace, claimed that wind has no colors. That is a blindness we both share.
>
> So before you decide to lower the curtain on your play in the desert, wait awhile. Soon it will be possible, using innovative technology, to change places in the simplest way. Jackie says it will be just like translation software: a quick shift of the cursor will open up a window displaying a column of options, and with one click we will be able to pick our perfect place.
>
> Allow me to be sentimental for a moment, and to make a promise, although it does not obligate you. We will meet one day in Isra Isle or in some other refuge where we will follow our wandering children. After all, we are all responsible for one another, are we not? If I could be a watching eye, or row backwards down the Niagara of time, I would restore life after life to life before life.

I wouldn't even need oars.

And now, before we restart everything, let us make a toast.

ON THE morning of September 15, 2001, Jackie Brendel walks the streets of Manhattan pinning signs to tree trunks. She got Simon T. Lenox's picture from the website that is continuously updated with new missing people. For some reason the printer refused to print the image in color, and so Simon T. Lenox looks out from the trees in black and white.

She had trouble describing their relationship to the commissioner, and only after it was ascertained that he had no family was she allowed to download the picture and undertake the search.

A canopy of darkness slouches over the island. What Jackie Brendel breathes in is not rainclouds, but charred dust scattered by the wind. It rips her to shreds.

She does not cry. Not yet. But her hair has turned white.

Her pocket is weighed down by a plastic frozen waterfall, which was delivered by FedEx to the apartment at Eighty-Seventh Street, corner of Third Avenue. The sender was unnamed, but the package originated in Grand Island, New York.

She has no idea what the purpose of the object is, but likes to inhale its slight whiff of tobacco and feathers.

The day will come when she will try to find out which stranger threw this memory-javelin at her from afar. Perhaps she will hire him to say Kaddish for someone who died alone.

Unless . . .

The wild-haired woman touches the folds of her stomach.

People nod their heads at her on the street. Some cross the line and hug her, others gather around her to pray, each to his or her Creator. One person shakes her hand and says in fluent Hebrew, "You should have no more sorrow."

Exhausted, Jacqueline Winona Brendel pins the last picture to a tree trunk so that her raven—white or black—will not fly off in the wind.

She strokes an invisible stain on Simon T. Lenox's face.

PART TWO

Ararat

SEPTEMBER 1825

The world is filled with remembering and forgetting
like sea and dry land. Sometimes memory
is the solid ground we stand on,
sometimes memory is the sea that covers all things
like the Flood. And forgetting is the dry land that
saves, like Ararat.

—Yehuda Amichai,
Translated by Chana Bloch and Chana Kronfeld

I HAVE never learned to identify the tracks of Jews.

From the day I was born beneath the thundering waters, you, Father Raven, began pointing out the signs for me. Pay attention to the torn path among the ferns, my daughter: a white-tailed deer must have made its way through to the watering hole. When a cluster of leaves suddenly fell on your head, it was a sign that a falcon had taken flight from atop the white oak. Everything that has been here has left traces. The world remains just as it was, but only at first glance.

Not so the tracks of Jews. For those you gave me no signs.

What is revealed to me now is not a vision, but what came before what came before. My little hand is in your big one, and you hold it over the quivering line along the riverbank but do not let me separate the water from the earth. Then you dip my hand in the water, as if to sever it, but there is no pain.

We left our own tracks on the banks of the Niagara on that distant day: the moccasin prints of a man who walks with difficulty, and beside them the skipping marks of a light-footed girl. As we walked away from the water, you pointed to the spot where a black bass had flapped its tail after accidentally leaping out of the water. I said that even a fish does not leave its home without a struggle, and you marked traces of white thought in me. I asked if the fish's spirit was still inside him when he jumped back into the water, and you laughed. I never doubted you again. I was young and my memory was paltry.

I did not know then how deeply the sickness dwelled in your bones. To conceal your weakness, you made up a game: you were a grizzly bear and I was the hunter who lures him down the path through the ferns, where the white-tailed deer passed. I played in the thicket, far from your fading voice as you tried to explain that people, both pale-skinned and red, draw a border between themselves and the earth in order to defy the day when they must return to it. You tried to teach me the secret language of the world, but all I could see was an enchanted land, a wonderful playground where the black bass and the dove and the raven danced in circles created just for me. Only in your absence was I forced to learn, alone, how to track the javelin that cannot be caught, and decipher its signs. Tonight the winds carry tracks I have not learned to identify. A Jewish chief sails in my canoe, and the burden of his body slows my journey to the island.

WE SAILED from Buffalo, a flourishing village of white men. A local name. For me it is temporary, though Lady Lenox regards it as a permanent settlement.

I row in the dark and the Jewish chief gazes at the black horizon, probing blindly for an outline of landscape. He arouses compassion in me. Soon we will arrive, I say. Don't you trust me?

Even if I were to close my eyes, the waterway would open up for me and beckon my canoe to its home. I keep rowing, marking traces of fear in my passenger's silence. He huddles in his overcoat like a young boy setting off on his Vision Quest. But my passenger is a man, and he has sailed many waterways and crossed many worlds. He sat for six days in the grand parlor at Lady Lenox's mansion and boasted of his travels, while all the dignitaries of Buffalo gathered around to gape and stare.

But on this night, the seventh since his arrival from New York, the gateway to the east, he grips the sides of my canoe as if it were a cradle. Perhaps he is afraid I will drown him, or perhaps his people are not accustomed to a woman navigating their boats.

I tell him: The Great Spirit will guide us. I do not tell him that your bones lie there, Father Raven, waiting for their final burial.

You, my daughter, are the last one. You must preserve our island, embraced like a bird in the arms of the Niagara.

On that distant day you dipped my little hand in the quivering line between water and earth, and made me swear devotion to the grassy lowland.

I row down the river of memory to what came before what came before. A father sheds his feathers and prepares his daughter for visions. You asked me not to defy them, lest I suffer from the afflictions brought by the white men from their distant lands. But I was terrified by the uninvited images that entered my spirit, and I envied the pale-skinned ones for their refusal.

I was the last of the last ones, and I was unable to keep my oath to preserve the island beneath my wing. Tomorrow it will pass to its new owners. The Jewish chief purchased it at full price, and at sunrise he will declare it the legal estate of his tribe members and will gather them from all the worlds.

There are other islands in the world besides this small strip of earth that juts out of the water. It does not sit in a great sea that draws adventurous seamen in search of mysteries. Nevertheless, this island is my home. For me it is the whole world. And for the Jewish chief? Nothing. A tiny patch scratched with a nail on the scrolls of paper the white people call "maps." Without them they cannot take even a single step. They wrote the white name of the island in slanted letters above the stain on the map: "Grand Island." Except that their maps do not show the traces scattered around this land, nor even the downy meadows that turn golden in summer, or the rustling canopy of foliage that comes in winter. The coyotes, the raccoons, the doves, and the ravens all move in their circles with the maple and elm trees. Everything in its place, as though there were no Buffalo, no America, only this island alone. And now it is the chosen land of this man, my enforced heir.

A Jew.

Had I not insisted, he would not have set foot on it at all.

WE APPROACH the little bay, and I hold out my hand to help the Jewish chief off the rocking canoe, but he rejects my hand and loses his footing between the water and the land. He waddles like a wild goose and quickly scrambles up. If his feet were small like mine, I would give him my moccasins and walk barefoot. But he is a large man and I am a little dove.

He did not even ask my name when we set off, but he told me his, twice: Mordecai Manuel Noah. I looked for the markings of a chief on him, and found no colorful feather crown nor the strips of metal that the pale-skinned men adorn themselves with after battles.

I say: Welcome.

He replies: On whose behalf are you welcoming me, Girl? This island is empty.

Is the Jewish chief poor-sighted or hard of hearing? How can his senses not detect the island residents rustling among the foliage, in the water, on the land? How will he lead his tribe if he cannot identify tracks, and how will I impart the essential lessons to him in one night?

AT THE end of every summer I leave Buffalo and row to

the grassy lowland. I do not know who gave the island its red name, all those countless moons and suns ago. At the end of every summer Lady Lenox gives me her blessing for the journey, to the master's chagrin. He fears I will not return to the mainland, and my lady will have to work the cornfields alone. From me she learned how to grind flour in a hollowed tree stump, how to strike a copper vessel and then stand silent as a scarecrow to frighten the birds away—to protect the fields from invaders with our own bodies. There, in a bower, perched above the sea of young corn-cobs, we wove a thread of friendship. Last winter, when the snows piled up outside all the doorways and we had to stay in the mansion for many long days, Lady Lenox asked me to call her by her Christian name. But I did not dare cross the line.

She has never asked what I do on the island alone at the end of summer, and I have not told her how in my mind's eye I enter the longhouse built by my forefathers and fore-mothers, walk through the meadows and prick up my ears to hear the ancient people sighing. The Huron and Neutral and Seneca people babble in the currents and whirlpools, declaiming the Iroquois Nation pact that protected the gateway to the east and the gateway to the west.

What came before what came before will not be recorded in the white people's books.

I LODGE the canoe's stern on the bank, lay down the slip-pery oar, and roll up the mat that covered my lap while I rowed. The water reflects the glimmering wampum beads on my belt. I grip the belt, which will protect me from the unknown.

As soon as he arrived at the mansion, the Jewish chief began to wave his deed of ownership around. At first I thought he was using it as a fan, but in fact he was displaying his entitlement to a valuable property, as though he had won a rare treasure.

Lady Lenox turned to me: That is your homeland, is it not? She did not wait for an answer.

My lady's husband took the deed from the Jewish chief and fingered it as he does when he examines the silver fur of a grizzly bear and bargains with the Inuit hunter who came all the way from the expanses beyond the great falls. He spent a long time examining the small, crowded writing on the paper and finally decreed: You are a lucky man, Major Noah. You know how to pull the right strings. Then he winked: You Jews . . . As if he had said: You Indians.

Land is not property. It was given to all creatures for custody, I said, boldly expressing a red thought. The men in the parlor rolled their laughter out like barrels.

Master Lenox whispered something to the Jewish chief and then turned to me. As always, he spoke to me slowly and deliberately.

Land is merchandise, Girl, just like the corn you help us grow, in return for which we give you shelter. This is the New World. But you would not understand that.

He addressed the guest again: How much did you pay, Major Noah? That's a bargain! If we had known Grand Island was up for sale . . .

Then he began pacing back and forth, making calculations. He had not yet given the deed back to the guest.

Perhaps there are other lands on the market, Lady Lenox opined. Lands one can buy for cheap, because no one wants to live or die in them. A land of exile, like Elba or Saint Helena, where the deposed Emperor Napoleon was sent, ten sun cycles ago.

The men's laughter echoed through the parlor again.

Suddenly Master Lenox tensed. His white thought turned even paler and he exclaimed: So close to us . . . An island of Jews . . .

He put his hand to his musket rifle.

That is when I told the chief: I will take you there.

A LAND of exile.

A land of exiles . . .

Jews. What are they? Who are they?

Do Father Raven and Little Dove not have the right to know who their heirs are?

A desired land. A piece of paper the white people pass from hand to hand.

I write my thoughts down in a little notebook, which I stole from my lady's escritoire. I keep it well hidden in the leather pouch on my belt, next to the pipe, lest her husband find out that I can read and write.

THE JEWISH chief pushes his way between the ferns, spraying us with beads of last night's rain. The night raptors open their beaks, and I refrain from replying to the eagle owls so that they do not think I am their lost mate. To reassure the Jew, I explain that if a coyote were lying in wait for us in the thicket, his smell would have reached my nostrils by now. I can even pick up the scent of my lady's husband from behind the door when he tries to break into my room at night.

Earlier this evening, in Buffalo, as I pushed the canoe into the currents, Master Lenox stood on the staircase with his feet apart and warned the Jewish chief about red women. Who knows what they're scheming? he said. She'll lead you into a pit, and in the morning she'll come back and tell us you were devoured by wild animals. She'll throw down your overcoat, ripped and soiled, and demand the island for herself.

But the Jewish chief turned his back on him, sat down in the canoe, and handed me the oar.

Now, on the island, when we finally emerge from the

thicket, I tell him: A land cannot be bequeathed with blood. Then I drop to the ground.

AT THE end of every summer, when I reach the island, I get down on my knees, which are swollen from rowing, and unload my longings for the island I have not set foot on since winter. On clear days I can see it from the window of my room in the mansion, far away in the distance yet almost within reach. In the rainy season the island blurs in the river's mist, and a great fear overcomes me: perhaps the grassy lowland has sunk into the water's depths and I have done nothing to save it.

If I had a lot of money, like the Jew, I tell myself, I would face the governor of the State of New York and buy back my island. But that is a futile notion: our tribes have dispersed, and even if Chief Red Jacket were still in this life, sated with moons and suns, he would not even recall his own name.

At the end of every summer, I kneel down on the shore. Were Lady Lenox to see me, she would quickly cross herself in fear. Countless times she has asked me to go to church with her, but I have avoided it.

Tonight a Jewish chief watches me. I thought he would throw the javelin of his faith at me and call me a heretic, but he keeps his white thoughts to himself.

I slowly stand up and my mouth is full of words. Trampled grass, broken twigs, crushed needles, droppings, patches of urine—tracks that lead nowhere, yet they are tiny circles of life. The earth is not sacred, I once wrote in my notebook, but those who dwell on it are so easily desecrated.

The Jewish chief leaves his clumsy footprints on the earth's rain-softened skin, while I tread lightly with my dove-toes. One can walk that way for hours without tiring, leaving no visible tracks. The Jewish chief tries to mimic my gait, but in vain. From time to time we bump into one another, and he quickly moves his body away from mine.

A red woman.

The whites stare at me, and there are always those who try to touch.

How pale Lady Lenox looked to me when I came to Buffalo ten sun cycles ago. I thought then that she was ill.

If only I could learn how to forget.

But you, Father Raven, pierced me with the javelin of remembrance, and bequeathed me the wampum belt. Our predecessors were the ones who gathered the white and purple shells on the shores of America and threaded them into the tale of our history in this world. The belt will always remind you of who and what you are, you told me, like the white man's Book of Books. But the beaver of time gnawed at the belt, the beads unraveled, and I learned how to write my memories using white people's letters.

I found the notebook one day during the great snow, in my lady's escritoire. A binder of thin pages, easily torn out, like a flock of memories gliding and swooping. At first my letters were heavy and clumsy, bleeding ink on the paper and on my fingertips. Later I learned to turn the quill into a needle that threads the word-shells. I write, though I do not know if there will ever be a reader.

WE PROCEED, but I keep glancing back surreptitiously.

The Jewish chief is neither young nor old. He is in that moment of life when self-satisfaction stands as an unwavering dam between childhood wounds and the beginning of bodily decay. His hair is the tone of reddish sand, and the nose beneath his high forehead slopes down like an eagle's beak. His sideburns are long and his lips are fleshy, and he constantly lowers his eyes, as though afraid I might perceive his weakness. Are these the features of the Jews?

We will know how to recognize them anywhere, and we

must protect ourselves from them, said my lady's husband to those gathered in the parlor. This was on the second day of the guest's visit. A coyote in human clothing. If that is indeed the true nature of the Jew, then I have walked into a trap. I should not have tempted him to sail in my canoe. After all, a man can inherit an island without stepping foot on it. He had initially intended to hold the ceremony on Grand Island, but was forced to change his plans when he learned there were not enough boats in Buffalo to transport the guests to the island. He spent six days in the mansion, devising the ceremony as though it were a coronation. Until the day I opened my mouth in the parlor, he did not so much as glance in my direction. Only when I offered to accompany him to the island did he freeze for a moment, survey me from moccasins to braids, and acquiesce. Perhaps he wanted to ensure that he was not risking his money on a dubious scheme.

He bought himself an island just like Master Lenox buys black slaves in the southern states.

When I suggest turning back, the Jewish chief refuses. It might be his pride. My lady's husband says that is a quality of his tribesmen.

Why this grassy lowland, unknown far and wide—why was it chosen? Was there no other land under the wings of Wakan Tanka that could be given willingly to the Jews?

My red questions stir in my mind, but I do not write them down, only tighten the wampum belt against my body.

THE ANIMALS track us, but the Jewish chief disregards them, as though there were no living creature in the world apart from him. We find shelter, and I explain to him that we must wait. Only after waiting for an unknown length of time will the island's residents welcome us, although suspicion will still hover over our heads.

To my surprise, the Jewish chief concurs. He seems to slowly open up, but I do not know if his ears can detect the woodpecker tapping, the branches creaking, the crickets chattering, and the crow calling.

I tell him: If you do not learn to recognize these sounds, you will not survive, here or anywhere. From within the fog in my head a voice thunders out: They are a race of survivors. But the Jewish chief's lips are sealed.

Where did that voice come from? An uninvited vision? Mine or his?

It is doubtful that the Jews are graced with a talent for visions. After all, they are white men.

Despite the fur of darkness that envelops us, I do not light a fire. It is buried in a shell in the leather pouch on my waist. Before leaving, I took an ember from Lady Lenox's kitchen. It burned my fingers but I did not speak the pain.

We must wait, I tell the Jewish chief. We must breathe the darkness together like a pair of scarecrows.

He stomps his feet like a caged animal, but finally submits.

The theory of traces, I tell the Jew, is a struggle between those who try to hide any trace of their identity and those who insist on displaying it like a scalp for all to see. I also tell the chief that any traces can be erased with water. The strongest smell is the smell of the prey's fear as he flees, galloping toward the quivering line between water and earth. I have learned to recognize my own smell of fear, and it is emanating from me now as though I were a cracked canoe. We lean on the slippery tufts of grass, and the foreign man whose hair is fiery puts one hand on his heart and rocks back and forth like a sheaf of corn in an approaching storm.

Who is the Jews' helping spirit? Perhaps he has turned his back on them and that is why they must find themselves a new island?

ON THE third night of his visit I served the guests their dinner and curtseyed, as Lady Lenox taught me. Her husband pointed and said: You are a very fortunate girl. Had we not brought the gifts of progress to this land, you would have drowned in the darkness of ignorance, worshipping stones and animals. And who is your raven? A filthy bird who pecks at carcasses. You should thank us, Girl. Let us all drink to the New World!

The guests raised their glasses, and Lady Lenox also drank. Her cheeks were flushed and she joked: Now I'm a red woman, too.

How does my lady's husband know about the Raven, my helping spirit? Did my lady disclose my deepest secrets to him? I believed she was my friend. Last winter, when the great snow piled up, we wove a thread of friendship, and she even asked me to call her by her Christian name.

After the meal I washed the goblets. The Jewish chief's was still full of firewater. I poured the liquid into a pit. I will never taste that fire; that is what I swore to you, Father Raven. As soon as I arrived at the mansion, my lady's husband tried to make me drink. He wanted to part my lips, and promised me joy and forgetfulness.

But I insist on remembering.

And sorrow insists on being.

HOW THEY flattered the distinguished guest, practically scrubbing the Jewish chief with their smooth tongues, glorifying his many titles as if they belonged to them: Major, Attorney, American Consul to the Kingdom of Tunis. He had recently been appointed Sheriff of New York. The Jewish chief showed them missives he had received from Presidents John Adams and Thomas Jefferson, and the guests passed them around and clucked their tongues admiringly. Lady Lenox even read out loud from President Adams's letter: "I have had occasion to be acquainted with several gentlemen of your nation, and to transact business with some of them. I wish your nation may be admitted to all the privileges of citizens in every country of the world."

The Jewish chief was delighted. He clapped his hands and showered praise on Lady Lenox. How fluently you read, he said. You are blessed with many talents, my lady. You could take the stage and play the lead part in the play I have written, a heartbreaking love story that takes place during the Revolutionary War. An American revolutionist woos the daughter of his adversaries who support the oppressive British rule. It is a spectacle replete with effects of thunder and blood. It was hugely successful on the stages of New York City. Has my lady ever had the pleasure of visiting the theater?

The Jewish chief promised to seat her in the front row. After the show, he would invite her backstage and show her how these effects of thunder and blood were created.

"Do not extend your hand to foreign mercenaries, who have crept in amongst the brave people fighting for their independence," he quoted boastfully from one of his plays. In between courses, the Jewish chief scattered a fabric of words, eager to gain their approval, or his own.

My lady did visit the theater once, and returned from New York alight with excitement. This is what she told me when she came home: A man stands on a raised stage and persuades the people sitting opposite him like scarecrows in the dark to believe in something that never happened. When the rector of Saint Paul's Cathedral announced the distinguished visitor, my lady's husband wrinkled his nose and only conceded to host the man when the rector slipped a few bills into his hand. But my lady's excitement was boundless. She ordered me to polish all the silver she had brought from Virginia as part of her dowry, and to lay fine woven blankets on the canopy bed intended for the guest, as though it were a bridal bed.

For six nights in Buffalo, the Jew did not close his eyes. Through the door I could hear him crying and laughing intermittently.

THEY URGED him to report the latest gossip from Tammany Hall, and wanted to know who had helped his election campaigns for the important positions he held. The Jew fell into the trap and could not resist boasting. He told of how he had freed Americans held in slavery by the Bey of the Kingdom of Tunis. He was destined for greatness from his youth, he explained. George Washington himself had been a guest at his parents' wedding. The chief also noted that he dined twice a month with Governor Clinton, and was his confidant. Was he not the most glorious Jew in America? He was regularly mentioned in newspaper headlines: Mordecai Manuel Noah. He repeated the name twice and opened up the latest newspaper on the table, among the dishes, as evidence.

The guests cheered, and Lady White gave him a few dagger-sharp smiles. Was he in the mind to marry soon and produce a few little Noah children for the world?

It was not yet time, he replied. He had yet to find the right match. He winked at Lady White and rolled up the newspaper.

Then the women were sent away and the men lit their cigars and filled the parlor with smoke as they lounged among the glass and china cabinets. Master Lenox insisted on walking the guest around the room to show him his cherished collection: white-tailed deer horns, the heads of boars, raccoons, and turkeys, and a taxidermied dove and raven. He told Noah how he had hunted the two birds on the day he married my lady. No one will ever forget that ceremony, he said. The bride's veil billowed up in the gust coming from the great falls, and the groom tied it around her neck so that it would not fly away.

A woman likes to be bound, he explained with a loud chuckle, and recommended to the lauded journalist from New York that he write down this piece of advice and disseminate it.

The Jewish chief grimaced, but I could not read his thoughts. Only moments before, he had found favor with Lady White and Lady Ransom when he professed his support for women's suffrage. But upon hearing Master Lenox's sentiments, he remained as quiet as a black bass.

The Jewish chief did not let go of the title deed for even a moment, keeping it buried deep in his tunic, close to his chest. I could have stolen it without him knowing. He asked to retire to his room, and apologized to his guests, explaining that he needed to finish writing his speech for the ceremony. Lady Lenox told me to prepare his fine clothes, and I followed him to the guest room, two steps behind, my head bowed. He handed me a robe and asked me to clean it. I held my breath. This shade of crimson was appropriate only for the elderly Seneca chief Red Jacket. A cascade of silk flowed between my fingers.

Finally the Jew spoke to me: The day will come when you will tell your children that you witnessed this occasion, the dedication of the Jews' island of refuge.

What have they suffered that they require refuge? Were they shot at with musket rifles? Were their teepees and wigwams and longhouses burned? Were they forced to drink firewater and have their visions trampled? Or perhaps they suffered no wrongs, but like the other pale-faced men they have concocted false pretenses to justify ripping out another portion of the earth's flesh for themselves. This is what the black boy, Simon, a servant at the mansion like me, says. He was born in America, but he looks to what came before what came before—to Africa.

"Everything-thieves," Simon calls the whites. And what shall I call the new invaders who suddenly emerged from the guts of an unknown continent claiming to be persecuted?

I shook the robe and a slight whiff of dust reached my nostrils. It was borrowed from a theater wardrobe, Lady Ransom's husband told the guests. They showered the visitor from New York with smiles for six days, but I heard them gossiping behind his back. Beneath all the honorable airs bought with money and scheming, Master Lenox claimed, the Jewish chief was first and foremost concerned for his own people. Lady White's husband concurred, and said the Jew had failed in his mission in Tunis, since the ransom he paid the Bey for the American hostages was excessive, and eventually he was disgracefully removed from his post as Consul. Lady White's husband was even able to quote from Secretary of State James Monroe's letter: "At the time of your appointment, it was not known that the religion which you profess would form an obstacle to the exercise of your Consular functions."

How fluent was his reading. He too, like my lady, deserved a part in the theater.

I MOVED among them and they did not bother to obscure their defamations.

Serve the food, Girl. Clear the dishes, Girl. Go to your place.

But where is my place?

Your voice crosses the eternal hunting ground, Father Raven: You are the last one, my daughter. Go wherever you go, just as long as the island is preserved in your visions. But there is no shaman left to guide me. I wear the clothes of the white people, I speak in their tongue, and I am forced to conceal my red visions.

A WHILE later, voices were raised.

Mordecai Manuel Noah was appointed Sheriff of New

York? Scandalous! Are we to allow a Jew to order the hanging of a Christian? Lady Ransom's husband was outraged. Such a thing must not be permitted. Master Lenox expounded: Noah probably elbowed his way into the lofty position through bribery and extortion. Eventually he will open up the prison gates and let murderers and thieves out onto the streets. The notorious Mordecai Manuel Noah.

I stood with my ear to the door. Could this Jew be both a despicable creature and a transcendent being at the same time?

I could hear the chief's voice coming from the guest room, where he was reciting his speech, but I could not decipher the words.

I CONTINUED to eavesdrop on the dispute in the parlor.

Lady Ransom's husband suggested appealing to the highest authorities regarding the deed of title. Why should such a valuable asset be given to the Jews without a struggle? Having extricated Grand Island from the savages' grip, and repelled the impudent demands of the British and the French, shall we now give it up so easily, a free gift to the Jews? The nation of money changers would do best to be dispersed throughout the world. After all, even in the New World there must be some limits to their greed.

Lady White's husband said: If they gather in one place, the Jews are liable to gain power, and eventually they will rise up against us, break out of the island's borders, and with their plentiful funds they will try to purchase Buffalo, New York State, and even all of America. A continent of Jews . . . What a horrifying idea! Have we not enough on our hands with the herds of heretics we have here? Must we now have the Jews on our tail too?

Lady Lenox's husband finally hushed the crowd. It is precisely when they are all in one place, he explained, that we will be able to keep an eye on them. The Niagara River will seal them in, and the great falls will block their exit route.

Upon hearing this reassurance, the dignitaries settled back into their smoke-filled parlor seats. It will be a reservation, Master Lenox explained. And the Jews will enter it of their own free will. The perfect cure for an Old World affliction.

It was only the rector of Saint Paul's who sided with the Jews, enumerating their positive traits. They are a hard-working people, he said, enterprising and diligent, and most importantly, the Jews obey authority and will submit even to the harshest decrees. They are as soft and supple as the white oak tree. A fine raw material.

It is true, he continued, that the Jews have some well-known flaws, and the Old World attempts to repair them came to naught. But the New World gives us a chance to completely alter their nature. Under our patronage, they will turn the island into a flourishing port of commerce, the Niagara will blossom, and we shall all be rich.

The rector declared, finally: It is better for the Jews to be a tool at our disposal rather than the other way around.

Every Sunday when Lady Lenox goes to church, the rector urges me again to join her, demanding that I kneel before the Christian chief and his virgin mother. But I am steadfast in my refusal. I will not alter my faith, despite the rector's ire. Why does he not demand that the Jewish chief abandon his faith? Because he is fond of the Jewish chief. The rector sent his carriage to a Cleveland quarry to bring back the stone that the Jewish chief will unveil tomorrow on the island as a monument. It is inscribed with letters in a forgotten language that no one understands.

It is Hebrew, the rector explains to the guests, who have by now begun to yawn. The language in which their Book of Books was written, from right to left. Perhaps that is the root of their troubles. They held onto what came before what came before, refusing to forget. Our duty is to sever the Jews from their past, which weighs them down. In the New World they will be our loyal adherents.

There was finally a hum of approval in the parlor. I stood by the mirror in the hallway, wearing a silk robe that did not belong to me, gazing at my reflection. It was as though one of my foremothers had suddenly appeared to face down the warriors, wearing her soft fur, gold and silver hanging around her neck, a wreath of feathers and gemstones on her head. As the tribal leader, she had the power to decide whether or not to declare war. The hoards cheered and waved their javelins, roaring deafeningly.

That is when Lady Lenox came upon me. Instead of reprimanding me, she tugged at the silk hem: Keep your distance from the Jew, Little Dove. Recant your offer to take him to the island.

I told her: At the end of every summer I row home.

She let go.

Forgive me, Father Raven, for not having yet found the strength to fulfill the tribal custom. This is my last opportunity; after tomorrow your bones will lie in a foreign land.

I took off the crimson robe and informed Lady Lenox that it was spotless. Then I put on my wampum belt, slipped into the Jewish chief's room, and told him it was time to leave.

All that came before.

THESE ARE the traces of our village, I tell the Jewish chief. We climb up the hill and pass the plots where corn, beans, and pumpkin no longer grow—the "three sisters" without which our tribes have no life. Then we cross the remains of the fences that surrounded a group of tunnel-like structures. Only the visions bring me back to the cool darkness that pervaded in the longhouse, with smoke from the cooking fires curling out through the openings. The light would seep inside through little portholes, caressing the beds of dry twigs and leaves. On either side of the central corridor were dwellings separated by lengths of hide. Many families nested there, and when a new couple arrived, we would build an extension on the end of the longhouse.

My vision fills with the laughter of children playing Snow Snake in winter, although I never had the chance to run along the frozen course and throw the javelin-snake.

The soft, pliable maple tree branches that served as the structure's frame have collapsed, and only one length of elm bark, of all the ones that covered the longhouse, stands up from the ground like the tip of a tomahawk.

The Jewish chief detects the other traces himself. A mat made of reeds sown together with a bone-needle and a thread of plant fibers, a cracked cooking kettle, a wicker basket, a pebble earring, a bear-tooth hair clip.

The traces are deceptive. Some might mistakenly think we left only days ago. A faint whiff of black bass roasted with roots and bulbs still comes from the kettle.

They came before us, Chief. Despite the heart's inclination to overflow and remember them more beautiful and kinder than they were, I will not adorn them with feathers of glory. In this place, in its multiple worlds, they rustled, flowered, and withered. Some loved, some hated. One took revenge, another made peace. They gave birth, they buried parents. Cycle after cycle, man and woman, they matured, they went into the forest to seek their helping spirits, and returned to the village with new names. But I did not go on my Vision Quest. The village was abandoned and we were left alone on the island, Father Raven and me, Little Dove.

No place is completely empty, I tell the man beside me. We all hover in little circles reflected in our wide eyes. Sometimes it is our turn to go outside, and sometimes to come inside. Life after life. Life before . . .

The Jewish chief will soon try to dam my flood of

thoughts. Like my lady's husband, he will say: Here is a redundant relic of the Old World. But instead he picks up an object and places it in my palm. His fingers breathe warmth through the clods of earth, but a chill runs through my body.

What is this object? the Jewish chief asks, and I take a step back.

A broken spear, its flint tip still sharp. If the Jew is injured, I will be blamed.

You fool, you senseless dove. The New World and the Old World are one and the same. Did the Huron not decimate every last one of the Neutrals? And were the Huron themselves not slaughtered by the Senecas? The Niagara River ran red.

That is the color of my skin.

The Jews will inherit that, too.

THAT IS your homeland, is it not? Lady Lenox asked on that summer day in the fields.

We were standing in the bower overlooking the cornfields, and the island hung from the river's neck like a pendant. We stopped beating the copper vessels, and I alerted my lady to the subtlest rustles: the beating of a butterfly's wings, a spider spinning its web, a goose feather in flight.

Her limbs grew increasingly rigid. I urged her to relax, but she resisted, spreading her arms out wide as she gazed at a flock of birds.

Suddenly her husband fell upon us and almost beat her for adopting savage customs. He threatened to throw me out of their home. Lady Lenox got down on her knees and pleaded on my behalf. Her husband put his hand to his musket rifle and spat at me: A hundred years from now, there'll be no trace of you.

That is your homeland, is it not? Those were the first words I wrote in my notebook. Now I wonder about my lady's intent. Is one's homeland the place where a person evolves into life, or is that a choice made in adulthood, as one chooses a fateful name? Perhaps it is also your memory, Father Raven, that plays tricks on me, and the land that was given to my mind's eye is not at all the homeland where our ancestors lived. Am I entitled to call my island "home," even though I do not live in it permanently? Even though from sun cycle to sun cycle it becomes more of a dream? I am flooded with another person's nostalgia, captive to the visions that insist on visiting me. You said: The visions will guide you. But the doubts have been planted.

A fictitious homeland. A longed-for land that never was.

If land is not property, then anywhere may be considered a homeland, and the Jewish tribe may therefore adopt the island even without a deed of ownership. The Jew is free to settle in whichever land he desires. Why, then, does he insist on drawing borders for himself, when he has already managed to obtain a measure of power that I will never achieve?

Perhaps that is the Jewish tribe's virtue: they have turned their foreignness into a javelin.

LAST NIGHT in Buffalo, I stood at the mirror, wearing another person's crimson robe, and the reflection stated defiantly: This is your true nature. The dove, too, longs to be a coyote. Nothing distinguishes you from this chief. You both entrench yourselves in secrets about suffering and draw power from them.

Now, by the ruins of the abandoned village, the ancient voice returns to unsettle my mind. Throw the javelin, Little Dove—it is still sharp—before the island's new owners destroy it. Here come the Jews to disinherit you from your earth: Shall you lower your head in defeat? You are the daughter of the daughter of prideful warriors, and your foremothers are the women who chose the chiefs and determined, with a wave of the hand, who would live and who would die. How will you look back at what came before you? You will turn red with shame. Throw the javelin now, Little Dove!

I repel the voice that growls inside me and toss away the flint blade.

A land is not inherited by blood . . .

A land is not . . .

A SUDDEN chill descends from the river, and the Jewish chief shivers. I gather stones, arrange them in a circle, and dig a hole in the center. I send him to gather firewood and he returns with maple branches and hands them to me with an imploring look. Perhaps this is how the Jews build shelter for freezing days.

The chief throws the maple branches into the circle of stones. Then he leans over and straightens one of them so it does not breach the border. Meticulous, like Lady Lenox's husband, who devotes his Sundays to polishing his rifle collection. The black boy Simon stands beside him, handing him the cleaning tools and looking down, fearful of the whip.

Despite the darkness, I recognize the maple. A perfect tree, resembling a bird in flight. At the end of every summer I sit at its foot and look up. Each limb has its reflection on the other side: leaf facing leaf, bud facing bud. When the maple leaves take on the tone of sunset, I know autumn is coming and it is time to return to the mainland.

In early spring, when the snow still covered the ground but the sun was beginning to warm the bark, our people used to collect the maple's sweet sap. But now summer is dying, and those who come after us—whoever they may be—will not write in their notebooks: Here sat a man and a woman and quenched their thirst for sweetness.

If I were to give the Jewish chief a drink . . .
His breaths are so close.

I REMOVE the ember from my shell and throw it into the circle of stones. The twigs ignite and the crackling hushes the water's rustle. How do the voices of my land sound to a stranger's ears? Are they a blend of languages he cannot decipher? Tomorrow the Jews will drown out the quiet tranquility of the grassy lowland with their forgotten tongue that no one else understands. What is their bond with this island? Is it possible to bundle up the history of a tribe and float it down the river in a canoe like cobs of corn?

Throw the javelin, Little Dove. This is your last chance to save your land from the trail of tears. Push the Jew into the flames, drown the stranger in the waters, restore your stolen home. So many strange deaths; the Jew's fate will never be discovered.

It is not the voice of the ancient War Mother that I hear, but that of Master Lenox loading his musket rifle with gunpowder.

THE FIRE burns vigorously but does not throw off sparks. The Jewish chief holds his hands close to the flames and draws their heat as if it were golden maple honey. He has removed his overcoat and his eyes shine brightly. The smoke blurs my senses, and for a moment I, too, am a daughter of the Jewish tribe, sailing behind my chief to a dream island, persistently murmuring foreign phrases. In my spirit's eye I dance between water and earth and call to the newcomers: Be whoever you wish to be, as long as you fill my island with compassion, for the world is emptying out. It is your turn to go inside and our turn to go outside.

If only I could trace the route I will take from here into the future. Will I bother to interpret tomorrow the traces I left yesterday? The indentation created by my toes is deeper than the one left by my heels, for I lean forward to fan the flames with a branch. The earth is marked by the fringes of my leather dress, made of hedgehog quills I gathered with my lady near the cornfield. On the nights of the big snow I sewed them into a dress, but no eye can detect the blood that dripped from my lady's fingers. She begged me to teach her the method. She said we were sisters . . .

The Jewish chief's face turns red from the fire. In the morning our tracks will be found: a wave of clear ashes in the heart of a circle of stones. The maple is better for burning than any other tree, and anyone who sniffs the ashes will inhale its wonderful aroma. The trackers—whoever they may be—will write in their notepads: At the fireside sat a man and a woman and warmed their bones together.

We must continue, I urge the man. The night is short and we will not have time to tour the island from one end to the other. Suns and moons spent with the pale-faced people have made me an impatient creature, like they are. I have inadvertently been swept up by the white time. You, Father Raven, will rightly flap your wings and say: That is the price paid by those who throw off their place in the world as though it were a dried peel.

If the Jew thought he had bought a large island, he is about to be bitterly disappointed. Perhaps I will force him to admit that his mission is doomed to fail, since the estate I am bequeathing him is more meager and tiny than his people hoped for. Will he tear up the deed of title? Perhaps he will tell me: It is your turn to stay, and my turn to leave.

You fool! Be wise, red woman. Your thoughts circle around your head as though you have drunk from their barrel of fire. The whites will never give up an abandoned land. They have already tried to rob it even without a deed.

We approach the remnants of huts that belonged to the homeless people who squatted here six years ago. My lady's husband joined the expulsion forces led by the Niagara sheriff. In the middle of the night the sheriff knocked on doors to recruit volunteers. When I opened the door for him, wearing only my nightshirt, he pushed me aside and I tripped on the stairs. Master Lenox was already preparing his musket, and Simon rolled the barrel of gunpowder for him. The master was so eager to take part in the expulsion that he whipped Simon's back to make him go faster. His finger is light on the trigger and he has good aim. On Sundays, on his way back from church, he shoots wild pigeons and the treetops shudder. The boy Simon carries the dead birds to the kitchen, where I am instructed to cook them for dinner.

WHEN I told Lady Lenox that our people ask the hunted beasts' spirits to forgive us, she gaped. How odd your customs are! Why would you ask forgiveness from those who are meant to be prey? The lesser creatures have no spirit. When will you learn, Girl?

She had already forgotten how on the nights of the great snow she asked me to call her by her Christian name.

On Sundays, after the hunt, I stir the pot in the kitchen. But I shall never taste the stew of dead birds.

I offer the Jewish chief a handful of sweet hickory nuts, which I gathered by the fire.

If I were given the day after this night as well, I would dig a cooking pit and feed the chief with baked horsetail reeds, tiger lily bulbs, and dried blueberries. If the foreigners find the island's flavors palatable, it will be the beginning of their love for this place. Perhaps I will teach the Jew to fish like our boys do, when they go out at night with burning torches to draw the black bass to the surface.

How will the foreign man learn how to love the land he has been matched with by law? Or perhaps it is better to impose hatred upon him, for then he will fold his tail in and leave.

It is easier to bequeath hatred than love.

In my vision, the Jews are cloaked in white fabric and wear black wreaths on their heads, and they chase the spirit. Perhaps they, too, seek prey. But from whom will the Jews ask forgiveness?

I want to tell the Jewish chief that in our red time, before and after do not compete with each other. Because what came before is occurring at this very moment, and what comes after has already happened. But why should the Jew learn from me? Even Lady Lenox did not heed my teachings.

ON THE fifth day of the guest's visit, I was ordered to clear the table so that the diners could spread my little-big island out on it.

Six and a half dollars per acre. That is what the Jew paid. Was it a fair price or an excessive one? The diners tried to evaluate the land's future value and the profits it might generate for the investor. Barrages of numbers were fired into the air.

Why should only the Jew profit from the deal? Lady Lenox's husband asked. In their visions, the guests chopped down all the white oak forests and divvied up the loot as though they were portioning out a bear carcass. Skin for you, bones for me.

If only my helping spirit had graced me with the courage to upturn the table and break the mirror in which my foremother foments a bloody war.

The Jewish chief was in his room all this time, working on his speech. Behind the door I heard the words "My persecuted brothers and sisters." He repeated them, underscoring, like a chorus of one.

Were I given the authority, I would give the grassy lowland to the black boy, Simon. He and his tribe deserve a homeland far more than the Jews do, to replace the one they were kidnapped from.

THE WANING moon peers out from shreds of clouds, and its silver reflection quivers in the water. As a child I wanted to carve a canoe out of it and sail up to the sky. The Jewish chief takes a handful of dirt from the spot where the light strikes. That is where he will place the flagpole. After the ceremony he will hang the flag of the Jewish state, a sister to the other states of the union. A white eagle will wrap its wings around the six points of the Jewish star, which will patch the darkness with yellow.

God, bless America.

Blessed art thou our Lord who sanctifies Ararat.

The Jewish chief turns my finger into a quill and writes the name in the dirt, using their forgotten language, from right to left. The Jews thereby choose a name for themselves, too, but they are elderly now, and perhaps it is too late to establish a new fate.

My wampum belt tells us that all the earth is one large island, hanging by its four corners from straps of leather. In time, when the leather ages and fades, the island will fall into the water and sink. The benevolent Wakan Tanka and her loyal aid the Raven will fish it out, and life will start over again.

I STRETCH the borders of my vision to the Jews' next incarnation. This, too, is your heritage, Chief—a whole spectrum of greens: from the bright green of the jagged elm leaf, to the scales of the white cedar. If the Jewish chief does not learn to distinguish between them, he'd best ask for his money back and cancel the deal.

He shelters beneath the glorious elm, which bows its

top like a canopy. I cover my face and whisper: Wakan Tanka, the most perfect of inventions.

The Jewish chief pulls off a branch and touches the leaves. Then he says: I cannot see colors.

These are the traces of Jewish eyes, Father Raven. My forced heir is half blind. He sees only in black and white and shades of gray. He cannot distinguish between a duck's reddish feathers and a crane's brown plume. And my skin—what color is that to his eyes?

Does he find my island beautiful? For even if he is color-blind, that does not mean he cannot see beauty or love. But if he does not see the redness of his cape, how will he know to protect himself from the blood?

The Jewish chief's hands are soft as silk when he hands me the elm branch.

I tell him: Welcome. And I finally mean it.

As though he is completely blind, I take his hand and run it over the all-remembering wampum belt. The white men came and traded beads and coins, and looted memory.

These are the annals of the island, Chief. The lowland was covered with ice and had no abundant grasses. In those days no mortal dared to cross the border of the deluge, the massive screen of water that rushed down between the worlds. Those who came before us stood above the cliff, looked out at the island, but did not enter it. Young girls were thrown from the heights of the Niagara to appease Wakan Tanka, but the Great Spirit did not want human sacrifices. The water kept pouring down—a warning sign, a monument to the flood that washed away life before life.

And these are my annals, Chief, though they have not been threaded in the wampum belt, nor written in any book. In the Cave of the Winds, deep in the falls, I was brought into the world. Had she not become pregnant and borne me, my mother would have counted many more suns and moons in her life. Father Raven anointed me with warm buffalo fat and bundled me—a day-old newborn—in the colorful blanket woven by my mother. Then her body was carried away in the current. Her place of resting is unknown. Her name was Maid of the Mist.

Last summer I visited the Cave of the Winds at the foot of the thundering waters. I sat by the baskets and clay pots and waited for the spirits to come, but the vision refused to visit me. I walked around the grotto holding a pine branch torch. The water-drums beat against the shell of rock, and I continued in vain to search for Maid of the Mist. The Cave of the Winds is empty, Father Raven. Tomorrow at sunrise the Jews will fill it with their barren spirits. I only hope they do not dry the falls, for without them, how will we remember what came before what came before?

I follow the spears of letters that the Jewish chief draws in the clean maple tree soil. Lady Lenox taught me how to read and write during the great snow, and I in turn taught Simon. Otherwise we will not survive, I told the black boy.

Simon replied: You have merely been singed by the fire, while I have been charred. That is why my skin is charcoal.

I shall not utter the rest of my annals.

I LEAD the Jew to the mound at the foot of the Trail Tree. East of here is where you rest, Father Raven. We shall never know which passerby planted the tree to guide the lost.

I tell the man at my side how my father died slowly, as though a beast had invaded the trunk of his tree. In vain I gathered herbs and concocted potions. I am not a medicine woman, and the ancient secrets are lost. We were alone on the island, and there was no one to teach me which javelin to throw into the disease. Father Raven grew emaciated, and I tried to stop up his cracks with pine resin. He dropped his wings and his feathers turned white. I carved him a stick out of maple wood and led him to the beautiful spots he liked. Finally he covered himself with the colorful blanket that my mother wove and said: Let go, Little Dove. It is only for your sake that I cling to this life.

Before I could claim my fateful name, my father was taken by Wakan Tanka. I was so angry that my thoughts turned pale. I violated my pact with the Great Spirit and rejected life after life. I beat my fists against the tree trunks, pulled off the foliage, and cursed the island that had ceased to be my home. I wrapped White Raven in wildflowers, then rowed the canoe to the white men's village across the river. That day, Lady Lenox took me into her home. Her husband announced all over Buffalo: We got ourselves a slave girl. And that night he tried to touch my flesh. The black boy, Simon, carried my handful of belongings to the small chamber next to the kitchen and retreated to his place in the barn, among the animals. Then I saw for the first time the traces of the whip on his back.

Ten sun cycles have passed since then. At nights I dream of returning to my vibrant village and placing my mat and my cooking pot in the longhouse. I dream of children competing with the Snow Snake and gathering shells for a new wampum belt.

Now I return to bring my father's bones to their final burial. May Wakan Tanka and the council of spirits forgive me, for I have been a rebellious child.

Go, leave your homeisland, I heard a strange voice say, and I obeyed, like a scarecrow in the dark.

Now I sit at the foot of the Trail Tree, a javelin's throw from a red-haired man, and the waterfall of my tears is blocked.

I TAKE the elm branch from the Jewish chief and separate the leaves.

Find yourself a home, lest you are forced to rely on strangers.

That which you did not have time to say on earth, Father Raven, you insist on delivering from life after life. In my vision you try to shelter me with your wings, and the cascade of your white feathers falls on my head.

You were a girl, and now you are a woman. The day will come when your children, too, will leave you. He who inherits sorrow will bequeath sorrow.

Here is your borrowed homeland, Jewish chief. Welcome to the people of the water. We are floating people, muddy and slippery, while you emit dryness, as rigid as the bark of the white cedar. Perhaps the Jews come from the arid place they call "desert," whose thirsty dwellers pray day and night for a few tears. Tomorrow they will come onto my island, and what will they be then?

Isra Islers.

And I—what shall I be? I have already been exiled, after all.

Perhaps the island seems more beautiful and greener to me now because I view it through the loss.

Find yourself a home.

I hear your voice, Father Raven, echoing between the walls in the Cave of the Winds.

To the Jewish chief I say: We must watch over the fire, so that it does not erupt from the circle and consume us all.

AS WE sit by the fire, he begins to tell his history.

From the beginning, his tribe members were transients. Many suns and moons ago, the Great Spirit told their first chief, Exalted Father, to go forth from his homeland. Wakan Tanka promised him a faraway land, and entered with him into a covenant of borders.

Why was the ancient chief Exalted Father tempted to

leave his familiar place? Why did he exchange a secure property for an unknown land?

The Jewish chief explains that the traces of these events have been blurred, and in any case he must tell his story quickly, for darkness is retreating.

Exalted Father took his second wife with him on his journey to the promised inheritance, but he abandoned her on the way. She wandered alone in the wilderness with her little son, seeking compassion, and came to be known as "Alone in the Desert." Wakan Tanka looked down kindly with Her one eye, and the thirsty wanderers survived. The little son gripped his javelin and swore revenge.

After Exalted Father's death, the tribe was led by his son, He Laughs, and then by his son's son, Yaakov. Yaakov was extremely cunning, and even as a child he managed to disinherit his twin brother, Red, from his birthright.

Are you telling your story, or ours? One twin destined to follow, and the other was red?

The Jewish chief smiles. His voice is pleasant, as though he has already delivered these words countless times. I thought: My people cannot rid themselves of uninvited visions, while the Jews hallucinate them through words.

The transients clung to Wakan Tanka's ancient promise, and although they were repeatedly uprooted from their land, the promise became the resin that bound them together.

The Jews' traces are so meandering that one night is not sufficient to recount them. In the book Lady Lenox takes to Saint Paul's Church on Sundays, some of their wanderings are recorded. Countries whose names I have never before heard are mentioned. In Goshen they were taken as slaves, and their chief, "Drawn From the Water," went on to be their savior and parted a red sea for them.

Perhaps your people bathed in that sea, and that is why

your skin turned red, says the Jewish chief. His smile flickers through the jagged elm leaves.

The chief also recounts how the tribe carried the stolen bones of their forefather, Yaakov, to his final burial place in the Promised land. That is what he willed.

When he was still alive, he changed his name to "Struggles With God." Did the third chief, the grandson of Exalted Father, decide to rebel against the Great Spirit by refusing to pursue the ghost land anymore?

The Jewish chief is reticent.

So much sorrow.

They had a land and they lost it.

I, too, am about to lose my homeland and walk the trail of tears.

To the Jewish chief I say: It is good that your tribe had time to bring the bones of Struggles with God to final burial. They dug a pit for their forefather in the parched earth. Perhaps even then they were disappointed. Who would want an arid land, a wilderness? Perhaps because they were thirsty and their souls were scorched, they began to harbor doubt—and that is a bird that no scarecrow can frighten away. Perhaps they got lost on the way and the land they reached was not the promised inheritance.

They had a land and they were exiled from it. Or perhaps they have an innate urge to roam, and will never be tied by their umbilical cord to any property. The yearning to find a proper resting place gnaws at them like the sharp teeth of a beaver. Even the name of the land they once possessed was derived from Yaakov, who became Struggles With God: *Israel.*

"Provoking the Spirit."

That is the name I would give to the land.

Let go. Loosen your grip.

First rest, then inherit. Or possibly the other way around.

Look at them, Father Raven: The descendants of Yaakov, who was renamed Struggles with God, are taking shortcuts. Land and borders—will these truly ensure their existence on the earth? They will have to learn our ancient secrets, because their teachings are not enough. What else in the New World will turn out to be false?

But the Jewish chief is determined to fulfill Wakan Tanka's ancient promise. He will gather them in from all the continents, in all the colors of the rainbow that his eyes cannot perceive: black and white and brown and yellow and even red. And although he has not undergone purification in the sweat lodge, where a canopy of steam rises from hot stones plunged into ice water, the chief's vision blazes. From the eternal hunting grounds, the spirits watch the Jewish shaman weave the future-history wampum of the island. Fortresses whose turrets will pierce the clouds, an invisible web strewn with villages larger than Buffalo, more massive even than New York. A longhouse more beautiful than any. A spring budding at the end of an unimaginably long winter.

The Jewish chief halts his flow of speech.

Spring Bud. That will be the name of their city. He envisions them milking the forests, rolling barrels of resin down the Niagara. A land of buffalo milk and maple honey.

May they not drown themselves in all this sweetness, I whisper. The Jewish chief pretends to be deaf.

The rustles and hums will be replaced by rattling machines, which will bisect the distant landscape. Even in the celestial routes there will be giant eyes.

He counts the members of his tribe in the millions. At least six will be able to gather on the island.

I say: That number is beyond my comprehension.

In his vision, the Jew builds a huge bridge that will join the island to the mainland. Those who come after us will be tempted to forget that the body of land is surrounded on all sides by water. At the foot of the Trail Tree they will build their house of prayer, and it shall have a golden canopy. Women and men will sing together to glorify the New World. A huge mass will gather here. They will sail in canoes, on rafts, and even walk across the river, because the Niagara will be parted for them. Instead of dry bones, they will bear on their backs their Book of Books.

And where do you write down what came before you? asks the Jewish chief. How will you remember who you are and where you came from without your own Book of Books?

My unraveled belt. Perhaps this Jew will help me gather up the beads. Who am I and where shall I go? Master Lenox always takes the trouble to remind me. One night during the great snow he banged on my door with his rifle. He wanted to drown me in white seed.

The couple has no children. Lady Lenox fears he will banish her if she does not give him an heir. She asked me to gather medicinal herbs for her, to open up her womb. In her desperation, she went into the forest on the first day of spring, alone, to find her helping spirit. In the evening she returned, full of sorrow. I did not find the Christian spirit, she said. Who will carry on our name?

When the moon completes its cycle, Lady Lenox shuts herself in her room and I take out the blood-soiled linens and wash them in the Niagara.

I block my door with wooden logs in fear of my lady's husband. The black boy Simon sharpened a knife for me, which I keep hidden in my nightgown.

In Buffalo they gossip that the Lenoxes will have no heir.

COULD IT be that the Jews do not deserve their own place? That they were imagining a promise never given? It was not Wakan Tanka who misled them, but they themselves who misinterpreted the vision.

I tell the Jewish chief of the covenant between the six warring tribes, from east to west. Many suns and many moons ago, they were visited by the Great Peacemaker, who brought them the message of repair. He gave them the first wampum belt, which was beaded with the tribal constitution. The warring factions united and became one Iroquois confederacy, and they buried their javelins under a tree in the state of New York.

Is Mordecai Manuel Noah another Great Peacemaker?

I make do with a small peace.

Desired haven—A promise that was never made and never shall be. Yet the Jews sit in their theater, reveling in its fictions like scarecrows in the dark. Why concern yourself with them, Little Dove? Do not fall into the trap. This man was not chosen to be a chief. He undertook this mission of his own accord, leading his tribe—and you—astray.

It would have been better to float barrels of gunpowder downriver in the canoe.

If it cannot be mine—it cannot be yours either.

The flood will wash away life before and life after.

I push away the visions of the ancient war mother, which pulsate in my arteries.

Facing my reflection in the mirror in Buffalo, I professed: My love for the island that was my home is what leads me now to hand it over to strangers, to ensure that its traces are not lost.

THE JEWISH chief embraces me, asks me to call him by his three names, and reveals the terrifying vision that rattles his sleep. For six nights, Mordecai Manuel Noah did not shut his eyes in the canopy bed. All the calamities that befell his tribe when they were transients were nothing compared to the horrors that would come.

I tell him: It is only the war mother enflaming your dreams. She has despaired of me, and so she has crossed over from the mirror to incite you instead.

In vain I plead with him not to thread his frightening vision into words. But the Jewish chief is already swept away. His feet trample the dirt, his nostrils flare, his red stubble turns gray, and the shards of his vision whip at me. Soon I will be what I already am to him: a gray woman.

I shout: Stop, Mordecai Manuel Noah! A vision is not a decree. Sometimes it is given to us so that we may know how to get away.

But the Jewish chief cannot escape the deception. In his mind's eyes he sees his people shoved like cattle into man-made grottos, suffocating in a colorless, odorless vapor, and there is no trace of the Dove or the Raven, no helping spirit to pull the people out from the deluge of ashes, and their names are lost forever.

As the night begins to lighten, we shiver inside one another, but not from cold. Mordecai Manuel Noah unbuttons his tunic and takes the title deed out of its hiding place. His voice echoes all around the island when he vows to provoke the Great Spirit. Tomorrow he will impose the reparation on his tribe.

There is no other Ararat. This is not the land that was promised, and yet . . .

I lie at the foot of the Trail Tree, gripped in the arms of a strange man, and the dam of my tears breaks open. Even on the day you left me, Father Raven, I was not able to cry.

I slowly remove my belt, bereft of its beads, and cradle the living dead man in my arms.

We lie together on the damp earth, on a bed of ferns under the canopy of an elm tree drizzling traces of rain. To the waterfalls' distant roars, we add our moans—mine above and his beneath. Traces of seed are buried in the ground. The island dwellers' nostrils will detect the act that has a name.

I wet his Jewish skin, secretly seeking traces of sorrow or joy, for he laughed and cried intermittently on those nights in Buffalo.

He holds me to him, almost suffocating, and whispers in my ear: Your lady's husband lies in wait for you. You belong with me.

An island for you and for me.

Then he tries to give me the deed of title, whispering: Someone must beg forgiveness from the prey's spirit.

I refuse to take the deed. When he comes back—this is what Mordecai Manuel Noah promises—we will deposit it together for eternal safekeeping in the museum of tribal history that will be built in Ararat.

MORDECAI MANUEL Noah shuts his eyes and falls asleep in my lap, and I adorn his red hair with feathers. If Lady Lenox were to see us she would say: That is a theater costume that was borrowed for the ceremony.

The earth now bears the imprint of our bodies. Traces of love must be passed down, Father Raven, for if they are not, what will remain once we are gone? A hollow filled with bodily fluids is an appropriate gift for our lady earth. The white men came from faraway and persuaded themselves that they were the earth's masters. But the earth was graced with immeasurable patience. She will bundle us all in her bosom, and in her benevolence she will grow weeds over us.

I secretly reach into Mordecai Manuel Noah's pocket and leave my pipe there, as well as a small bundle of tobacco leaves.

The joys of little peace . . .

Wherever he goes, he will take the pipe with him.

AS HE sails around his islands of dreams, I whisper: A new land is a *shidduch.* You cannot be expected to love this patch of earth as much as I do, for I was carved in its image. Perhaps after one or two generations the Jews will stop being strangers here, and those who come after you will be a limb of the landscape, like the maple, the elm, the black bass.

And the seed inside me.

Perhaps she will be . . .

Araratian.

Lady Lenox's womb is barren, while inside my own body tonight a journeyer has been planted.

One night during the great snow, when we had to stay inside, she asked me to call her Jacqueline. Her eyes shed tears as she held my hands, looked this way and that—to make sure the master was not watching—and wept at her bitter lot. In my mind's eye I can see her adopting the fruit of my loins as though it were her own, cradling a baby on the banks of the Niagara and protecting her from disasters.

THE DAY rises. A few pale red drops followed by a rushing white throng. No mortal can fully perceive the colors dissolving into one another.

Mordecai Manuel Noah's feather-breaths flutter. How modest my own visions are, compared with his. With a single utterance he will guide an entire nation down the Niagara, dreaming-warring his glorious fictions in black and white. Soon he will wear his borrowed robe and impose the reparation on his tribe.

In his sleep he murmurs words in their forgotten language, and I caress his red eyelashes. Perhaps when they shed their place, the reparation will occur and their bitter lot will be sweetened. In my invited vision I see children rowing canoes all the way to the waterfall, where the rainbow refracts in the bridal veil. I have seen young mouths—white, red, black—gaping at the spectacular sight, a spell that Wakan Tanka casts to momentarily quell all fighting. The little Jewish mouths will also gape at the rainbow. But how will the half-blind man know that this miracle of colors truly exists?

The colors reveal themselves so suddenly, so different from one another, yet inseparable.

On the nights of the great snow, when we were at home together, Lady Lenox wanted to know how Wakan Tanka strings beads together into a necklace in the sky. The white woman opened her dowry chest and took out some glass beads she had received as a wedding gift. She scattered them on the table and said: These beads crossed over from Venice in the Old World, a city built on water. She asked me to thread them into an amulet for her. We held the string together and she repeated after me: A white bead symbolizes age, a green bead announces growth, and a yellow bead is a sign of maturity. The most precious of the beads, red, the color of life, was threaded last.

On the first spring day, when the snow thawed, Lady Lenox slipped away into the woods, wrapped in a grizzly bear fur and wearing the amulet around her neck. But since losing hope of finding a helping spirit to open her womb, she has stopped wearing the necklace.

I have stopped trying to explain the secret of waiting to the white woman, but to Mordecai Manuel Noah I whisper: Perhaps the members of your tribe understood that waiting interminably is tantamount to giving up on the promise. In their persistent demand that Wakan Tanka redeem the deed, the Jews confirm their faith in the Great Spirit. Tinged with doubt and scorched with disappointment, it is nevertheless an act of faith.

THIS IS a moment of grace. A moment to savor the island's tranquility before it becomes a bubbling Ararat, a theater of blood and thunder. One day I shall take the highway to

New York and see a play. I will sit like a scarecrow in the dark, watching visions created by flesh and blood. But no applause or cheers echo through my mind. Rather it is the hum of the river, a body of water in whose depths the black bass multiply and from time to time leap out of its borders. My mother, Maid of the Mist, was carried away in the current, and Mordecai Manuel Noah's father also disappeared without a trace.

An equal decree for bequeather and inheritor.

In Buffalo they say that on the last day of summer, when the thundering water swirls in the splendor of twilight, a woman's shadow appears in the opening of the Cave of the Winds, her perfect belt threaded with white and purple shells, and she holds a javelin. Others swear it is a pipe.

I have not seen her.

Lost Maid of the Mist, who will fish your name out from the Niagara of forgetting?

EARLY IN the morning, the river is calm. This is my favorite hour, when the day dwellers slowly awake and the night raptors retire to rest in the treetops. The switching hour, when the creatures are still free of strife and quarrels.

Our fire has died out, but I withhold sleep from myself. Without me, the Jew might miss the grand occasion. No power in the world can sabotage his vision now, because this stubborn man is determined to found his Ararat, whether here or elsewhere.

I should wake him, for the yellow light is already trickling in. Soon it will turn red and there will be no more difference between him and me.

I once thought the sun was a canoe and its rays were oars. You did not have time, Father Raven, to tell me who the rower is, and why he rows to the dark side of the sun. I have missed so many things. Am I not a hostage of fear and blame? That is my part of the inheritance.

Before he closed his eyes, Mordecai Manuel Noah told me about the man who was once the chief of all people, before they separated into nations and tribes, colors and continents.

In their Book of Books he is called "Righteous in his Generation," while in my wampum he is "Rows Without Oars." Countless moons and suns ago the land was covered with a layer of ice, and people slaughtered each other. When the ice began to run red with blood, the Great Spirit decided to shatter it, but she promised the ancient chief that he and his sons and his son's sons would survive. Our forefather gathered his few possessions, carved a canoe out of elm wood, and began sailing. He had no destination.

Rows Without Oars could not understand why he survived the great flood alone. And although Wakan Tanka was fond of him—according to the Jews' Book of Books—he challenged the Great Spirit, because she had obliterated life before life. In his desperation, he cried out: It is not too late to teach the hunters to ask the prey's spirit for forgiveness!

He threw his oars into the water and they became a dove and a raven.

Rows Without Oars shed tears, creating his own waterfall, and the sinking world wept with him until it ran out.

The traces of this story must be passed down from generation to generation.

ON THE mainland across the way, preparations for the ceremony have begun. The people of Buffalo scamper along the quivering line between water and earth. Lady Lenox takes her finest clothes out of the closet and prepares to leave for Saint Paul's Cathedral, where the state of the Jewish tribe will be publically declared. She stands at the mirror. Soon she will call me to help her dress.

I rock the man in my arms. His body is heavy and my

flesh stings. Get up, Mordecai Manuel Noah. It is my turn to leave and your turn to enter.

His eyes, as they open, are as pure as those of a bear cub I once found in the field after his mother was devoured. Disoriented, he does not know where he is or in whose lap he has found refuge. He fingers his red stubble, which has grown overnight, and he finds the amulet around my neck. It is the one I threaded for Lady Lenox, which she tossed aside like an empty vessel after failing to find her helping spirit. The boy Simon found it in a pile of feed in the barn and gave it back to me.

He was the first person on the mainland to call me by my name.

On the night I arrived in Buffalo, the black boy slipped away from his dwelling and stood in the doorway of my chamber with a bowl of mush. At first I could not distinguish him from the charcoal night. I was terrified by the faceless voice. Until that day I had not seen skin colored like his.

Simon asked softly: Why are you a little dove?

I told him: That name is only a temporary guise, because I have not yet chosen my fateful name.

I did not tell him that I had lost faith in the magical healing powers of a name.

I am the only one who calls Simon by his name. To everyone else in Buffalo, he is "boy." That is what Master Lenox shouts when he chases him around the village.

There are nights when the black boy crosses the threshold of my room and I clean the bloody sores on his back. His eyes spark when he asks: What will happen when I turn white and I am an old man? Will I always be a boy to them?

Simon is not his real name, either, for that was lost in Africa.

If I could write down his history, I would gather all the beads in the world for him.

ACROSS THE way, on the mainland, the boy loads the cornerstone commissioned by Mordecai Manuel Noah from a Cleveland quarry onto the carriage. The Jewish chief told the stonemason to engrave the date: September fifteenth, 1825 years since the birth of Chief Crown of Thorns, the fiftieth year of America's independence, the second of Tishrei, 5586 since the creation of the world according to the Jews. At the head of the stone, in their ancient language, he engraved the transients' most sacred whisper:

"Hear O' provoker of the Spirit, Wakan Tanka our spirit, Wakan Tanka is one."

I turn over the canoe, which was hidden in the thicket, and show Mordecai Manuel Noah how to hold the oars.

He asks fearfully: What if the oars are lost in the current?

I tell him: You can row with your hands, as did the ancient chief of all of us. His defiant cry to Wakan Tanka pierced my first vision. I received it on my first night on the mainland, immediately after being welcomed by Simon. I spread out my mat in the chamber next to the kitchen, filled my inherited pipe with tobacco leaves, and then my vision erupted from the smoke. First I heard Rows Without Oars shouting at the Great Spirit. Then I saw him rocking on the surface of the great flood. Together with him I shouted: Wakan Tanka, you and I remain alone! Shall this be called a world?

In my vision, the Great Spirit asked for forgiveness from the hunted, and promised to recreate herself. Rows Without Oars' hands were as swollen as a pair of dead fish, and they almost fell off from the pain, but he kept rowing until the waters calmed.

Ever since then, the Great Chief has demanded that Wakan Tanka keep her promise.

That is the vision that always revisits me.

SAIL AWAY, Mordecai Manuel Noah, to your Ararat.

I would like to tell the man in my arms: Your tribesmen would do best never to come to this island. They should wait interminably for Wakan Tanka's promise to be fulfilled. For if Ararat does come true, they will have to recreate themselves. They should be transients forever. When the storm comes—signs of ashes blackening the horizon—they must hurry onwards. Wakan Tanka directs the circles of roaming, and sometimes one circle overlaps another.

So much sorrow.

I do not say a word of all this to Mordecai Manuel Noah. Who will remember a chief with three names in the world after the world?

He hugs me, almost suffocating, and presses the deed of title between us.

Wait for me, Teibele, he says.

That means "Little Dove" in their Jewish language, which is merely a temporary guise for the language that preceded it, a robe borrowed to serve them during their interminable wait, until its turn to leave.

Teibele.

I adopt the name, which no helping spirit chose for me, but rather a flesh and blood man.

You wait for me, Little Dove, with a jagged elm leaf in your beak. Seemingly a perfect tree, yet the leaf is lopsided and its two lobes are never identical.

I carved the canoe from an elm trunk. I found it lying at the edge of the forest in the beginning of spring, the day Lady Lenox went to seek her helping spirit. The trunk was still covered with ice, but beneath the ice it was starting to bud. My hands were covered with blisters and my blood seeped into the wooden flesh, but I kept planing the face of the trunk back and forth.

When I returned from the forest with the canoe on my shoulder, Master Lenox laughed: Are you planning to sail away in a log? You'll never reach a safe harbor that way! When will you learn, Girl?

That night, Simon left his bed in the barn, intending to throw himself off the great falls. I hurried after him in my canoe, though it was not yet finished, so that he would not become one of the floaters whose faces are erased by the water. The canoe was starting to sink when I dragged the boy's body in. The water came in through holes and cracks. We were swept in the whirlpool and almost capsized, but I breathed into Simon's mouth until his life was restored.

I shouted: We will not leave the world without a struggle!

Had Lady Lenox seen us, she would have spat out: That is how you tempt Satan.

The black boy said: I wanted to die and now I owe you my life. From here on out, it is in your hands.

I anointed his scars with buffalo fat and promised him happiness and forgetting.

Now let go, Little Dove. The night is over and the tribal custom must be done. I must bring your bones, Father Raven, to their final burial.

When Mordecai Manuel Noah has dug the grave, he says: My Teibele, save room for me beside the Raven's bones. The last Indian shall lie with the first Isra Isler. Pray for us.

I UNFASTEN my belt, feel for the empty shell, and know that my womb is full.

If she is born, I will name her Winona.

She will be your granddaughter, Father Raven. A little

first-born Araratian. That is how the Indian name will make its way among the transients.

Will Ararat be able to prevent the trails of tears? The day will come when all the worlds will lament the miserable people who were lost in the plains of ashes, their names unknown.

On the mainland, the procession departs from the Buffalo courthouse, proceeds along Main Street, and arrives at Saint Paul's Episcopal Church. It is led by members of the city council and the husbands of Lady White and Lady Ransom. Then come the Masons with their array of decorations, and behind them an artillery company with the canons that will fire the honorary salutes. Master Lenox is also at the fore, wearing his polished musket, and the boy Simon carries his barrel of gunpowder. A crowd has gathered on either side of the street, as though it were a parted river. Such a scene has never occurred in the frontier town of Buffalo, and it will be recounted even in great New York.

In my invited visions I see parents urging their children: Do not forget. As though memory can be commanded. The day will come when you, in turn, will tell the Araratians who come after you that you were present on this occasion, when the roaming circles of ancient tribes overlapped. The day of exchange. It is such a rare and elusive moment that there are those who spend their lives anticipating it.

You will know happiness, too. The parents will try to spare them from the sorrow.

But the children of Ararat—Winona, Simon, and Jacqueline will be their names—will open their eyes wide like scarecrows in the dark, an audience at a play composed entirely of thunder and blood. I, too, have trouble distinguishing between the cannon fire and the lamentation of the falls, traces of the great flood that once destroyed life before life—the vestiges left by Wakan Tanka so that we will always have sorrow, if only under the guise of happiness.

That is the true legacy. It does not bestow any entitlements.

Sometimes the falls sound like a reprimand and other times like mad laughter. On rare winter nights, when the whole world is frozen, they fill their mouths with ice. That voice is now swept away by the sounds of the musicians and drummers who accompany the procession.

At Saint Paul's Church, there will be organ music and a choir singing. The rector will read from the Book of Books shared by Christians and Jews, and Mordecai Manuel Noah, a citizen of the United States of America, glorified yet infamous, will step up to the altar. Beneath the image of Chief Crown of Thorns, he will declare himself judge of the transients, and will order a collection of three shekels or one Spanish dollar from every Jew in the Old World and the New World. Reparation fees.

In all the newspapers in the two worlds, the Chief's appeal will be published, and in one newspaper in Vienna in the land of Austria it will appear in their ancient language, which will briefly open one weary eye.

Isra Islers, land gatherers, put on your moccasins and return to Ararat.

I have invented it especially for you.

THAT IS how it is in my visions. They have no borders.

The wind circles around Father Raven's clods of earth and carries the voice of Rows Without Oars: You wait for me, Teibele.

What will I do, my beloved Noah, with an empty beak?

PERHAPS I shall be fortunate enough to tell my daughter how the ancient Chief of us all set his oars floating over the great flood. At first they became javelins, and then the

Dove and the Raven pulled out the land that had grown weary and sunk. They strung it between their beaks, and the circle of life was healed. A slippery blink of time during which Wakan Tanka's promise was fulfilled.

The girl Winona will thread another bead on the all-remembering wampum belt, while I seal the pages of the white notebook.

I told Lady Lenox that the Raven and the Dove were the ones who taught the act of love to those who had been recreated. The cornfield danced in the wind and I wanted to drown in it. Lady Lenox looked out at the horizon with her scarecrow eyes and said: I did not know.

Before he left, I put my amulet—beads in all the colors—around Mordecai Manuel Noah's neck. He dabbed at his eyes. It's just the light, he explained, like a child caught in the act. Standing in the canoe, he opened his clothing and cast his waters into the Niagara. Then he quickly sailed away without looking back.

The sun dips down in the pale blue sky, and the canopy of vapors above the falls poses as a cloud. Opposite, on the mainland, there is a public celebration. Master Lenox leads the revelers to the Village Inn, where they will promise each other happiness and forgetting. My lady will drink to the New World, and she will stop looking for her helping spirit.

When her husband kicks her, he calls her by her nickname, "Jackie," and I cover my ears.

I am the last of the last ones. The true heir. I scatter a bundle of prematurely red elm leaves over the first burial site in Ararat, and outline the borders of a proper resting place for the Jewish chief whose eyes cannot perceive the colors but whose visions are as colorful as a rainbow. He bequeathed them to me.

One day someone will point to this spot and say: The cemetery is the foundation of everyland, the place where the borders between the dwellers of below and the dwellers of above are erased. The Raven, Wakan Tanka's loyal aid, joins life before with life after, which the whites call "death."

We are not really parting, Father Raven. I will reach you in a circle with all my children. The future Simon, the future Jackie, and my little Winona, they will all stand here one day and enjoy a game of Snow Snake. They will spin legends in which we are the heroes. They will lavish praise upon us, although we were no better than they are. I only hope that one day the Isra Islers smoke the tobacco in the pipe I hid in Noah's clothing.

A small peace is enough.

IT IS possible that I hallucinated this strange and knotty night, and that the red-haired red-robed Jewish chief is nothing but a piece of my theater, a sorrow-quelling belt whose beads I threaded out of loneliness. The illness I have been afflicted with has no cure.

Ararat is empty again, but its invisible dwellers—the one in the earth and the one in my belly—fill it with their presence.

I shall wait, as I promised, for Rows Without Oars to return. An interminable wait, but for me it will pass in the blink of an eye.

Even if he does not keep his promise, I kept mine, Father Raven. You will never again be torn from your spirit-provoking land, which is sown with the traces of Isra Islers. When they journeyed, they were accompanied by a little dove whose feathers have turned black.

I take off my moccasins, dip my feet in the quivering line between water and earth, and ask the spirit of the prey for forgiveness, on their behalf.

PART THREE

Isra Isle

SEPTEMBER 2001—AN ALTERNATE STORY

I was thinking about the Falls, and I said to myself, "How wonderful it is to see that vast body of water tumble down there!" Then in an instant a bright thought flashed into my head, and I let it fly, saying, "It would be a deal more wonderful to see it tumble up there!"

—Mark Twain, *Adam's Diary*

I'M SKIPPING out on you again, Jake, but I swear this is the last time. This job—let's call it a mission—is going to take care of our future. I was in such a hurry that I didn't have time to pack a suitcase. Didn't even take a toothbrush. I'll buy one on the way, and you can add it to the junk piled up in the darkroom, which you call a *boydem*. I hope you won't take advantage of my absence to chuck it all out.

Believe me, Jake, it was a spontaneous decision. An irresistible impulse, to use the legal jargon. I didn't call a travel agent, didn't even book a room. If I'm lucky I'll get a discounted ticket; tourist season is over, thank God, and all the kids being dragged around the sites by their parents have finally gone back to school.

So listen to me, Jake, before you change the locks and count me out for good. There comes a moment when you have to take a gamble. The slightest hesitation or delay could mean that the tracks are erased, and then it's a lost cause. I'm not going to come home with my tail between my legs like I did last time.

That son of a bitch Lenox woke me up when he called.

We'll pay any price, Simon, he said.

His voice pecked at me through a cloud of Jack Daniels. I was in the middle of a nice dream about swimming in a puddle of money. And then Lenox starts kissing my ass, like he always does, as if he were going to show my photos in some upscale gallery.

Turn on the TV, now! he yelled.

Every channel was showing the primary results, and her face was all over the screen. She had that grin her consultants told her to use, very aware of the importance of the occasion, and she wore a designer outfit that Lenox helpfully informed me was red, to match her trademark red hair. While Lenox nattered on and I started shoving my camera into the bag and strapping on my lens case, I noticed something shining right at the presidential candidate's neckline. At first I thought it was a technical glitch in the broadcast, but then I picked up a lighthouse signal in the rhythm of her breaths, a tiny light flashing on and off. And that's what convinced me that I had a real chance this time—because I could smell her fear, too.

The smell of fear, Jake. There is no sharper perfume.

Job, did I say? Mission? Let's settle on "professional challenge." To disrobe the lady of all her theatrical costumes and expose her for what she is. A fair deal for the voters.

Lenox kept up his dizzying stream of flattery: You're the only one who can shadow her, Simon. Stake out the house and the campaign headquarters; get past the security detail, bribe whoever needs to be bribed. We'll cover all your expenses. Just get us the picture.

He spoke in the first-person plural, like he and I were partners in some grandiose plan that would alter the course of history. I was completely awake at this point, and my dream about the puddle of money began to seem real. I saw us bathing in a cascade of dollar bills. It would be like getting a windfall inheritance from a relative we didn't even know existed.

How much are your promises worth, Lenox? I asked. Because last time you strung me along and ended up not buying a single shot, after I worked my ass off for you chasing that porn star whose silicone implants burst.

Lenox said: I give you my word, Simon. You've got two

days. A rare window of opportunity, as politicians like to say. Then he laughed out loud, brimming with self-satisfaction. This is your lucky chip, Simon!

I didn't tell the son of a bitch: It's a good thing I'm the pursuer and not the pursued. Because who wants his picture spread all over the front page with his hand down his pants? Although, let's be real: a photo of me, no matter how embarrassing, is not going to topple a presidential candidate, and whatever we do or do not do within the narrow confines of our options is not going to reverse history.

I was still zapping through channels, trying to catch a rerun of the primary results. I had to make sure I wasn't wrong, that the shiny spot at the candidate's neckline was more than just a digital illusion or some new eyesight problem. While the pundits splattered their clichés about the crossroads of American democracy and the premature—or belated—maturity of the voter, all I could think was that her image consultants had made a big mistake. If I were them I would have vetoed the glimmering pendant—the candidate's Achilles heel. And that's when the penny dropped: This time, Jake, I really have a chance to make it.

Lenox yelled: Get off your ass, Simon, before it's too late!

It's the only US state I've never been to, and everyone says it's a special place. You're in on this too, Jake—it's your chance to take a journey to your roots and go back home, all through my camera lens.

So this is it, partner. I'm taking the first flight I can get to Isra Isle.

HOME. WHENEVER the word comes up, I think of you. Home is the place you leave with a slam of the door and swear you'll never go back to. You once told me that I could never understand what it's like to live on a tiny stain of land. Despite the massive bridge and the underwater tunnel that connect the island to the mainland, the journey was a deeply ingrained experience. Unlike New Yorkers, Isra Islers are prisoners who willingly enter lockdown, allowing the watery gates to slam behind them for the rest of their lives. The island dooms its residents to constant humidity, you told me. Green poison. Not that I've ever been fortunate enough to see green. Maybe that's why you dry yourself obsessively after every shower, sometimes even going through two towels.

When we first met, and we didn't yet know that we would be together, you described yourself as a swamp creature. I didn't understand what you meant. I thought you were being self-indulgent, using the emotional blackmail so typical of your generation, which has elevated self-searching to a religion. But that's exactly what made me fall in love with you, Jake. You are a man-island flailing inside your own maelstrom, and not a day goes by when I don't pinch myself to make sure that I, of all people, have been chosen to be your bridge to solid ground.

So don't change the locks in our apartment. I didn't leave a note, or a message on the machine, because I knew you'd try to stop me from leaving. Not because you find this kind of assignment despicable, and not because you particularly care if I screw up the presidential candidate's skyrocketing career, but because I'm about to set foot on the thereplace that represents all the things you turned your back on. Don't worry, Jake, I won't be seduced. I'm immune to the spell cast by the island of Jews on its inhabitants. There's no chance I'll start wearing a Star of David with elm leaves around my neck, like the candidate does.

And don't bother looking for your old laptop. I borrowed it to download some background material. That son of a bitch Lenox didn't even offer any help with research. All he said was: Ask your Jewish boy.

Before I have time to type anything, the flight attendant pounces and asks me to turn off my laptop so it doesn't disrupt the navigation system. I'm dying to pee, but the seatbelt sign is on and the pilot is chattering about flight altitude and freezing temperatures. There's a headwind, so we'll be landing a little late, which doesn't matter because no one will be waiting for me there. Just the oppressive shreds of your memories. How can someone loathe so much the place where they were born? Most people I know are nostalgic for what they call their "homeland," and that is especially true for the other island natives, which makes them the butt of countless jokes. Sometimes I think what's hiding beneath your loathing is . . .

What are you hiding there in your *boydem*, Jake?

Such a unique word you Jews gave the world. You see? Isra Isle was not in vain.

Boy Damn.

The flight attendant wheels the beverage cart in my direction. I'm tempted to buy a little bottle of Jack Daniels, but I resist.

It's on us, she says.

There's no such thing as a free lunch, I reply. What do you want for it?

She laughs and rolls the tiny bottle between her fingers.

Sorry, honey—what you want, I can't give you.

The plane is practically empty, but the row behind me is humming. A gurgle of voices comes from under a tangled blanket—the kind they give out at takeoff, assuring passengers that they are freshly dry-cleaned. When I finally get up and stumble toward the toilet, I notice a braided head bent over and a man softly moaning under the tangle of fabric: Don't stop, Keisha, don't stop!

Her braids swing back and forth. On the seat next to them I spot a glossy brochure, which I read out loud, disturbing their romp: "Honeymoon Special! Niagara—Gateway to a Happy Family!"

Jake, if only you could see Keisha and her groom, acting like there's no one else in the world. And that's a fantasy of yours, isn't it? You said you didn't want to die without experiencing transatlantic sex.

Hey, Keisha, baby. Enjoy the fuck, because you have no idea what's in store for you. The day will come when you and he will draw blood from each other. You'll tear each other to shreds just over the toilet seat. How fortunate, Jake, that in our home it's always up.

I'M SURE you're having a fit right now, standing in the middle of the empty apartment cursing me to hell. I know, I promised I'd stop summoning up ghosts and digging into your past. As far as you are concerned, the Isra Isle chapter is over and done with. God, how much energy you invest in defeating the beat-up term *homeland.* Why can't you just ignore it? Just regard it as a concept that neither adds nor detracts. Why can't you just tell yourself, once and for all: Okay, that is the place where I came into the world. So fucking what?

Take me, for example. What connection do I have with Africa? Do I have some innate yearning for a place I never knew, even though it was branded onto my forefathers' consciousness ever since they were kidnapped, chained, and sold into slavery in America? I don't even ask myself what would have happened if Abraham Lincoln had been born earlier and ended slavery in the previous century.

Think about it, Jake. An individual finds himself on a certain point along the continuum of time, and he has the power to overturn the entire course of events. Except I don't argue with history, because what's the point of playing what-ifs? If the deck had been shuffled differently, would the suffering of millions have been spared? Not necessarily, because sorrow is destined to come, no matter what. And anyway, these are dangerous questions that lead nowhere.

A yearning-refusenik, that's what I am. Unlike you, who never truly rid yourself of it. Since we are now separated by a barrier of digital signals, I will allow myself to tell you what I can't say face-to-face: When I get up in the middle of the night to pee, I hear you dreaming. I have no idea who you're arguing with in those pictures that whirl around in your head. One day I won't be lazy, and I'll write down the strange words you mumble into the pillow in who-knows-what-language. Whenever I ask you in the morning, you deny having dreamed at all.

You never told me about how you left home.

THE MANTEL of clouds unravels and I hold my camera up to the plane's dirty window. The pilot announces: In three minutes we will land at Ararat Airport.

I can already see the Triplets piercing the clouds, and I take a picture of them for you: Mordecai, Manuel, and Noah. A hundred floors in each tower. Amazing to think they were built around sixty years ago, a little after the Empire State Building. But no one jumped out of these buildings during the Depression in the last century. Jumping off the falls was always a more appealing option. From this vantage point, the square Noah hides the tubular Manuel; and Mordecai, the triangular tower, overshadows them both. The cluster of buildings transmits a continuous flicker that a viewer from above might interpret as distress signals.

SO WHAT isn't Isra Isle?

An independent sovereignty. A religious enclave. A penal colony. An autonomous state. A quarantine area. I'm sure I've missed something.

When I was searching the Internet, I even came across an antiquated term, *ghetto*, which hasn't been used since the Middle Ages.

Let's assume for a moment that some paparazzo far more talented and audacious than I am is really lurking out there. It's doubtful he would resort to these dry definitions. Best case, he'd melt at the beautiful landscape spread out beneath him. Most likely, he wouldn't notice the difference between this place and any other.

Still, what *is* Isra Isle?

A city of refuge, you said. A biblical concept. It's too bad I didn't listen to you. Now I'll have to go back to that ancient book I never bothered to open. I recall only a few boring history lessons in school, on the reservation where I grew up. Arguments and disputations that have surrounded the Jewish question for almost two hundred years. I have no desire to delve into the issue of which constitutional amendment is still valid, and what legal rationale the legislature used to maneuver Isra Isle into the federal union. A long-winded debate that has preoccupied generations of freeloaders.

If that son of a bitch Lenox would at least help out with the research. "Listen to her media interviews"—that was his only advice.

It doesn't take much imagination to yawn out the questions they ask on the current affairs shows. Is the United States, in the third millennium, expected to contain within it a state with its own explicit religious identity? How does running for president accord with the fact that you view yourself, primarily, as a member of the Jewish people? Does the fact that you are an Isra Isler conflict with your duty to lead the American people impartially?

Blah blah blah.

Her win is really incredible, given the crushing loss predicted in the polls. The reality sinks in and I suddenly lose confidence in my ability to track her down. The assignment doesn't seem all that easy anymore. It's not inconceivable that Lenox insisted on sending me because all the other photographers said no. Devious bastard. How do I always walk into his traps?

My ears are stopped up from the altitude change and my bladder is bursting. I get up again to go to the bathroom but the flight attendant blocks the aisle and lets out chirps of wonder as she gazes through the window. Although she works this route regularly, she says she always holds her breath at the sight, considered one of the most beautiful in the world. Dozens of poets have waxed lyrical over it, and the Internet overflows with graphomaniacs' homages. Only when you look at it from above can you see that Isra Isle really does resemble a bird. Don't miss the lights and colors show! she gushes. She even has the nerve to reach over and aim my camera at the laser beams pointing up from the falls, cutting through the mushroom cloud of spray that hangs over them permanently. You told me about how the water droplets refract the light, creating a colorful splendor visible from anywhere on the island. When you were a boy you thought it was the pillar of fire and smoke that had accompanied your people on their wanderings. I thought I recognized a longing in your voice, although of course you denied it.

We both ignored the word "colorful."

THROUGH THE curvatures of glass, the beams of light are just a pair of spears, signposts pointing the way to the island so that no one—including the satellites circling in space—misses the glorious jewel in America's crown. Who said the people of Isra Isle are too modest?

My camera captures the airplane's reflection in descent, as though it were a canoe trembling in the water. But I'm not sure the picture will do justice to the original. I hope you will overcome your urge to delete the images I send you, and stop trying to understand what things looks like in black and white. I'm sick of hearing the hackneyed question about whether I see the world as a huge darkroom, and it doesn't help when I explain that darkness and light are a matter of perspective. On our first night together you asked if I felt that I was missing out on something. I said: Let's talk about things in terms of what is gained.

You can't have forgotten.

True, color-blindness is not something I'm in a rush to put on my résumé. Lenox is convinced that my disability is precisely the reason I manage to capture details that other paparazzi miss. Colors blind the senses and cause a loss of focus, he likes to opine when he introduces me to the junior writers on staff. He makes me seem like a circus freak, but I admit that I enjoy seeing the young mouths gape. I've bedded a few people thanks to the illusion that I am able to see things beyond their perception.

Until you came into the picture.

Lenox, ingratiating himself as usual, has already sent me an e-mail. The minute I switch on the computer, his giant letters gallop across the screen: Good luck, Raven. After you, the flood.

WE APPROACH landing and the plane is engulfed in miniscule drops. Zero visibility, no point in taking pictures. This is neither splendid nor colorful—just a *boydem* of water hanging in the sky. You once told me that to you that mushroom cloud hovering so close to Isra Isle always seemed like a sign of disaster.

One that happened, or one still to come?

All right, Jake. Enough with this.

The engines are stilled and the handful of passengers quickly deplane. Keisha ties back her tangled forest of braids, and the groom hauls their new luggage, price tags still hanging. Their blanket is tossed on the floor and the groom trips on it. Keisha suddenly turns around and glares at me: Enjoy the show, pervert?

To my credit, I will say that I didn't even flinch. I thought of you. Not wanting to die before you try it. I wanted to hug this bride and groom, to comfort them in advance and offer council: Don't fight about the toilet seat. Wait a while longer.

In the end I didn't have time to pee.

So WHY did the candidate decide to wear that pendant after spending her entire campaign demonstratively avoiding any identity markers?

While the plane was still taxiing on the tarmac, I had time to scan the official photographs from the election site, and I found no Star of David with elm leaves around her neck. Logic would dictate that now, at the finish line, before the voters make their final decision, it would have been all the more prudent to play down the ethnic distinction and stick with the "All-American Candidate" line. So why did she decide, against her consultants' advice, to put herself in the line of fire and expose her weak spot? Perhaps she secretly wants to fail. You know, a self-destructive bent, that quality so typical of your nation. It seemed to have been completely eradicated, but suddenly, after generations, the tip of the iceberg peeks out from the water.

Or maybe she realized she was reaching the point of no return? That's understandable. Between you and me, the fact that the most powerful political seat in the universe is suddenly within arm's reach could curdle the blood of the most courageous candidate, much less an undistinguished former senator and the governor of the tiniest state in the union. I can already imagine the political analysts musing in tomorrow's papers: Does the candidate have what it takes to govern a superpower? To lead countries and nations across a giant chessboard and make critical decisions that could affect hundreds of millions of lives? I would also get cold feet if I were in that position.

At Ararat Airport, as I race the moving walkway to the bathroom, the Isra Isle logo rushes past on the walls: a six-pointed star with a blossoming elm branch in its center. So obvious. An overused icon, milked of any trace of meaning.

For our anniversary, I considered buying you the pendant on a nipple-ring at Tiffany's, but I quickly dismissed the idea. I knew it would end up in the darkroom, which I call a *boydem* now too, along with the disposable toothbrushes. I can see you now, as through a hidden camera, waking up to find my side of the bed empty. You shake your dreads out in that involuntary move that turns my stomach. Convinced I've abandoned ship, you curse the night we met. We've already agreed that it's pointless to argue with the super-matchmaker who amuses himself with strange pairings, because we will never get his sense of humor. And yet, we can still laugh at the joke. You and me and our unbridgeable gaps. On paper we are complete opposites. Beyond the differences in age and color—which are plainly visible, even to me—we have an argument that has been going on since the night we first met, at the club. You claimed the impulse to wander has been in your DNA ever since some hyperactive forefather of yours got the bug and made journeying a way of life for your people. You declared that a two-hundred-year stop on the most bucolic island in North America is just a dot in the evolution of a people, and cannot negate the centuries of persecution and harassment that came before. A vicious cycle that must be broken. And you want to drag me into it and prove that the journey from Africa to America made me a serial victim, too. Except that I dropped out of the worldwide suffering contest; I have no aspiration to win a gold medal for victimhood. After all, there will always be a new contestant who overshadows his predecessors and takes center stage to present the wrongdoings he has suffered. And that sounds a bit like a pissing contest, doesn't it?

So instead of dwelling on what differentiates us, I chose to connect with you, with the assumption that we would never become one body. Maybe the only lesson I've ever internalized during this journeying life that I—and not any mythological forefather—chose is this: that at each station it's best to gather up little gifts scattered on the roadside, rather than get bogged down in a swamp of grievances. Sorrow and loss will always outweigh joy anyway. It's my own little course of affirmative action. I'm not going back to what came before what came before.

Listen, Jake. It's good that we mark our borders—where you start and where I end. That way we don't get mixed up with the concept of "ownership." Freedom of movement. It cost me a huge effort to obtain it. To journey from one place to another is for me a privilege, not a punishment. Just like the tracks you change effortlessly when you DJ. I wish you could adopt my attitude, instead of constantly settling scores retroactively and trying to grab onto some imagined freedom.

There is no doubt that my agreeing to go to Isra Isle is not only because of the fat check Lenox offered. It also stems from my need to face your fears, which flow into me. What is it about Isra Isle that threatens you so much? What is the secret of this zigzagging love-hate relationship?

Your grandmother's death . . .

We won't talk about that now.

I TOOK a picture for you of the boulevard of elm trees that leads from the airport to downtown. From street level you can see the Triplets, with their peaks hidden in the clouds.

I hope you'll appreciate the photo, because I almost sprained my neck to get it. I also got a shot of the candidate plastered on an electronic billboard, her arrogant expression alternating with the campaign slogan dreamed up by a slick strategic advisor: "Emanuella Winona Noah—The Future Is Already Here."

A torn election leaflet lies on the floor near the rental counter. I skim the bullet points of her résumé: An island native. Educated at Legacy of the Mothers private school. Graduate of the theater department at Yale University. Joined the foreign service and served as ambassador to Northern Africa. No mention of her family pedigree. That must have been on the bit that was torn off.

By the way, I rented a Grand Cherokee, your favorite car. Maybe that will tempt you to join me? The sleepy rental agent said there were two available, and asked which color I preferred.

I flipped a coin.

When you and I stand facing the mirror together, what I see . . .

Two gray men.

THE AGENT hands me the keys ceremoniously, as though he were the angel at the gates of Eden. What was it your grandmother called the island? "The Fulfilled Land."

Maybe because I fail to respond enthusiastically to the wonders of the Grand Cherokee, the agent discloses: *She* just landed here an hour ago. In her private Gulfstream jet.

I'm not sure whether the Isra Isler is boasting of the lauded native daughter who will soon take up residence in the White House, or warning me about her. When I simply ask where the bathrooms are, he seems insulted.

I end up peeing next to an elm tree in the parking lot. At least there I don't have to contend with the airplane bathroom faucets, a malicious invention that cruelly separates hot from cold.

Sitting in the hotel—a grand suite on the fifty-eighth floor, courtesy of Lenox—I sip a bottle of Jack Daniels from the minibar and stare vacantly at the scenes passing by outside the window. Isra Isle is not a ghost ship hitting the shoal of your childhood, Jake, but a place with longitude and latitude lines, a specific datum-point on the map, which only your peculiar night visions have distorted into superhuman dimensions.

Even the sternest critics have to admit: Isra Isle is a success story. The embodiment of prosperity and abundance. From here you can also see the chain of man-made islands built to house the exploding population. Your grandmother said it was the most popular place in the history of American immigration. And it isn't just the Jews who have applied to settle here since the state was established in 1825. Yes, I checked the records. That is the first piece of information that comes up on the official site.

How fortunate that Isra Isle existed by the time the Nazis rose to power in the last century, so that your grandmother could be swiftly granted "persecuted" status and sail to America on board one of the rescue boats. Think what could have happened if the Jews hadn't had a ready-made island shelter. The Jewish people's fate could have been as bad as that of the Gypsies, the handicapped, the mentally ill, and the homosexuals.

What would have happened to us if . . . ? It's horrific to think about.

ON OUR second night together I dreamed we were standing naked in a concrete cell. Suddenly the roof tore open, but it wasn't the sky . . . There was a shower of gas . . . You clung to me, and I hugged you . . . People around us were praying, but I couldn't understand the words.

I didn't wake you, Jake. I don't want to be responsible for another of your nightmares. I remember very clearly what you told me when you stepped down from the DJ stand at the club that night. The age of persecution is over, you said. Jews are no longer in any danger. The island of refuge has fulfilled its purpose and the mission to save the Jews is complete. *Rest and inheritance.* That was the phrase you used. Whereas the continued existence of a separate ethnic framework is a threat in and of itself, because it is precisely the segregation that reinforces a sense of persecution and prevents rehabilitation.

I have no idea in what *boydem* you keep your "right of return" document, if you keep it at all. I could sell it and make a fortune.

Do me a favor and have a look at the photos. I managed to get a decent shot of the West Bank, with all the yachts docked in the private marinas.

I down the rest of the bottle in one gulp, and the warm liquid spreads all the way to my bladder. I wish I could photograph six million Isra Islers sleeping, snoring, fucking, tossing and turning, trapped in a nightmare about a cement cell and a sky-roof tearing open. Someone stands at the window and pokes his tongue out at his own reflection. Another screams in pain or sorrow. Another masturbates, or cries . . .

Who the fuck cares that right at this moment some poor guy is ending his life in horrible loneliness?

And me? Someone might be watching me right now, pressing the . . .

SHIVERS. I drape myself in a scratchy blanket that smells like fabric softener, and blow circles of vapor on the windowpane. A new dawn is rising on Isra Isle, Jake. When I say the name out loud, my lips make another circle. A professional challenge for the window washer.

Isra Isle. Your notoriously argumentative people took so long to settle on a suitable name for the island of Jews. What was wrong with Grand Island? Ararat is a nice name, too, if you don't take the romantic biblical connotations too seriously. But you had to preserve your brand, celebrate your status as eternal rebels against Yehowakan Tanka. And all because of an ancient forefather who wrestled with God.

That is the explanation issued by the computer for the chosen name. I have no choice but to do my own research. Son of a bitch Lenox could have offered some help. I have no expectations from you at the moment.

One day that God will rebel against you.

Send me a word, partner. I need to know that you're less angry.

I WAKE up with no idea where I am. Like jetlag, although there's no time difference between your thereplace and my hereplace. There isn't supposed to be any physiological response to this journey.

Floating in space, I am unable to move my arms and legs, and they tingle like thousands of shards scratching me from inside. No, it's not the island's magical influence, but a combination of exhaustion and stress. Unlike you, I do not find hidden meanings in my dreams. All they are is a random collection of sights and sounds filed down by the brain. They have nothing to do with communications from some prior or future existence.

Life before life or life after life? I have no idea what your grandmother was talking about. I think she was just disoriented at the end. I rolled some tobacco leaves for her, and when Nurse Valentina wasn't looking I added a bit of marijuana, to ease the torments of dying. Grandma Brendel was the only old lady in the Home for the Hebrew Aged in the Bronx who smoked a pipe. Even at the very the end she wouldn't give it up, ignoring the nagging doctors. When Nurse Valentina told her she was shortening her life, your grandmother laughed out loud and sucked in the smoke exuberantly. To me it seemed she was reenlisting a militia of strength. But her expression was slightly glazed, as though she was already floating down a river, looking for a safe spot to anchor.

I rearranged the pillows around her neck, which was so gaunt, with skin as shriveled as parchment. I wanted to take a picture of her for you, but the sly coyote was on her guard, making sure I did not immortalize her. It wasn't because of the illness. She never wanted her picture taken. She claimed my eye was purposely seeking her moments of weakness. Unaffirmative action.

I didn't argue.

Suddenly, from within the tent of pillows, she sharpened her eyes at me in a lucid, chilling look, and asked in heavily German-accented English: Where the fuck am I?

Would you believe it? Grandma Brendel, at the age of eighty-six, used the F-word!

We laughed so hard. She even tossed up one of the pillows I had so carefully positioned, and the feathers leaked out and started flying around the room. We made such a ruckus that Nurse Valentina burst into the room and started scolding us. Grandma Brendel put her in her place: Don't you dare hurt my grandson's goy lover. A deluge of white feathers landed on us both, and your grandmother howled with laughter. Her false teeth danced around in the two arcs of her mouth-cave.

Dear lord, Simon, just don't go turning white on me!

And then she said: What a pity you two won't have any children. Then she asked me to smoke with her.

The taste of her pipe. Fragments of tobacco and marijuana. Nurse Valentina FedExed me the pipe when your seven days of mourning were over. No, it's not in the *boy-*

dem, in case you decide to go looking. Your grandmother told me she'd found the pipe behind a heap of stones in the old cemetery on Isra Isle, right after she came to the island. Hand-carved. An original work of art.

She also gave me her will during that smoking ritual. You'll have no choice but to read it one day. Who knows, maybe Grandma Brendel left us a castle in Germany? We'll have somewhere to live our life after life.

I can't believe I'm writing all this. Maybe the journey between places really does addle the brain. Where the fuck am I?

I HAVE to put some order into this chaos.

Grandma Brendel was not born in Isra Isle, but for her it was the only refuge. It was irreplaceable.

Jacob Brendel III is a native of Isra Isle, yet he has disowned it because he wants to rid himself of the "persecuted" label once and for all.

Emanuella Winona Noah, a descendent of the visionary of the state, is the governor of Isra Isle and a candidate for president of the USA. I'll hear what she has to say soon. I signed up for a press tour with the candidate through the "landscapes of her homeland."

And me? Does the fact that I am in a relationship with an Isra Isler mean I can take on the contents of his *boydem*? Or perhaps this particular Isra Isler, and no other, was, is, and will be my home . . .

My bladder is bothering me again. Remind me to make an appointment with the urologist when I get back. Of course I'm coming back. I told you, I'm not disappearing. Just temporarily absent.

THIS IS the only time I will see her face-to-face, with no barriers. The truth is, I prefer taking secret photographs. It's doubtful the candidate will reveal much at a tightly supervised media event. Emanuella Winona Noah chose to begin the press tour at the Memory Site—the plot of earth where the first settlers arrived after the founder published his appeal to "Come en masse!" I take a picture of the original pole where, after the Civil War, they hung the flag—stars and stripes with a tiny Star of David in between. I also document the wooden pier where the boats bringing pioneers from Tunis docked, and which was reconstructed on the occasion of Isra Isle's hundredth anniversary.

How do I sound, Jake? Could I pass for a tour guide? I might send some of my pictures to *National Geographic* to generate some income. Or maybe I'll settle in Isra Isle. Don't panic, I'm only joking.

The candidate picks an attractive position next to the ancient cornerstone of Ararat. Her hand just barely touches the glass dome built to protect the inscription from the ravages of time. The staged photo op projects both determination and fragility. She looks polished, well groomed. She is roughly my age.

As predicted, she looks different than she does on television, but I assume her glowing personality is merely a sophisticated theatrical stunt. Politicians are graced with a Niagara of charm. Naïve citizens believe they have found someone who can touch the deepest part of their soul, but a small circle of confidantes knows the truth about the displeasure and self-worship in which the public's beloved wallows. A full *boydem.*

Boy-dem. I like that word. Like a pair of deadbolts slamming shut in your mouth.

The wind from the river musses the candidate's hair, but she does not fight it. She's going for the natural look—probably the consultants' idea. Every so often she pushes a stray curl away—red, they say—and turns her face to the wind. Although there is not a cloud in the sky, I feel a constant spray of water, and my camera lens is smudged. Perhaps these are sediments from your grandmother's hallucinatory visit to my foggy mind last night in the hotel. Tobacco and marijuana . . . What I wouldn't give right now . . .

Forget it. I have to get back to work. This job could secure our future.

SHE FLASHES a series of tailor-made smiles at the cadre of journalists huddled in the small square, although she carefully avoids projecting any imperiousness or conceit. Her accomplishment, she seems to be intimating, is no political sensation but a completely natural course of events. After all, the Jews are Americans in the fullest sense, and Isra Isle is proof that there is no contradiction between religious and communal uniqueness and full participation in national politics.

Jesus, how often can you rehash these hollow clichés? Who knows how many rehearsals preceded this debut performance.

But she is not about to rest on her elm leaves—a joke inserted by the speechwriter—because now she faces the real battle, against the incumbent president.

Any questions?

Although I adjust my lens to the strongest close-up, I cannot locate the pendant. Where is it? Did her advisors make her remove it, or is the ancient icon buried deep down? I can't afford to get any closer to her. If she imprints my face in her memory, the whole mission will be jeopardized.

WANT TO hear a joke I heard on the lawn at the Memory Site? And this one wasn't planted by a professional speechwriter.

So the Jewish woman is finally elected president, and she invites her mother to the swearing-in ceremony at the White House. The mother complains: I can't come, I have nothing to wear. The president elect sends her a top fashion designer. The mother grumbles again: How will I get there? The daughter sends Air Force One to pick her up. So the new president's mother sits in the front row, waving at her daughter as she is sworn in on the Bible. Suddenly she elbows the national security advisor sitting next to her and says: "With all due respect to my daughter, this is nothing. My son is a doctor!"

Admit it, Jake. A particularly bad joke. But the *New York Times* political correspondent can't contain himself. First he makes sure no one is watching, then he farts out a series of giggles.

I hope you're at least smiling. I'm dying to take a picture of you at this rare moment. Grandma Brendel told me that when you were little, still living with her on the island, you promised that one day you'd grow feathers. Medicine was not one of your aspirations, although I suppose one could view DJ'ing as a form of healing.

I wish I'd known you then. I would have tried to spare you some of the sorrow.

Let me tell you something very clearly, Jake: I'm willing to fly after you even if our destination is nothing more than an imaginary thereplace that exists only in your imagination. I thank the super-matchmaker for bringing us together. Maybe we're not such an unlikely couple after all. Are you laughing now, Jake? In embarrassment, or at the bad joke? Laugh, my partner, because I've never seen you cry. Not even on the night I told you . . . I had to get you there on time, drag you by the hair to the old age home in the Bronx. I myself didn't understand that the old lady was dying. I didn't want to . . .

THE TOUR continues.

The herd of reporters pads after the candidate to the longhouse. I finally get the opportunity to enter the gates of the holiest of holies. She is surrounded by a ring of Secret Service agents, and there is to be absolutely no photographing. I squeeze in at the edge of the crowd. We are led inside with a reverential air, and despite the prohibition I turn on my camera under my windbreaker. They can kiss my ass, these Isra Islers with their holy sites.

The space is dark and cool, and I suddenly have the peculiar feeling that I've been here before. Even the herd of blithering journalists fall silent at the spectacle.

The candidate stands directly beneath the opening in the longhouse ceiling, as if under a spotlight. Her voice gradually wanes into nothing but moving lips. Behind her, like a screensaver, single frames fade in and out: a feather crown, a beaded seashell belt, a curled side-lock, moccasins embroidered with strange letters . . .

Where the fuck am I?

Are you feeling okay? The *Times* correspondent jabs my ribs with his elbow. It's suffocating in here, isn't it? And the audiovisuals . . .

So that's all it was. An audiovisual show. Special effects. Thunder and blood.

I was so swept up that for a minute—you won't believe this—I thought maybe Grandma Brendel had bequeathed me her talent. "Visions," she called them. After all, she always wanted to compensate me for my impaired eyesight.

So that's all it was. High-tech stage tricks. What a relief.

The reporters applaud, like students flattering their teacher even as they undermine her authority. I step back and furtively snap a few pictures, without the flash. I doubt anything will appear, but I like pictures of darkness. Something always shows up, it's just that sometimes you need a whole lifetime to identify the traces.

Click click click. I can't get the moccasins out of the frame, and I stare like an idiot at the imaginary tracks glimmering on the marble floor.

Distress signals . . . I think you're exaggerating. If you were here with me, you might show some compassion for the place where you were born, rather than keep making unreasonable demands of it. A country is no substitute for parents. Freud and Jung didn't come up with any intricate psychological theories to explain "geographical deprivation."

Between you and me, Jake, what does Isra Isle really amount to? It's a miniscule, powerless entity, which had, at one time, every justification to ask the world for protection. Sheltered under the broad wings of the American eagle, it created a display of sovereignty. Lenox would sum up the deal as a win-win situation. The world was satisfied, the Jews flourished undisturbed, but you keep wallowing in your swamp of resentment. Now, after almost two hundred years of patronage, with no threat hovering over the Jews' heads and the world showing signs of recovery from the cancer of racial hatred, it's time to call it off. Your bitter argument with Grandma Brendel . . . God, when I think of how you yelled at her: Don't pass on your Jewish anxieties to me! If you'd known how little time she had left, would you still have refused . . .

I volunteered to be her heir instead of you.

Now, with my feet finally on the land of Isra Isle, I see no point in bringing the curtain down on this harmless little performance. Who would you hand the keys back to, Jake? To deliberately dismantle Isra Isle would contradict our natural inclination to preserve existing frameworks, if only for reasons of nostalgia. Not that I'm belittling nostalgia. I can't even throw away my disposable toothbrushes because they are attached to some elusive moment in my journey.

I see you waving your fists at the television and wishing the mother of all defeats on the candidate: You motherfucker! Again the Jews rear their heads. Compulsive trespassers. Why can't they overcome the urge to keep provoking a supreme authority?

This sentiment—in a less refined version—is whispered by the reporter standing next to me. I have no idea who he works for. He writes down the candidate's speech in his notebook and hisses: I hope the president pummels that redhead.

My camera has yet to capture any hint of faltering in the candidate. You should support Emanuella Winona Noah, Jake. Go volunteer for her campaign. Her victory may be what ends up making your dream come true: Isra Isle will lose its uniqueness. It will be woven, like a dry piece of bark, into the cultural rug of the new world, surviving in records as a passing episode. Why do you waste so much energy trying to bring things about prematurely? In this life or the next one, Isra Isle will cease to exist.

QUESTION:

What about the claims of the original Native Americans? They argue that the Jews imposed themselves on Grand Island, and seek to prove that a deed of title, even if legal, does not confer a bond between nation and land. The natives demand that the Law of Return be applied to anyone who has been an islander for generations. They also want an official apology.

Answer:

This is a petty petition put forth by a marginal underground group. The petition was rejected out of hand by every court of law, and I believe the ruling of the International Court in the Hague . . .

And about the apology . . .

HEY, JAKE. Your forefathers could just as easily have purchased any other island. Maybe it's not too late to put a tender out on eBay: country wanted. Willing to compromise. Prefer empty land or uninhabited island. Cut-rate prices.

I start up the Grand Cherokee and drive away. The Memory Site flutters in my rearview mirror.

Those who try to place borders around memories—are they afraid that without fences and barriers, memory might be washed away?

On my résumé I will write: Born and died on a memory island.

Don't worry, partner. I have no intention of dying before my time. Besides, I haven't kept my promise yet. An airplane. Transatlantic sex. Remember?

VILLAGE INN. The most famous restaurant in the Niagara Falls area. You need to make a reservation two weeks in advance; but a press pass, like a diplomatic passport, gets me in. The waitress leads me to a side table. A Noah campaign button is pinned to her lapel, and she distractedly runs her finger over it as she hands me the menu.

I spread out my notes under the starched napkin to review what I've gathered so far. You'd be surprised how cooperative a campaign staffer can be when you pose as a potential donor. I even found out what the candidate's favorite dish is: roasted black bass with pearl onions and corn pudding. The waitress warmly recommends it. She has just served the dish to the famous diner, who is sitting at the finest table in the restaurant—next to the window looking out on the river—talking to someone who really does look willing to scatter his money in the wind. At a nearby table, sullen Secret Service agents sip Diet Cokes.

Fortunately, I am allowed to drink on the job. So I order a Jack Daniels and a medium-rare hamburger. The waitress is clearly disappointed by my refusal to try the Indio-Jewish cuisine: It offers a unique blend of flavors, and the chef is internationally renowned. Perhaps the pumpkin soup with dumplings, or chopped wild goose liver with bulbs?

No thanks. Just the burger. And don't forget the ketchup.

I squeeze the grayish condiment onto the even grayer burger and think about you. You would have badgered me with a detailed history of ketchup, including which chemicals it contains and why they decided to keep it red. An ancient relic from hunting days. Blood stimulates the appetite.

It's a good thing you're not here with me at the Village Inn; otherwise you'd have managed to ruin my meal. The candidate is eating heartily, and a circle of waiters dances around her. I could get a shot of her gaping mouth, teeth dotted with fillings, but since hunger is not considered a weakness sufficient to sabotage a political career, it's not worth the effort.

Ketchup drips on my work papers, which note her private residence, the campaign headquarters, her schedule for the next two days. It's packed with events, which means the two of us will be running around like chickens with our heads cut off. I try to savor my last decent meal. From now on, it'll be snacks only. Don't be jealous, Jake.

Roasted black bass with pearl onions and corn pudding. That's what I should have ordered.

When I try to wipe the stains off, the ketchup soils the starched napkin. I notice that it's printed with a stylized image of fish formed into a Star of David. I have a feeling the waitress is watching me reproachfully, as though I were a misbehaving child. Fuck her. It's not like ketchup won't come out in the wash.

I remember what you said very clearly. Even though the island was handed over without bloodshed, there was great sorrow.

AT NIGHTS, when I come back to bed from the bathroom, you lie sprawled between the sheets with your limbs askew—in my absence you have managed to invade my side of the bed—and I stealthily slide my hand over your outline, an unscarred robe of flesh, and I want to break into your dream to pull the sting of sorrow out of your body. The defective gene.

Your grandmother asked me to protect you from yourself.

Her will is in the darkroom. Open it, Jake. Please. Maybe now, while I'm gone, is best.

HOW DO you like it? the waitress asks, even as she glances over at the dignitaries' table, ready to pounce.

I look out and see the shadows cast by the Triplets on the Memory Site. Was whoever came up with that name trying to put his finger on something that lies beyond the site? Or perhaps it was meant to underscore the border between what is worth remembering and what is . . .

Memory forfeiture.

You probably think I've lost my mind. I promise: I'll pull myself together soon.

Who said memory is a fixable defect?

LET'S MOVE on to the next question:

Isra Isle has reached saturation and the island is full to capacity. What about the rest of the Jews in the world who might define themselves as "persecuted" and come knocking on the island's doors?

Answer:

It was the constant wanderings that constituted a threat to the welfare of the Jews. The existence of Isra Isle as an official refuge eliminates the vestiges of aggression toward them. Isra Isle was, and still remains, an effective preventative medicine. It is the New World dam that stops the flow of Old World racism.

Our time is up.

CHECK, PLEASE.

How much?! Unbelievable. These prices! For a hamburger?

The waitress brings me a little goblet of warm maple honey for dessert, on the house. That term always makes me uncomfortable—an ostensible act of generosity that alludes to exactly the opposite.

We didn't really build a home, Jake. We left our longings for home hanging in midair, hovering between earth and sky, an abandoned satellite that keeps circling in an endless loop.

The candidate and her entourage are also served warm maple honey, but she insists on opening her wallet and handing out bills, so that no one can claim corruption.

I leave the waitress a generous tip inside the soiled napkin and rush out after them.

A FLOATING home. That's what Grandma Brendel said the island was for her. She never got used to the abundance of water and never let you go near the riverbank. On your bar mitzvah, when you set off alone in the canoe headed to Niagara Falls, wrapped in a prayer shawl, she waited on the bank for four days and nights. Everyone said: It's the tradition. What are you worried about? All the young boys and girls go on their maturation journey and come back safe and sound. But her dam of fears was already broken. For the first time in her life, she sought a helping spirit. She prayed, not out of faith but from fear.

All night I sat next to her at the Hebrew Home for the Aged. She moved there only to be close to you, but you didn't visit her even once.

No, this isn't emotional blackmail. Just stating the facts.

I stroked her thin, withered hand. The marijuana was working as a temporary painkiller, but it did not diminish Grandma Brendel's ability to row back and forth in time. She remembered birds gliding above her. She did not recognize them. How could she? She wasn't born on the island, nor did she die there.

The light grew dimmer, and from the window I could see the quivering strip of the Hudson. I still hoped to take a picture. I remember saying: Without that island you wouldn't have survived. The adoptive parent is sometimes much more of a parent than the biological mother or father. And she said: How will you know if you don't have a child?

I said nothing. I turned off my camera.

Then, when it was almost dark, Grandma Brendel wrote her will, and right there and then she had Nurse Valentina witness it. I still have a faded image in my brain: an old Jewish lady standing on the quivering line between water and earth, cursing this rite of passage. She was afraid to lose her Teibele in the flood.

What language did she curse in?

Maybe in the foreign words you murmur in your sleep.

How do you say *fuck* in Hebrew?

THE UNIVERSITY of Ararat-Niagara's website proudly announces three students who signed up this year to study Hebrew in the department of ancient languages, where it is taught alongside Latin, Ancient Greek, Gaelic, Aramaic, Eskimo-Greenlandic, Kaweskar, and the language of the Tuscarora tribe, which is recently undergoing a revival.

"The fortunate students will be able to read the Book of Books in its original language." Brilliant. Sign me up.

The site also notes that Hebrew letters are engraved on the Ararat cornerstone, and on the acknowledgment plaque at the memorial for DeWitt Clinton, the New York governor who gave his blessing to the island of refuge.

A zoo for extinct languages. Come on, kids, let's visit the Hebrew cage!

You can force pandas in captivity to breed, but how can you pass down a linguistic genome?

Making love in Hebrew—what a bizarre experience. Why don't we try it some time?

You never told me whether you were graced with the promised vision on that bar mitzvah voyage to the falls. Maybe when I get home I'll have the courage to ask you if Yehowakan Tanka really did gift you with wisdom and strength.

I spy on the entourage outside the Village Inn. When the Secret Service guy opens the limo door for the candidate, his hand seems to linger just a moment too long. The vehicle pulls out onto the street, and my Grand Cherokee tails it.

Isra Isle is humming with traffic. Now I understand why the island is considered one of the most crowded places on earth, almost as bad as Gaza District in Grand Palestine in the Middle East. How did they pack so many Jews into such a small area? Not to mention the Indians who arrived with the Trail of Tears expulsion, demanding—rightly—an official reservation, based on the Jewish precedent. If the Jews deserve it, why not other persecuted peoples?

Except my black forefathers, who were not included in the hotly contested category.

Despite the limited space, people drive courteously. No one honks or cuts into lanes. I merge into the flow of cars, making sure to use my turn signal, and wave keenly at the driver who passes me.

But you mock the feigned serenity. For you, Isra Isle is just a way station, like the truckers' rest stops along the freeways. Underneath, you said, there is a fundamental unease, perhaps because of the smoldering humidity, or the mushroom cloud of spray that always gets in your eyes. I have a suggestion for you: take a deep breath and inhale the negative ions that saturate the air. Rumor has it they dispense horniness. That must be the reason I'm chasing you with my e-mails and pathetic landscape pictures, even though it's quite possible you aren't there anymore.

An empty house. I don't want to think about that.

I've always been convinced it's the chase that you enjoy, because what would you do if the promise actually came true, God forbid? But now I'm starting to understand that what you're striving for is in fact a breach of the promise. So tell me, my Jake, which one of us sees the world in black and white?

I SLOW down and follow the limo into Spring Hill, a charming suburban neighborhood. It's no wonder real estate prices are skyrocketing. Let me live in the candidate's mansion and I promise you I'll give up the journeys forever.

What was it Grandma Brendel said? Rest and inheritance, not necessarily in that order, although she didn't own any viable assets. She moved lightly, free of objects. All she brought to the Hebrew Home for the Aged was her pipe. That night, when we smoked together, she asked me to communicate with the previous smokers of the pipe. I thought it was the drugs talking, but her eyes lacked the usual glazed look. The old woman seemed to be summoning what came before what came before. The room started to spin and the walls evaporated, as if someone had struck me with an axe. Truncated scenes. Curly sidelocks and moccasins. Someone rowing upriver in a strange vessel. I was certain it was just the marijuana.

Now my mind is completely lucid, and yet . . .

The dead are like a screensaver.

So what did she leave us, your grandmother? Let's not compete over who misses her more.

Here's another joke I heard, from the waitress at Village Inn: Why is the Jewish woman running for president? Because God's job is already taken.

Hah hah.

Why aren't you laughing, Jake?

THE ELECTRIC gates of the estate swing open, and the limo glides inside. It's a pity I can't tell from here if the Secret Service guy is taking advantage of the opportunity to touch the candidate's hand for too long again. Her schedule says: R&R.

The hunting hour. Now I just need to position myself.

What nickname do your family members use for you, Emanuella Winona? Your ex-husband who popped up out of nowhere this morning to support his ex-wife's candidacy; your daughter who avoids the media, secluded in an ashram in Free Tibet; a secret lover of one gender or the other . . . What goes on in your *boydem*? Even Lenox likes using that Jewish word.

Damn you, boy, damn.

Between you and me, the tabloid tycoon once quipped, what's the difference between politics and entertainment? Candidates who entertain the press are beloved, and so they're willing to pay a fortune to joke writers. And if the punchlines fall flat, they can play the saxophone, or burst into the studio on a Harley . . .

And Ms. Noah? What is she scheming over there in her grand *boydem*? How will she show the public her "true nature"? Lenox might suggest that she jump off the falls in a sailboard.

If I peel off her costume, I might actually help her. The weakness might end up being the javelin that launches her. Lenox would say I'm one of those paparazzi who try to cleanse their conscience by turning prying into an ideology. Fuck him. I'm willing to be that biblical prophet whose name I forget, the one who came to curse and ended up blessing. Back in the day, when I'd just started at the paper, I told Lenox: If you want to hunt a buffalo, you have to use tricks, and even that doesn't guarantee that the beast won't respond with his own ruse. Lenox shot back: You're a clever son of a bitch, building in your escape route from the get-go.

LURKING OUTSIDE your home, dear candidate, the prowler is in action. Incidentally, it was Lenox who gave me that nickname. I wanted "Tells with Pictures," but he claimed that wasn't commercial enough. A name, he explains to junior reporters, is simply a promotional tactic, a marketing ploy to increase distribution. In the tabloid headlines, he branded the candidate in giant letters: "Rows Backwards."

The front of her estate faces the water. A Federal architectural style, which combines Indian motifs with North African tones. Not that I can identify the Tunisian light blue that adorns the doorframes and window lintels, but I believe the people who say it's there. The same color is painted on the yacht bobbing in the private anchorage. I photograph the name on its side: *Boy of the Mist.* It seems Ms. Noah has plenty of capital to finance an election campaign.

Why "Rows Backwards"? Remind me to ask that tabloid son of a bitch what he was thinking.

Spring Hill. Home. The more I repeat these words to myself, which were meaningless last night, the more loaded they sound. A sort of whispered spell.

The official website notes that the colonnade was modeled on the biblical Temple and augmented with feather decorations on the finials. I don't take pictures, because I'm not interested in using up valuable memory space on something so trite that you can see it on any architectural website.

Megalomania, you said. And you're not the only one who lambasts the ostentatious display. Above the gates, in ironwork—of course—the Noah family emblem: a seven-oared candelabrum topped with a bow-shaped tomahawk.

I have to find a stakeout position. I choose my tree, based on the angle of its top branch, which affords a visual line straight to the windows. I find a hollow in the trunk, right where the branches split off, and that's it: a maple *boydem*. I see but cannot be seen. And I don't mean that I've become invisible. On the contrary—I move clumsily, but observers will not perceive me: they see but do not see, because for them I am but a leaf, a tendril swaying in the wind, a bird.

If I were the creator of this story, I would put my hero in the same position forever, and his ass would have to slowly get used to the protrusions poking his flesh. Sometimes I think that our tale, from its beginning—although its end is still unclear—is a wild invention. Lenox thinks we'd make a good tabloid story.

WHAT'S WORSE, a kike president or a nigger president?

That's not a joke; it's a riddle. I can't remember where I heard it.

Give me a sign, Jake.

I'm writing to you so I don't fall asleep on the tree. I have pins and needles all over my body, but I'm afraid to move in case I drop my camera and laptop. I am enveloped in foreign sounds: chirps and hums and taps and rustles and wails and bellows, a language not taught in any department of ancient languages. If I had lived here two hundred years ago I might have understood something. That's what happened to your uprooted grandmother when she adopted a home, not necessarily out of longing but as a refuge. She claimed that if Isra Isle had not existed, she would not have gotten out of Germany in time. If I could crumple the ruler of time, I would go back to those dark days and establish a shelter island for homosexuals, and one for Gypsies, and another for the disabled, and for the mentally ill, and one for blacks. An archipelago of the persecuted. Maybe it's not too late to shake the tectonic plates and remap the planet?

But if I had lived on the island of blacks, how would we have found each other?

Journeyers. That is the only tribe I choose to belong to.

Is ISRA Isle a city of refuge? I get so bored in the tree hollow that I find myself digging through the Bible. Unlike those lucky ancient languages students, I can only read your Book of Books in translation.

So that's the precedent? The Old Testament? Are you sure the State Visionary wasn't a little muddled when he predicated his plan on some ancient command to found cities of refuge? Maybe Mordecai Manuel Noah was so excited about exploiting the real estate potential that he bet the whole pot, unwittingly risking all of your lives. After all, cities of refuge were designed to contain accidental killers so that they would not become victims of blood vengeance. That is what it says in Numbers, in Deuteronomy, in Joshua, and in Chronicles.

I admit it, Jake. I got carried I way. I had to make sure I wasn't wrong.

Listen carefully: the Book prescribes three cities of refuge on either side of the river. And any obstacles in the refugees' path must be removed; no mound or valley or river may hinder them. Although it's not clear that the Niagara would have presented an obstacle for your grandmother. For you, she would have parted it in two.

What should really concern you, Jake, is that someone might conclude from the biblical concept that you are all nothing but murderers—they'll ignore the part about "accidental." Maybe instead of voluntarily dismantling Isra Isle, as you suggest, we just need to update the basic definitions. I trust your people's improvisational skills, Jake. If you ask me, it's better to be categorized as persecuted than as murderers, even if only accidental ones.

And what about those people who were unjustly persecuted—why weren't they attended to first?

On second thought, I like how those biblical forefathers tried to break the cycle of vengeance in any way they could, and prevent further bloodshed.

My inbox is empty. Where have you disappeared to, partner? You can't deny me the right to worry; anxiety is not the exclusive property of the Chosen People. Maybe that's what Grandma Brendel left me. I would also like to be gifted with wisdom and strength from some great spirit. Maybe it's not too late to go through a Jewish rite of passage. After all, the falls are within reach. Can you see me canoeing on my own, wrapped in a cloth, summoning my helping spirit? Who will wait for me on the shore?

The urn containing Grandma Brendel's ashes . . .

You're not saying anything, but I suspect that, wherever you are, you are responding to every word.

What's worse than a Jewish president?

A female Jewish president.

The Internet is filling up with jokes. Millions of users in an outburst of creative humor. It turns out, by the way, that your stand on the presidential race is not uncommon: support for the Isra Isler candidate among your people is at a low. Many of them claim they would rather she run for vice president. A glass ceiling for Jews, because even the sky has a limit.

One more thing I forgot to tell you, Jake. In the days of the Messiah they will add three more cities of refuge to the six existing ones. Does that mean the expansion of borders will in fact lead to an increase in accidental murderers?

Dying to pee. Can't hold it in.

THERE IS some movement in the windows, or perhaps it's just the shadows from the maple tree. The light fades, but sunset lingers. Imagine what a prowler aiming a high-end lens at me would see: a ridiculous creature peering out of a treetop full of honey resin for springtime, leaking. If the watchful eye has a sense of humor, it will assume this is just a defect of nature. Some asshole who can't control his bladder. But if it's a righteous and uncompassionate eye, which is far more likely, it will turn me over to the authorities for trespassing, and I'll find myself rotting away in some pit until Lenox deigns to rescue me. Or maybe the eye will be naïve enough to believe that the drizzle is the first rain. After all, it's September, even though the sky is cloudless. My pure bodily fluid soaks into the earth covered with dry leaves. I don't want to die before we have a chance to . . .

I don't want to die at all. So what?

I see the two of us in my mind's eye . . .

An airship. Unknown destination.

Go forth to the child I shall give you.

A transatlantic flight, the two of us cuddling under a tangled blanket. Your body gives off heat, the real gift you got from the Great Spirit. I put my head in the hollow of your back, above your beautiful ass, two mounds that make up a perfect landscape. For me that is the most promised land. We will hover for eternity between water and earth.

You see, partner, despite my impaired vision, or perhaps because of it, I can capture sights other people miss. Even if our story is an invention that goes against every grain, I prefer it to a putative tale that follows the familiar track.

In my vision I see us making love from right to left.

THE LIGHTS come on in the mansion. A door slams shut. A hand opens a window. A human shadow flutters. If the candidate and the Secret Service guy are using the break for a quickie, then the act that has no name is occurring outside of my lens's range. I can understand her desire to make love before moving on to her next challenge. It is not an unusual weakness, and the match between those two is no more improbable than our own.

The night we met, I remember wanting to get out of the club because of the electronic throbbing, frequencies to which you attach sublime significance. My skin was being ripped off, piece by piece. This is what it feels like to be scalped, I thought. I really struggle to understand why, in your new world, a party has to involve a herd-like gathering, collective addiction to chemical aids, and a planned epileptic fit designed to quell the sorrow of loneliness.

But sorrow will come, Jake. There's no escaping it.

I told you—or rather, I had to scream over the din in the club—that in my old world, dancing was a series of measured steps, back and forth, back and forth, eventually selecting one single partner. Your collectivity made me feel the full brunt of my loneliness.

I only wanted you.

You stood in the DJ booth, captain of a raft, swirling the human mass toward a destination only you knew. I aimed my lens. Your face crumbled into grains with only the pupil a focused island. To this day I have not looked at the pictures I took that night in the club, and they take up valuable memory. I don't know why you agreed to leave with me. There were more beautiful options, and certainly younger ones. I tried to joke: we were both born in the last millennium. It's a good thing you didn't say we'd both die in the next one. I don't know what prayer your people say over the spirits of the dead.

LIKE AN idiot, I stood there with Grandma Brendel's urn, carefully removing it from the FedEx packaging with both hands.

Across the way, the gates open and the limo starts its engine. My lens picks up a different Secret Service agent opening the door for the candidate.

Why are you afraid to read your grandmother's will, Jake? Is it because you might find out, God forbid, that someone loved you without limits?

THE MAPLE hollow has suddenly become comfortable. The prickling twigs are gone, and my un-athletic body has molded into the shape. I am tempted not to move at all, to become an extension of the tree and settle in until spring. The thought of them tapping sweet resin from me . . .

Unfortunately I am tied to the candidate's tracks. My obligation to the assignment, or my fear of Lenox, overcome the temptation to set down roots. Let's go camping together some time. They say Beaver Park is a perfect nature preserve. I hope those sharp-teethed beavers don't gnaw through the whole forest before we get there. We'll find a tree hollow for two.

Here's what really differentiates us: for you, romance is met with cynicism; whereas from my years of experience it is the most glorious, elusive gift one can ever receive.

You'll understand one day.

DARKNESS THICKENS and I have no flashlight. The Triplets give off a light mist that hides the stars, but down below there is a thick black swamp. I feel my way to the Grand Cherokee, which I hid in the thicket, stumbling through ferns and tree stumps at various stages of decomposition. My feet wallow in excrement. Every step seems to summon hidden creatures from the *boydem.* A pair of eyes sparks and vanishes. Let's hope there aren't any coyotes left on the island; they might want me for dinner.

Imagine Lenox's headline: Devoured on Duty. Disappeared Without a Trace.

The vegetation took advantage of the interlude, and my jeep is covered with a fleshy layer of leaves. I pull out pieces of bark stuck between the wheels and pollute the estate with a cloud of fuel when I turn on the engine.

This is the point at which the protagonist is supposed to promise: I'll be back. Such a sweet assurance, as sweet as spring resin. Fortunately, there is no obligation to fulfill the promise right now. Maybe I'll be back and maybe I won't. I can't make any promises. Always leave the voters in suspense.

A LITTLE feather flits around inside the Grand Cherokee and sticks to the mirror. I try to blow it away, but it insists on clinging to the glass, disrupting the picture of the lane behind me. When I dropped down from the tree, a winged creature took flight with a loud caw.

I hear your grandmother's voice: You must ask forgiveness from the spirit of the prey. And then the subconscious wave is cut off, perhaps because of the wind whistling through the open windows, perhaps because of the feather.

The old lady said some strange things on her last night. The thought that she would soon not exist, that I was only a substitute . . .

I take both hands off the wheel and salute the brave Jewish woman who was not, and will never be, my blood relative. She did not want to be pitied just because she was dying. It isn't fair to use emotional blackmail, because the victim is in the same boat, being carried to a place with no horizon. Rowing without oars, against the current.

I almost miss the interchange: I could have ended up in the little village of Buffalo by mistake and driven onto the highway in the wrong direction. But I'm not going back. Not yet. I promised Lenox I'd deliver the goods, even though both parties agree that a promise is merely lip service. Lenox and I are a pair of compulsive gamblers dropping more and more coins into the slot.

Before us, the flood.

ARE YOU Simon? I'm Zoe, deputy press officer.

A young woman with her lips, nose, and eyebrows pierced hands me the candidate's written speech and points to a few highlighted passages, to make sure I don't skip the main points.

The victory party is being held at the campaign headquarters. I make my way to the ballroom on the basement floor shared by the three towers. The ceiling is thick with balloons that bob up and down in huge clusters over the revelers' heads. One balloon bursts but the noise is swallowed up by the campaign jingle. I can't find the DJ booth. Volunteers in jeans and tattooed Isra Isle logos shower me with propaganda leaflets. A thin young man with braided hair and pockmarked skin winks at me and writes down a phone number over the candidate's portrait on a torn piece of glossy paper. There is a smell of election lust in the air.

The option of a different partner . . . A tiny contemplation flashes and quickly dies. I'm probably past the age for extracurricular activities.

You have chosen me.

We were both devoid of promise.

One gamble, and that's enough for us.

AT THE souvenir counter they sell carved pipes, T-shirts with images of the Triplets, wampum belts with lantern and oar patterns, and replicas of the Ararat cornerstone inside crystal balls. The nose-ringed Zoe tries to convince me to order tickets for the Snow Snake—the world javelin-throw championship. Instead of watching the live broadcast like the other millions, I could be sitting in the best seat in the VIP gallery. I could sell the pictures to sports magazines for a fortune.

Here are the instructions I downloaded, and this is the real game, not some computerized simulation for loafers. First you cut a branch off a hickory tree and plane it until it is as smooth as a fish. The spearhead must be slightly rounded and slanted upwards, and it's the tail that is supposed to be sharpened. The course has to be prepared, too. You drag a log over the snow to mark the track, and then you spray it with water, which freezes.

I can see you holding the snow snake in your right hand, supporting it with your left, sprinting forward and then launching it as far as you can.

Sound easy? Maybe to you, having been born here. For a moment I imagine myself among the children of Isra Isle, practicing the javelin throw year round, not just in winter. There is even a grove of hickory trees near the Trail Tree, grown solely for making javelins. It was planted facing east. I'm sure you know why.

As the herd of admirers, led by Zoe, roar their victory slogans, I download more and more data. Did you know it's believed that the journeyers brought with them an ancient version of the game? But researchers disagree on the type of spear used in the Jewish version. Try to get into my mind for a minute and see your past—a boy with a strange name and a pipe-loving old lady sliding over a thin layer of ice, launching snakes of fire and smoke. Which direction do you run in, Jake? Because when you turn around, forward becomes backward.

Since Zoe is watching, I aim my lens at the candidate as she bounds up onto the stage, and pretend to be amazed by the thunderous cheers. The room is incredibly crowded, stifling, but Lady Noah glides like a bass in water. Her pit stop in the Secret Service guy's hollow seems to have recharged her. I zoom onto her hand as she hushes the crowd, and click-click at the Snow Snake champion who skips over to the stage and stands next to her. For a moment they remind me of a pair of boats caught in a lighthouse beam. That smarmy athlete exploited the Law of Return and moved here so he could represent Isra Isle, and now he's making millions endorsing sports moccasins.

The enthusiastic Zoe practically throws herself at her idol, and her piercings tremble in the dark. Would you like an autograph? she gushes. You can give it to your kids.

I don't . . . We don't have kids.

Sorry.

She pulls a dry twig from my hair and laughs: Fall out of a tree?

LISTEN TO her speech, Jake. Who the fuck wrote this stuff?

> The United States of America is a chosen nation. We shall lead the world to new challenges, proudly carrying the torch of democracy, liberty, and equality among all the children of this earth. Our pillar of fire will shine in places still governed by tyranny, ignorance and xenophobia. America will fulfill its destiny—to become a light unto the nations.
>
> Let us look back to what came before us, to our fathers' fathers, who founded the great covenant of peace and announced to the world that "the time of great sorrow and terror is behind us." Just as the ancient Iroquois people buried their tomahawks and spears and vowed never to shed blood, so shall we gather into our circle the hawks who still nest in their dark hollows, and under the flourishing canopy of

leaves we shall renew the covenant together. We will all be peacemakers.

God bless . . .

Could she have written it herself?

THERE'S NOTHING to photograph. The glimmering pendant was just an illusion. Maybe it's time to leave this job and start snapping brides and grooms against saccharine backgrounds.

From the ballroom I send a quick e-mail to Lenox: I quit. Send someone else.

Zoe shamelessly peers at my screen to make sure I'm immortalizing the historic occasion. The Isra Isler's vision will be the lead story on every newscast. Zoe is fully convinced that a new era is dawning, that evildoers all over the world will soon drop to their knees and beg the spirit of the prey for forgiveness.

I resist dumping a bucket of ice on her naïve dreams. She reminds me of myself at that age. I was the joke of the reservation. A lone black raven among the reds.

I make my way to the doorway, which is blocked by a juggler wearing stars and stripes. Each of his three juggling balls is blazoned with one fluorescent word: Isra Isle—My—Place.

The candidate's speech is still blaring from the speakers behind me, and I suddenly sense that her message is unscripted. Perhaps Lady Noah is improvising a vision for us? After all, politicians have always been measured by their ability to advertise promises, just like the Great Spirit who chained that hyperactive ancient forefather to herself and sent him on a huge gamble. Maybe the candidate realized she was facing bankruptcy and had no way of winning votes other than by making her own promises.

What amazes me is that for thousands of years people have remained loyal to the Great Spirit and been mislead by her promises, even though—as politicians are wont—she has rarely kept them.

More Broken Promises. That could be a decent headline for Lenox's tabloid.

I FIND myself transfixed by the spinning balls and words.

My—Place—Isra Isle—Place—Isra Isle—My.

Stop!!!

We need to ask the heretical question: Why this place and not another? Much like the question of whether you really are the only one for me or whether I'm just banging my head against the wall. If I'd gone to a different club that night, I might have met . . . Or what if a different DJ had been spinning?

I was going to ask Grandma Brendel if it was a coincidence, or if life before and life after encode some sort of path that is beyond our comprehension. But I didn't have time.

WHEN I get back to the hotel I flop onto the bed fully clothed, stinking of animal droppings and rotting wood. Maple twigs have left gashes in my flesh and every muscle in my body is pulled. I don't even have the strength to close the drapes. Tomorrow I will drown in full daylight.

My resignation has not brought relief. Lenox will probably make me pay back my expenses. Fuck him.

What would we do without the wonderful F-word, the American language's greatest contribution to the world? Even Grandma Brendel let it slip like a ring of smoke before she died.

She is somewhere out there on the Jews' eternal hunting grounds now. It's a pity she didn't pass down a courage gene to her grandson, or to me.

What difference does it make whether or not Isra Isle keeps existing? Or whether the United States does or does not get a president with Jewish blood? Nothing will change the way the deck has been shuffled—and not by some great spirit, some mysterious Yehowakan Tanka watching over us from above—because we are incapable of switching courses and rowing backwards.

MY HAND is swollen and I need ice. I stretch over to the minibar, but the maid forgot to replenish the Jack Daniels. I'm so thirsty. This is how it feels in the desert.

Hug me . . . I'm dehydrating without you, Jake.

At least she didn't forget the toothbrush I asked for at the front desk. It's on the minibar, with a note: "Courtesy of Management." For all I care, you can throw out all the disposable toothbrushes and all the other dubious contents of the *boydem.* I'm handing back the keys, Jake. Getting out of the game.

A desire to fail?

Could be. But what I've gone through this time has worn me out. Still, my brain keeps zigzagging madly. I try to hold on, reaching a hand out from within the whirlwind. May Day. May Day.

A waterfall made out of unidentifiable material sits on the pillow. Like a congealed fishbowl Jell-O. The giant Niagara waves have been reduced to a handful of wrinkles, and the useless object glares at me like a grumpy old man. I don't know what got into me. I gave in to an urge to buy it for you, for one dollar, at the souvenir stand in the headquarters. You can throw your childhood landscape at me when I get back.

Jake, I am planning to use my nonexistent right of return. It's only been one day, but to me it feels like an entire lifetime. Life before or life after . . . Is someone else in bed with you now instead of me?

I don't want to die before. I don't want to die after.

The creator is sick of this story, too, because the forward-backward-forward track is driving him crazy. He's dying to shut his single eye. Just like me, he doesn't want to dream either, not even by mistake.

I let the bed cradle me as though it were that perfect hollow in your back, and doze off to the lullaby sound of the soft trickling.

I awake suddenly, completely lucid, and stare at the computer screen I forgot to turn off, which glows at me like a square moon. Your letters are anchored on the screen: Don't leave.

I'm washed over, Jake. A cascade of sudden bliss. Even if you are only saying it because Lenox made you try and stop me from quitting.

Through the naked windowpane, a field of light-crops flashes. I can't distinguish the Triplets' lights from the stars. In Isra Isle, it turns out, it's never completely dark.

Good night, my partner.

ZOE JOLTS me out of sleep to tell me I should be at the old pier by ten o'clock. It's unclear why I have been chosen to join the handful of lucky reporters who will get to immortalize the candidate's highly-publicized sailing to the falls.

I got up. I shaved. I brushed my teeth. That's what I would write in my essay about the school trip. I was a good boy, Jake. I even dried myself with two towels, like you do, to remove all traces . . .

Here's another version: I get up. I pee. I miss you. Instead of toothpaste, I brush my teeth with Jack Daniels, ordered especially from room service. Alcohol for breakfast? the waiter boldly quips, jeopardizing his tip. I make sure the minibar is full, send the waiter on his way, and type a message to Lenox:

A second chance is not a handout, fucker. You have to take it by force.

THE ODDLY named private yacht, *Boy of the Mist*, lurches up the Niagara and my stomach turns. The Jack Daniels starts dancing. I'm already regretting taking back my resignation. What do I need this forward-backward-forward pendulum for? Look at me. One wave of your finger and I melt.

Boy of the Mist. Maybe it's named after you, or some other boy doomed by tradition to go searching in the mist for a helping spirit and a false promise.

The candidate turns her perfect profile to me, so that I can shoot her at her best. Zoe hands out waterproof ponchos, which look dark gray and light gray to me, but to others are blue and white. When she offers me a life jacket, I refuse. I wouldn't be able to maneuver my swollen hand into the sleeve. Perhaps that is what calls the candidate's attention to me. She glares at me, and although I'm wearing the poncho hood, she has obviously engraved my black face in her memory, which means the chances of getting any incriminating evidence are slim. Maybe a miracle will happen and Emanuella Winona Noah will take off her designer suit and jump into the freezing water. Or maybe she's planning to conduct an ancient Jewish ritual at the falls—a collective bar mitzvah, where we will all wear prayer shawls to stay dry.

The two Secret Service agents project an arrogance that competes with the negative ions filling the air; it's probably because of the latest polls, which show a bump in the candidate's support after last night's speech. I'm the only one who isn't buying her goods. Her call to action only makes me want to retreat. I told you that night at the club: I don't want to be part of the dancing herd.

I take a picture of the two banks passing by in slow motion for you, and the ferns reaching their green probes into the pale water. I lean over and dip my bruised hand in. Foamy clusters lap at the pain. I have to be careful not to fall off the deck. A seafarer's burial—that's all the campaign needs. Next thing you know they'll be throwing the raven's corpse in, wrapped in a plastic bag . . .

There will be no trace of us. And who will be left to create our story?

I wonder how you withstood your coming-of-age journey alone. Why do they force frightened boys into adulthood, severing them from childhood with a tomahawk? It occurs to me that perhaps it was during that long-ago isolation when you decided to be a DJ. You wanted to make the trembling waters dance.

The candidate breathlessly asks us to listen to "the sounds of her childhood." This is where the media addicts get their dose of kitsch. She talks about her illustrious great-grandfather, who dreamed up the vision of Ararat on the water and proclaimed the Jewish state with extraordinary theatrical talent. A real Shakespeare. *The undiscovered country, from whose bourn no traveler returns.* Some say he was accompanied on his first sailing to the island by a mysterious Indian woman. She disappeared without a trace.

Yeah, right. Another fairytale to sell the voters.

BIRDS ACCOMPANY *Boy of the Mist* on its way to the falls. Like Grandma Brendel, I can't identify them. I think about the diminutive Jewish woman with the German accent, how she sailed in the opposite direction, holding a suitcase. She knew she would never again see her homeland. Unlike you, for her that was not a dirty word.

Go into the darkroom and read the will, Jake. It's not me

imposing premature adulthood on you. You and I know that border has already been crossed. Dependency—that's what you're afraid of. You see Isra Isle as a crutch, and you're a big believer in personal survival. Why carry around unnecessary items that could weigh you down and sabotage your chances of surviving intact?

But your grandmother told me that when she went into the longhouse for the first time and saw the family pods, for her it was suddenly home. Maybe not the ideal home, but the closest she could get. She took one more step and entered the heart of the circle, where Indian mothers used to feed their children and tell stories of what came before what came before, and the children passed the story on when they grew up. That is the real journey, the Jewish shaman whispered to me. I leaned over to be sure I was catching every word. Now I reconstruct for you, like a negative from an old camera, the vision that emerged.

We recreate the story every time. That's what Grandma Brendel said. Sometimes by mating two different species. And the story emerges from the celestial body after every flood, like a rainbow.

I will never see the colors. I've accepted that.

Read the will. Your grandmother wanted us so badly to have . . .

I told her: I'm afraid.

She started wheezing more loudly, more frequently, and I ran to get Nurse Valentina. When I got back her eyes were wide open, and it took me a while to understand that what was lying there before me was an empty shell. My black hand closed her eyes and covered them with white lashes. I deeply regret fleeing her final gaze. Perhaps her eyes reflected the undiscovered country she sailed to. I was paralyzed. Even sorrow dawdled. I wanted to say: Grandma, if there is life after life, give me some proof. But no words came out.

Nurse Valentina suggested that I pray. I told her: I have no idea what the Jews say at the time of death.

I phoned you, but I didn't dare leave a message on the answering machine.

WHAT ARE you typing there the whole time? Zoe asks—or scolds. You're a photographer, not a writer. Haven't you noticed we've arrived?

I can't hear Zoe or myself. Why do they give out ponchos and not earplugs? The computer gets sprayed again and again, and I shove it under my poncho. I leave the camera open, blinking at the white deluge.

Even your deafening nightclub, Jake, would bow its head before the Niagara trance. *Boy of the Mist* circles on its axis within the dimple created by the falls. The deck empties out and the herd of journalists retreat onto the glass-covered balcony. Even the Secret Service men are hunched over, out on the deck, but the candidate stands steady at the bow. Her head is uncovered. She does not put on her hood. Tufts of hair slap her face as she looks straight at the roiling wall of water. I'm not convinced the citizens of the United States would want a bedraggled woman dripping with water as their president. I snap shot after shot. Finally, the picture that will take care of our future. I've completed the mission, Jake. A perfect future.

Just at that minute I am overpowered by an uninvited spirit.

Fuck you, Lenox! I hear myself scream. It's hopeless to fight against a force more powerful than yourself. You are tempting the spirit!

I'm beginning to see some clarity. What is it that you people pass down in your genes? Jews, Isra Islers, Isra Isle-ites . . . Dear God, how did you end up being what you are?

The candidate still grips the railing, but then she starts

to slip and cartwheels her oar-hands in the air to steady herself. She is rowing backwards. Instead of snapping a shot, I find myself reaching out to catch her—offering a spear of black flesh. We both go down, two pillars of water, rolling together on the uneven deck, and I think to myself: What a way to go, holding on to Emanuella Winona Noah's pendant.

Through the mist I see a series of flashes. They're photographing us, I tell her. Someone's going to make a killing, and it won't be me.

The Secret Service men pounce on me and start kicking. The pendant rips off in my hand. My camera is broken. All the pictures . . . What will we leave behind?

They prop up the shaken candidate and aim their guns at me. I hold up the only pair of oars I have. I would like to choose how this story ends. This can't be it. They take my laptop, push me into the control station and handcuff me to the wheel. How will my words reach you now?

I'M GOING back to the morning after.

We lay in bed. I anchored myself in your wonderful back hollow, a place I had just discovered. I was the happiest Columbus. I didn't want to get up. I was barely breathing.

You spoke first: What's happening between us?

I knew that if I called a spade a spade you might pull away. I remember thinking to myself: You're such a coward, Simon. Trembling at the act that has no name, even though it has countless euphemisms. For me it was clear from the first moment. I saw you up on the DJ stand and I felt like a sailor on the mast who finally sees land. I didn't even know your name or that you were an Isra Isler. What difference does it make?

Go forth to whatever place you choose, and I'll fly after you. This island, another island. The world is a circular course of wanderers anyway, all chasing their own promises.

Since my computer has been confiscated, I have no way of writing the real thing. But maybe it's best not to put the words down like feet—black on white. Otherwise their tracks might disappear.

I will make love with you in whichever language you want. Even from right to left. How do you say "I love you" in Hebrew?

I AM wet and shivering. She is also wet and shivering. The candidate for the highest office in the world is a mere mortal. The Secret Service men wrap a blanket around her, and she shakes the water off her body like a grizzly bear.

We set sail again, this time in the opposite direction. *Boy of the Mist* jerks like a dance floor, and from where I lie, handcuffed, Isra Isle emerges from the mist crowned with a halo of spray. You ran away from this place. Didn't want to be under the canopy of disaster. What did you mean, Jake? We could have taken advantage of your right of return and lived a tranquil, comfortable life for the rest of our days. It's still not too late.

Zoe comes over to apologize. She hands me back my laptop and the memory card from my camera. She promises the lab techs will restore all the data.

I reassure her: There's a lifetime warranty that covers everything, including climate damages. Anything except fire. That consumes everything.

I get an official apology from the Secret Service agents, and they unfasten the handcuffs. They're probably afraid of getting sued by Lenox. It's hard to tell an enemy from a friend these days, says the one who touched the candidate's hand for too long. He seems very eager to boot up the laptop for me.

Paranoid, I tell myself. That's what happens when you get too close to Jews. Probably picked it up from his boss.

Your words slowly crawl across the screen and I stare at them, hypnotized. I don't need the crutches of vision to see you getting out of bed silently, going into the dark room, and taking the sealed envelope out of the *boydem*. You rip it open and read the will.

I know what you're going through, partner. The defiance reflex has been ingrained in you for generations. The fact that life before crosses the river of time does not obligate life after. Why are we doomed to be obedient children, to submit to the spirits' command? Go forth from your land and your homeland. Must the covenant be kept at any cost?

At the bottom of the will my signature appears. "I, who am not a relative and have no benefit or interest in the estate, hereby testify that the bequeather, being of sound and disposing mind, has signed this will in the presence of us both, after having read it and declared it her final will, willingly and without any duress or coercion." Nurse Valentina came up with the formulation, as if she were an experienced lawyer.

Tzippora Brendel asked you to scatter her ashes on the waters, but not the ones that tremble on the outskirts of Isra Isle. On the eve of her death the Jewish shaman recalled a different homeland, one that had almost been forgotten. Homeland, I remind you on her behalf, is not a dirty word. She did not want to be buried. For little spirit thou art, and unto little spirit shalt thou return, she said. You will hold the urn on one side and I'll hold it on the other, and together we will scatter her over the quivering border between water and dirt. We will drive to a dry, barren place on whose land she has never set foot, an island once renowned but forgotten when it was lost in the cyclone of journeys. We can name it ourselves, as if it were a child. We will travel to the lost country; Grandma Brendel hid her love for it in the *boydem* of her heart. Through the clouds of tobacco and marijuana she told me: Don't be afraid, Simon.

And perhaps all this is just my hallucinations. My vision impairment—a spreading affliction.

I UNCLENCH my fist and find the candidate's pendant in my palm. I'll be accused of theft.

Emanuella Winona Noah says: Keep it. You can wear it to my inauguration.

She came into the control station without me noticing, and waved away the Secret Service agents to ensure our privacy.

I minimize the browser window on my laptop—a joke site.

Is there anything else you'd like to photograph? she asks.

I say nothing.

She takes the wheel and starts up the engine.

Tomorrow we'll be spread all over the front page. A sharp transition from photographer to subject. Are you prepared?

She is short, almost as short as Grandma Brendel, and I feel like a hulking bison in comparison. She takes one hand off the wheel and opens the little window wide. The wind whistles in, mussing her now-dry hair. It has a particularly gray tone.

I'm going to do this in spite of them, she says. I will place my hand on the Bible and swear allegiance to the United States of America, and promise to serve all of its citizens and all the other sons of Noah.

She gives me a pointed look, as if I'm supposed to get the hint.

Me? A son of Noah? Since when have I been annexed to the family? The *goy* lover—that is my genealogical connection, according to Grandma Brendel.

The candidate puts my hands on the wheel, forcing a joint navigation. *Boy of the Mist* now sails on calm waters, with no traces of the rough ride from before. You should try it once, Jake. It's an addictive experience.

After the flood, seven laws were issued to all the children of Noah, Emanuella Winona Noah explains; to me it seems she's rehearsing her inauguration speech. She continues: It was a new set of laws, a moral scaffolding on which the human race would be reconstructed, to ensure that it would continue to exist without another flood.

An ambitious agenda, I say. I tell her about the website where people debate what to call the future president's potential spouse: "First Man"? Or maybe "First Doormat"? Whoever guesses the right name wins a lifetime subscription to *Racism & Prejudice Magazine*.

Emanuella Winona Noah scolds me, as though I were a misbehaving pupil: You're not listening! Any person who strives to fulfill the seven Noahide laws is a righteous gentile and earns a place in the world to come.

A lofty promise, Ma'am, but I doubt the voters will buy it.

I decide not to repeat the site's most popular joke. I wish I knew which commandments would earn me a place of honor—not in the world to come, but in this one. The idea that you and I are part of the same family contradicts my signed testimony on your grandmother's will. Now it turns out I *do* have a benefit or interest in the estate. Like it or not, we are connected, Jake. Even the site's winning joke, the one I didn't tell Ms. Noah, puts us in the same place:

Why do kikes and niggers stink?

So blind people can hate them too.

I TELL the candidate: If hatred can cross all borders and survive all journeys, then we need to strike out the current book of laws and reformulate everything from scratch. It's been too long since the flood and the new laws it gave rise to. We need to start over.

Emanuella Winona Noah turns the wheel and the *Boy of the Mist* falters. If we hit a shoal, it'll be her fault. I'm just a hitchhiker. That's exactly what Lenox wants; a disaster of Titanic proportions would boost his tabloid sales to new heights.

Be careful! I yell.

You should be careful too, Prowler, she shoots back. If you were interested in women, I would flirt with you.

She misinterprets my silence as embarrassment.

I hope he loves you back, she says. I don't tell her that there is always one who loves more and one who loves less. That is the only unbridgeable gap. I'm already preparing myself, Jake, for the day when you fly after some other raven to an enchanted and far more promising Ararat.

The woman with the wild red hair suddenly looks like a reflection of my future self. Perhaps running for president, like any other chase, is a painkiller against loneliness. After all, she and I both know there is no promised land.

Fortunately, her sense of humor saves us from wallowing in the mire any longer. She comes up with the perfect name for the president's spouse: How about "First Person," Simon?

I'll vote for her, Jake, and I'll drag you to the polls, too, so you can fulfill your civic right.

SHE REACHES one arm out the window toward the falls. They were there long before humans surrendered to their yearning for changing places, before bloody borders were engraved on the earth. All that beauty existed for itself, and still no price has been exacted for it.

You should visit in wintertime, Simon, when Isra Isle is bathed in white splendor, cleansed of any injustice that came before or may still come, and the Memory Site is turned into a skating rink. Even the trembling water briefly freezes, suspending its fury.

She tells me that the water is so immensely powerful that it is gradually wearing down the waterfall cliffs. Thousands of years from now the falls will retreat toward Lake Erie and eventually vanish. Isra Isle will be flooded and all its inhabitants will have to leave. A little patience, partner, and your prophecy will come true. One way or another, this island will become a hallucination.

You won't believe this: she gave me the keys to her estate and invited us to spend our honeymoon there. It'll be empty anyway, because the owner is relocating to a new address: 1600 Pennsylvania Avenue, Washington, DC.

The wind cuts through at me, and I ask her: Ma'am, do you know of another city of refuge for the Jews?

Her eyes turn hazy, and she acquires a hardened shell, like you, Jake. A different city of refuge? What are you talking about?

As I wonder how to explain it to her, she drops her hand from the wheel and pulls mine off, too. She leans into me, perhaps adopting the interrogation methods she learned from the Secret Service guy. The yacht starts to tip, and I stutter: It's a place . . . It disappeared without a trace.

The minute the words leave my lips I realize I've stepped over the line.

WE'VE BEEN anchored for some time now. *Boy of the Mist* sways back and forth, and I don't know if we're in high tide or low tide. Pictures of the candidate flicker across the wall in the yacht. A floating picture album. A girl with feathers in her braids. A student at her final play at Yale, playing Jessica, Shylock's daughter. A senator giving her first speech, wearing a wampum belt. An ambassador in a crimson robe, delivering her credentials to the King of Tunis. And the final picture: a mother and daughter running side by side on the javelin-throw track, with the Trail Tree in the background. I immediately recognize the pendant on the daughter's neck. A family heirloom. Her glamour shots are mediocre, Jake. She could do better.

The memory card in my camera . . . I have no idea if it survived. I always regret capturing a particular moment in my photographs. It always seems that I could have—if I'd only taken a different gamble—frozen a different moment, one closer to perfection.

A KNOCK on the door, and through the crack we see the worried face of nose-ringed Zoe peering in. The gap in the candidate's itinerary needs to be closed up. With the pendant still in my hand, Ms. Noah and I shake hands, and only then do I discover that the Star of David has come apart from the elm leaves.

No one knows exactly what kind of branch the dove brought back to the ark, says Emanuella Winona Noah. It's not even certain that it was a dove. The forefather might have just gotten mixed up. So many species and types in one ark. All the creatures were beautiful and worthy in his eyes.

Listen to the candidate's version of the story, Jake. It is not the one that is written in the Book of Books on which she will swear allegiance in Washington. I can only imagine the headlines Lenox would concoct: The Ark Lands on Ararat . . . A Rainbow Emerges in the Sky. And the subtitle: Pair by gaping pair, the creatures look up at the amazing spectacle . . . All except the dove. She was the only one whose eyes were blind to the vision, because they were filled with the raven, who waited for her on the quivering line between water and land.

I suggest to the future president that she work the tale into her inauguration speech. We're all paying royalties to a Lenox-like creator anyway, churning out season after season of a hit soap opera. And the ratings are sky high.

Afterwards, in front of Zoe and the Secret Service men, Emanuella Winona Noah teaches me your mourning prayer: *Yitgadal v'yitkadash sh'mei raba . . .* May His great name be exalted and sanctified is God's great name, in the world which He created according to His will. May He establish His kingdom and may His salvation blossom and His anointed be near, during your lifetime and during your days and during the lifetimes of all the House of Israel, speedily and very soon. Then she instructs us all to say "Amen" in a chorus.

I wish you were here with me, Jake. I miss your voice so much.

She lingers for one more moment before leaving. You have no idea, she says, how hard we worked to preserve the ghost language that serves as a cipher for prayers. There's a course offered in the Department of Ancient Languages at Ararat-Niagara University.

I wrote down the Hebrew prayer she recited, syllable by syllable, so that you can have the option of reciting it when we arrive at the lost desert we're going to.

YOU BOUGHT tickets to Damascus??? Which one? You don't have to go all the way to the Middle East. There's a Damascus in New York State, and another one in Pennsylvania, and they're not even that far apart. We could catch both in one day without any jetlag.

I can hear you laughing through the digital barrier: No. No shortcuts. You bought tickets to *that* Damascus, the one that was the point of departure for all the others. You paid full fare, on my American Express card. That's all right, Jake. I can afford to finance a folly or two. Speedily and very soon we will land in a sweltering, steamy airport, rent an off-road vehicle, and cross a border into Grand Palestine, heading toward the sea. Grandma Brendel did not specify a particular landmark, leaving us free to decide where to scatter her ashes. I don't think there are more than a handful of Jews in Grand Palestine. I couldn't find any organized community on the Internet. Not even a synagogue to speak of. Grandma Brendel said: Ten Jews are enough for a prayer circle. You can pray under the open sky, too, or anywhere your feet may carry you. The members of the Jewish tribe do not need marked places to address their serial promise breaker. Is there any more proof needed of the durability of the journeyers' memory card?

Maybe we'll search the desert for eight more Jews and join them to pray in Hebrew. May His salvation blossom, during your lifetime and during your days and during the lifetimes of all the House of Israel, and let us say Amen.

See? I'm an excellent student.

When I set foot on the ancient pier that was restored for the Jewish State's centenary, Zoe hands me the newspaper. The candidate and I are on the front page, falling onto the deck of the *Boy of the Mist.* Time perfectly frozen. I couldn't have done a better job myself. The headline says: "Lost Their Balance."

Lenox is having a field day. He sends me gleeful e-mails. His sales have doubled, even though he bought the picture from the agencies. But who cares when the paparazzi himself creates the headline and turns the candidate into the hottest story of the year? Your bonus check is in the mail, Prowler. Mission accomplished. And let us say Amen.

KILLING TIME before my flight. You're right: you can see the mushroom cloud from every spot on the island. I'm beginning to understand what you meant when you said there was always something lurking over this place. It makes it seem as if Isra Isle was isolated so that experiments could be conducted here, a laboratory where they can study how the wandering tribe behaves under permanent residency conditions. Something like the turtles on Galapagos.

I think about all the gullible immigrants who thronged to Grand Island, inspired by the promising name. But a quick walk around the island makes it immediately clear that this is merely a tiny patch in a river—not even a sea. I assume the pioneers hid their disappointment deep in the *boydem*, because who wants to admit to a mistake? Fortunately, your people were blessed with the art of improvisation, a mysterious quality that has not been thoroughly studied. It's too bad I didn't ask the candidate if her great-grandfather was the resourceful man who decided to pack them all in vertically, turning Isra Isle into an imitation of Manhattan. Of course it also emulates Gaza in Grand Palestine, the most tower-laden metropolis in the world.

Meanwhile I've had a personal appeal from Ararat-Niagara University to sign up for a new course they are offering next semester: The History That Wasn't. The message said: "We have been informed that you have shown a particular interest in the question of what would have happened to the Jews if . . . "

Who snitched on me? Is this the candidate's revenge, or Lenox's cruel joke? Or maybe it's your plot to ground me here—an eternal exile—as far away from you as possible.

Hey, Jake, the only island in the world you can exile me to is the island of the color-blind, in Micronesia.

University, at my age? You sweetly explain the history with a DJ's metaphor: Isra Isle is just a cover version, and if it were up to you there would be a remix that improved upon the original. Even Martin Luther King Jr.'s famous "I Have a Dream" speech has become a hit on the dance floors. Incidentally, they're selling it for half price at the music store on Clinton Avenue, corner of Devorah the

Prophetess. Should I buy you a copy? Or would you rather download it?

I amble through the ruler-straight streets, with the candidate's broken pendant in my camera belt. I was almost tempted to stop at the local Tiffany's and ask them to repair it. On President John Adams Boulevard, corner of King David, I was asked if by any chance I was the man from the sensational picture in the papers. I said I wasn't.

I've reached Javelin Woods, and I sit down under a tree and scan the first pages, my hands shaking. I think I saw a stain. In the *New York Times* it shows up on the candidate's cheek, and in the *Ararat Post* it's on me. A white blemish on a black island.

AN ISRA Isler boy runs on the track opposite me, practicing the javelin throw. Every so often I cheer him on. I would like to ask him if he's already celebrated his bar mitzvah, and which gifts he's expecting from Yehowakan Tanka at the end of his coming-of-age journey. But he slips away into the horizon.

I don't expect you to miss me back, Jake. Love only sails one way. Nevertheless, I'd like to believe that you are standing on the banks of our empty bed holding the tickets to Damascus, and declaring in sound and disposing mind that the act between us has a name. Maybe that's what it says between the lines of Grandma Brendel's will.

The wind in Javelin Woods whistles background music to your words as they flow to me from the computer. When did you have time to look up consolation phrases, Jacob Brendel III? Your e-mail says:

Ha'Makom yenachem etchem . . . May the place comfort you among the mourners of Zion and Jerusalem.

So it's the *place* that offers consolation? Could it be that Zion and Jerusalem are real places? Because I couldn't find them on the map.

WHAT'S YOUR name? the kid asks. His javelin is caked with dirt and leaves.

Simon. What's yours?

Liam.

Nice name. Does it mean anything?

Liam shrugs his shoulders, then offers me the javelin. Maybe he hopes I'm a talent scout recruiting for a college. He holds my camera and shows me how to grip the javelin. He takes me to the launching point and pushes me forward. Running and throwing at the same time is against the laws of nature. How did you do it, Jake? I run down the track that has been conquered by countless pairs of feet before mine. My poor bladder takes a few jolts, and the javelin drops to the ground like a removed prosthesis.

Disqualified, Liam announces, and runs over to pick up the javelin. Like many others, he mistakes me for a bird-watcher. I don't bother to correct him.

Think about it, Jake. A child of our own.

Despite my pleas, Liam refuses to give me a second chance. He tells me proudly how he once threw the javelin beyond the ancient cemetery of Ararat. Only when he stretches his arm out—muscular from training, bursting with youth—and points to the distance, do I notice the wavy row of stones peering out from beyond the woods.

Liam gives me back my camera without having used it. Failure, the little smart-ass informs me, is not something worth preserving in an album. Try to look for your helping spirit, he suggests; maybe you'll improve your performance. Even our candidate has one, and that's why she's going to be president.

The lens is covered with bird-shit. How have they already managed to crap on it?

The memory card . . . It's my only chance to pass something down.

Before Liam goes back to practicing, I put the candidate's broken pendant in his hand. Take it, I tell him. You might need it one day.

He thanks me politely, but I can tell that the moment I'm gone he'll fling both pieces as far away as he can. Now I regret not keeping the pendant for you. The nipple piercing could have connected the Star of David with the elm leaf.

ALTHOUGH IT'S not an obligatory tourist stop, I'm about to skip over the wave of stones bordering the ancient cemetery. Visiting here is not recommended. Even the State Visionary, Mordecai Manuel Noah, didn't find his final resting place in this ground. So who is buried here?

I can hear you scream at me through the screen, Jake. You would physically keep me from crossing the border if you could. The dead are not anywhere; that's what you told me when I came back from the Hebrew Home for the Aged. I wanted to hug you, to take away some of your sorrow, but you clutched your CD case against your beautiful body and did not let me come close. When you went to work, I hid the urn of ashes in the darkroom. I think that was the first time I called it a *boydem.*

May the place comfort you . . . Now I know what I was supposed to say to you, according to your custom. If that isn't a promise, I don't know what is.

Mourners of Zion and Jerusalem . . .

I have no idea where Jerusalem is, but we can visit Zion National Park in Utah. They say it's a geological wonder, with cliffs towering over the canyon in magnificent reds and whites. You can tell me how beautiful the colors are.

I GLIDE past the crooked headstones, twisted on their axes by seeping groundwater, and gaze at the view as though it were a theater set designed especially for me. An election leaflet flutters over a field dotted with fallen feathers:

"Emanuella Winona Noah—The Future Is Already Here." Yeah, sure it is. Like dead people have the right to vote.

Outside the fence, I recognize a small mound. Why does this place look familiar? Or am I having another uninvited onslaught . . . I'm not sure if I recognize it from what you told me about your journey home, or if Grandma Brendel is still stabbing me with visions from her unfamiliar land.

You came back early from your journey. Instead of waiting for dawn, you sailed home from the falls in total darkness. You didn't even know which way to row. There was not another soul there but you.

Two by two in the ark. That version softens the fear.

How did you withstand it? I ask you now. You were only thirteen.

Your answer comes immediately: Without fear, I wouldn't be who I am.

I give up, Jake. Sometimes I suspect that I willingly chose to be color-blind, because the alternative sets fear in my heart. Don't worry, partner. The Jewish seer cobbled together an island of refuge somewhere out there in the desert for you. An Ararat beyond Ararat. Just in case a flood of ashes should gather your defiant tribe into a cracked canoe once again.

STILL, SOMETHING bothers me, Jake: If America is the fulfilled land, why did your grandmother lose her faith in Isra Isle before she died? After all, the world strode confidently into the third millennium, recovering from the ills of racism and fanaticism. The age of great peace is near, as the candidate declared last night.

Before I left, Lenox told me about a delusional playwright who lived in Vienna about a century ago and came up with the madcap idea of establishing another Jewish state, in the Middle East. Just imagine, Jake: a branch of Isra Isle, like it's a hamburger chain. The poor man was subjected to mockery and became the butt of jokes, and his flourishing career was cut short. Lenox quoted from the newspapers of the era: A madman suffering from megalomania . . . The playwright whose name no one remembers today tried in vain to find a publisher for his manuscript, which he called "Old New Land." The book was eventually shelved. What happened to him, you ask? He disappeared without a trace.

History is not a pawnshop, I said to Lenox in my argumentative way. You can't deposit a country and then demand it back.

Lenox laughed. Why is it always theater people who go around dreaming up countries? They're the first ones willing to experiment with imaginary reality, as long as they can get their five minutes of fame.

The son of a bitch is refusing to pay my expenses for the Middle East trip, of course. To him it's just a wild goose chase. Grand Palestine is the sleepiest place in the universe, and the chances of hunting down a sensational headline there are about as high as the chances of winning the house at the casino. Send your idyllic pictures of the little village of Jerusalem to *National Geographic*, he suggested. Maybe they'll be interested.

HEADLINE: THE Homecoming. I go into the darkroom in my mind and try to organize the pictures. Be patient, Jake. It's your story—I'm just the paparazzo.

First picture: The canoe capsizes and you are washed up on the mound of earth. You're cold. You huddle in the dirt until you fall asleep.

Second picture: Dawn rises over Isra Isle. You wake up confused. You wipe beads of sweat from your brow. Not recognizing the place, you ask: Where the fuck am I?

Third picture: At the edge of the mound you notice a hickory branch sticking out from the ground. For a moment you think it's your javelin, but then you see the carved letters: *Teibele.*

That is how you found the name, lolling around meaninglessly in the earth. You liked the sound and insisted on using it. Grandma Brendel thought you'd lost your mind.

DJ Teibele. Glowing neon lights outside the nightclubs of New York and Ibiza. You said you wanted to spread circles of happiness from the heights of the DJ booth. That was your destiny, in a world without borders. The dancers—seized by youthful excitement—jolted me from side to side. I was almost crushed in the whirlwind, but I couldn't see anyone except you.

I want to grieve in your hollow, DJ Teibele. I want you to weep all your sorrows into me. I put on my headphones and listen to *Dark Side of the Moon* from your laptop. I'm surprised that you discovered the music of my youth. And I naively thought Pink Floyd had long ago fallen into oblivion. I remember pricking myself on the needle and bleeding onto the record.

One day I'll find the strength to tell you about my childhood as the only black boy on an Indian reservation. My first camera was a gift from a Jewish man who came to gamble at the casino and lost everything he owned. He said to me: Never mind, I'll start over again. Then he put a bullet in his head.

I try to photograph the anonymous burial mound for you, but the camera is dead. I pull out the memory card and toss the bird-shit-covered camera into the Niagara. It lands on the quivering line between water and dirt and sprays drops in my face. If little Liam could see how well I'm throwing now, maybe he'd put me on the Isra Isle team. The camera rolls like a feather, then surrenders to gravity, leaving behind a series of rings that slowly vanishes.

End of story. Full circle.

It was from you that I heard your grandmother's favorite Yiddish saying: "It's never too late to die or get married."

We may not be able to get married in this lifetime, but a child of our own . . . You can play him Trance music, or House, and I'll take him to the darkroom and teach him old-fashioned methods of creating stories.

House music. Home music.

I have no place other than you, Jake.

AT THE hotel's front desk I finally pick up my ticket back to New York. I couldn't get a direct flight, but I wasn't willing to wait. I got a seat on a United flight via Boston.

The Grand Cherokee is filthy when I return it at the airport. I can easily identify shreds of leaves, mud, tobacco, and bird shit. But there's something else, too. The forensic report will indicate traces of a nonflammable substance containing oxides and salts, left over from burnt animal or plant tissues. Ashes . . .

The rental car agent does not do a good job of hiding his anger: You should be ashamed of yourself. This is how you return something you borrowed?

I don't give into the guilt trip. I learned that from you.

The commotion is behind us. The candidate and her press detail have just taken off in her Gulfstream jet. On the counter is a stack of newspapers with the incriminating picture of me and her covering practically the entire front page.

The agent hisses: You couldn't get her, could you, you fucker? He charges me an exorbitant rental fee. I pay in cash and keep my mouth shut. I don't have time for another round in the victimhood contest.

Home, before it's too late. I could have driven back to New York, but I'm tired. Twelve hours straight on the road are beyond my strength, and the Tappan Zee Bridge interchange is so confusing. I've already been stopped there once, and they took my license.

SOMETHING TO drink? asks the flight attendant. I resist the complimentary Jack Daniels. I want to be lucid and eloquent when I get to you. I missed seeing the Triplets during takeoff because a mantle of clouds was hiding Isra Isle. The pilot announced reassuringly that it was just a morning fog, and conditions were clear in New York: low humidity, 77 degrees Fahrenheit. Perfect weather for an election campaign.

Admit it, Jake: we both found the journeys convenient, each for our own reason. Me, because all places are worthy in my eyes, and you, because the search itself is the purpose. Perhaps our *shidduch* of complete opposites is the only purposeful journey: countless tiny journeyers darting around, drowning each other in sorrow and joy.

I am thankful to the frothing, restless Niagara that remixed you. Your shrewd grandmother knew that I was willing to knock down my own borders for you, in sound mind, and declare myself an occupied territory by the act that has a name.

I asked at the Department of Ancient Languages. In Hebrew it's called *ahava*. Love.

DON'T FORGET to declare the urn of ashes. Otherwise we'll get arrested for smuggling at the Damascus border.

You can write on the form: "Fulfilled the right of return."

ON THE joke site, which is seeing heavy traffic, I found one that seems to have been written about you. An old Jewish lady walks along the riverbank with her grandson when suddenly a huge wave rolls in and sweeps the boy away. The old lady pumps her fists at the sky and pours out her wrath on the Creator. Since the great paparazzo cannot abide the cascade of human fury, he gives up the booty and sends the grandson back atop another wave. The grandmother hugs the boy and checks him from head to toe to make sure he isn't hurt. Then she shouts up to the sky . . .

You can fill in the punch line.

WE'LL ADOPT a child. Maybe in the desert across the Damascus border—the one the delusional Viennese playwright was aiming for—because the whole world is full of persecuted people, with or without official papers, and all we can do is try to pass down what little good there is in us. One day, in the afterlife, the boy—we'll name him Liam—will play with the disposable toothbrushes in the darkroom and announce that your music belongs to the old world, and that a javelin-throw championship is a stupid, unnecessary show of force. The color-blindness, thank heavens, he will not inherit.

Sometimes I regret the gift of the rainbow. It was given so that the Great Spirit could cleanse her conscience. If man had not learned to isolate red, perhaps he would not have shed blood so easily.

THE FLIGHT attendant leans over and hands me a note with a personal message from the cockpit. It came in over the radio from the candidate's plane, which is hovering on a parallel course. I type the message for you, word for word:

Seafarers believe that when a person saves another person from drowning, the two are bound by a covenant of blood. From there on out, the rescuer is responsible for the survivor's life. Take care of yourself, Prowler, because the future is already here. Yours, the debtor.

I DON'T want this forced *shidduch*. When we land, I will send Rows Without Oars an official protest letter and undo the covenant. What happens if she ends up at the destination she sought and finds a disappointing Ararat?

I touch Tzippora's little peace pipe, which I always carry with me in my lens belt. I will never part with it. That, I can promise.

THE PLANE is quiet, with no Keisha making love to her partner under a blanket. The passengers are asleep, and the only sound is the clicking of my keyboard. I try to view the photos I took, but a window pops up announcing system failure. I hope you kept the picture of Isra Isle from a bird's eye view. I can't accept that all this effort was for nothing.

I promised you transatlantic sex, remember? You and I will never make love in that language they teach in the Ancient Languages Department. In Hebrew we can only die.

IN MY invited vision I anchor in your hollow, run my lips over the body that packages the beautiful Ararat where you flutter, Teibele. Did you know, Jake, that a dove flies only in daylight? Noah opened the window and asked for a volunteer. I'm certain there was a terrified silence in the Ark, because after the raven disappeared no one wanted to risk their lives and go out to check if the waters had receded. The ancient dove—who knows what color her feathers were—was the only one who agreed to go out in the dark. Time was running out. She had no doubt that her partner was waiting for her, turning one eye to the future while his other was pinned firmly in the past.

THE PLANE approaches New York. September sun melts away the borders of darkness and the light blinds me, so that for an instant I imagine I can finally recognize the red that has evaded me all my life. A stain flits over my eyeballs and quickly vanishes.

The Twin Towers are right within camera range. What a pity I threw it away. I could have captured the flashes of light from the windows and focused on the faces of people waking up to a new day in this life, the only one there is.

I long for you, my love, so much that it hurts.

A circular motion. We plunge. Hard to breathe . . . The sky is covered with a mushroom cloud . . . A pillar of fire and smoke . . . A deluge of ashes . . . I'm scared . . . So scared . . .

My Teibele, don't wait.

Yitgadal v'yitkadash sh'mei raba . . .

*

JUST BEFORE sunset on the fifteenth of September, a young man walks along the strip of shore between Jaffa and Gaza. His backpack contains a Pink Floyd CD, an urn of ashes that passed a moderate security screening, and a disposable toothbrush bought at the last minute at the Duty Free in Damascus Airport.

The setting sun tints his four-day-old facial stubble with a reddish glow. His steps leave traces on the sand as he walks along the quivering line between water and earth, zigzagging to the water's edge and away. Behind him sits the profile of Jaffa, with its minarets, and before him the skyscrapers of Gaza.

The man is young, although not a youth. He still does not fully grasp the sorrow that whips at him like a sharpened spear. The constant motion he has imposed upon himself is a temporary armor. If he stops, even for a moment, he might plunge into the depths.

Although the twilight air is warm, he searches for branches and planks to light a fire, but he can find no trees. He makes do with a handful of dry weeds. He builds a circle, but instead of sitting by the flames, he walks around thc circle of fire over and over again. His coming-of-age journey flickers in his memory card. How did he have the audacity to deny his helping spirit and think he could create his own vision, one that did not depend on providence? He wants to pour out his fury and defiance now, but there is no one to defy.

In this place, the Great Spirit is called *Allah*, but the young man does not speak Arabic. Go forth. Was that an eviction order? Or a rarely granted permission to be an eternal journeyer, designed to repeatedly offer the choice of a promised thereplace?

Someone is following him. Not compassionately, for the watchful eye is unaware of Jacob Brendel III's desperate need for embracing arms. Rather, this eye watches him curiously. Strangers rarely come to this desolate place, which has sunken into blessed oblivion. And perhaps it is the oblivion that heals the plague of hatred between the tribes.

Night falls. Sunset is very fast here.

His body gives in to the jetlag, and the sharp transition from one place to another takes its toll. The young homeless man drops to the fine sand and shuts his eyes, but he does not sail into sleep. In vain he searches the darkness inside him for doves and ravens. They may not nest here, or perhaps even in the story their traces were lost. They circle inside the flood and cannot find each other's Ararat.

In the morning, the young man whose hair has turned white from salt will open the urn of ashes. It also contains a handful of charred dirt, which he gathered from the ruins as he fought with a policemen who tried to keep him away from the heart of the disaster.

On the third day, when it started raining suddenly, disrupting rescue efforts, Jake withdrew from the smoldering pit and refused to submit to the chain of comforters who tried to gather him in. At the last minute he managed to pick up a strange object in the shape of a frozen waterfall, which had not been consumed by the fire.

SHE WHO follows him, an elderly lady with a youthful expression, will sit by the fire in the morning—he will have extinguished the flame with a stream of urine—and try to comfort him with her words: "*Ayuni*, my eyes, they are before us and we are after them."

As is the custom of the desert people, the old lady will purify her hands in dirt and not in water, and she will explain to the refugee that the Arabic word for death means "redeeming the debt." Then the two will say a prayer from right to left:

Yit'allah wa'Yitkadash . . .

DJ TEIBELE leads himself in a dance along the shore between Jaffa and Gaza, scattering his traces in the wind.

Tel-Aviv, December 2004